Death Comes to Dartmoor

By Stephanie Austin

Dead in Devon
Dead on Dartmoor
From Devon with Death
The Dartmoor Murders
A Devon Night's Death
Death Comes to Dartmoor
A Devon Midwinter Murder

a&b

*Death Comes to
Dartmoor*

STEPHANIE AUSTIN

Allison & Busby Limited
11 Wardour Mews
London W1F 8AN
allisonandbusby.com

First published in Great Britain by Allison & Busby in 2023.
This paperback edition published by Allison & Busby in 2023.

A CIP catalogue record for this book is available from
the British Library.

10 9 8 7 6 5 4 3 2 1

ISBN 978-0-7490-2902-9

Typeset in 11pt Sabon LT Pro by
Typo•glyphix, Burton-on-Trent, DE14 3HE

By choosing this product, you help take care of the world's forests.
Learn more: www.fsc.org.

Printed and bound by
CPI Group (UK) Ltd, Croydon, CR0 4YY

To Katy and Phil

CHAPTER ONE

I left Ashburton at the fag-end of a long, hot summer. There were no murders in my absence. During the ten days I was away there were certainly some interesting goings-on, but no suspicious deaths. According to some of my more uncharitable friends, this was simply because I wasn't there. It was even suggested that it might be safer for the residents of Ashburton if I stayed away permanently. I think this is unkind. It's not my fault I'm good at finding dead bodies. And, as it turned out, whatever strange power arranges these things, was merely saving them up until I got home.

When you run two businesses, even taking a short holiday is not an easy thing to contrive. I had to time it carefully. The shop wasn't a problem. Sophie and Pat have looked after *Old Nick's* on a daily basis ever since it opened, and with the tourist season tailing off at the start of the new autumn term, it was unlikely that a shop selling art, crafts, antiques and second-hand books was going to be overwhelmed with business. In fact, our takings were so dismal whilst I was away it wouldn't have mattered if we'd hung the *closed* sign on the door.

It was the other half of the business – the domestic goddess half – which was the problem. I walk five dogs on weekdays, as well as clean for, and generally help out, a variety of human clients. It was making sure their needs would be taken care of whilst I was away that was the difficult bit. But I hadn't seen my cousin Brian for over two years, and I needed a break. He's my only remaining relative, my mother's cousin, which makes him either my second cousin, or first-cousin-once-removed, I'm not quite sure. He's always been more like an uncle to me, older, wiser, chummy and kind. He'd recently come home on leave before taking up his new diplomatic posting, so I popped up to London to see him, spending ten days in his flat. He was off down to Portsmouth for a week's sailing after that. He wanted me to go too, but I get sea-sick and anyway, there is only so much of Brian's hag-wife, the toxic stick-insect Marcia, that I can stand. I promised to visit him again later, once he'd taken up residence in Paris.

As it happened, things worked in my favour. My most ancient client Maisie, ninety-six and still counting, was to receive a visit from her daughter, Our Janet, down from the wilds of Heck-as-Like, or wherever she lives up north, so I was able to organise my holiday at the same time. I managed to subcontract the dog walking to Becky, who runs a mobile dog-grooming business. Mrs Berkeley-Smythe was away on a cruise and wouldn't need my services till she got back, and I knew my friend Elizabeth would keep an eye on Tom Carter. Everyone else, as far as I was concerned, could manage without me.

I haunted the markets of London, lusting after antiques I couldn't afford to buy for *Old Nick's*. I was determined to keep my money in my pocket, despite Brian's assurance that anything I bought could easily be buzzed down to Devon by carrier, no trouble at all. I went shopping with Marcia, resisting her attempts to drag me to the gym each morning, and we bonded, slightly. We don't really like each other, but for Brian's sake we did our best to get along. Why, after fifty years of contented bachelorhood, he had decided to marry a widow with two grown-up daughters, I don't know. To be fair, Marcia is probably an ideal wife for a diplomat. She's fluent in three languages, can organise a formal dinner party at the drop of a hat and apparently plays a fiendish hand of bridge.

At first, I felt energised by the buzz of London, the rush, but the excitement quickly wore off. I found myself longing for muddy lanes and birdsong. At the end of ten days when every day had been crammed with shopping and sightseeing, each evening spent at an expensive restaurant or a West End show, I was more than ready to come home. As my train headed back into Devon, I found myself letting out a breath.

From Exeter the railway line hugs the south Devon coast, passing red cliffs on one side and the open sea on the other. The train stops at Dawlish, where on wild nights sea spray washes over the carriages. During a storm a few years back, the rocks beneath the line were swept away, leaving the track swinging like a rope bridge a few feet above the churning waves. The track turns inland after Teignmouth, running alongside the lazy grey waters of the Teign estuary to Newton Abbot, which is where I got off.

Despite my determination not to shop, I'd come back from London with far more bags and baggage than I'd left with. I'd received several offers from people happy to pick me up from the station but decided I'd rather sneak back into Ashburton with the minimum of fuss. On the other hand, I didn't fancy the bus ride with all my baggage, so I compromised and took a taxi. My last little luxury, I warned myself, before I got home. The previous occupant had left a copy of *the Dartmoor Gazette* on the back seat, and I gave it a quick flick through to see if anything interesting had been happening whilst I'd been away.

Not much. Someone living in the village of Scorriton had lost her Labradoodle, convinced it had been stolen, and police were searching for three men who'd been spotted climbing out of the back of a lorry just disembarked from the ferry at Plymouth. Then, buried at the foot of an inside page, I found something fascinating.

District councillor and property developer,
Alastair Dunston, was granted a restraining order
against a member of this newspaper's staff at a
court hearing in Exeter today. The injunction bars
our reporter, Sandy Thomas, from being within
one hundred yards of Mr Dunston's home. Mr
Dunston was quoted as saying that Ms Thomas
had exceeded the considerable liberties afforded
to members of her profession, stalking him and
harassing members of his family. Ms Thomas was
also accused of causing an affray at a fundraising
dinner attended by Mr Dunston and was bound
over to keep the peace.

What had Sandy been up to? She can be a pestilential
nuisance, as I knew to my cost, forever pestering me
with questions when I'd accidentally got myself involved
in a murder investigation. It was she who saddled me
with the title of 'Ashburton's Amateur Sleuth', a source
of cringing embarrassment to me ever since. Merely the
sound of her breathy, Welsh voice on the phone was
enough to wind me up. But she was just doing her job.
She could be pushy, but I couldn't imagine her making
so much of a nuisance of herself that someone had taken
her to court. And what had Alastair Dunston been up
to that had aroused so much of her interest? I squinted
at his photograph. He was quite good-looking. County
councillor *and* property developer, that was a likely
conflict of interest for a start. But causing an affray, what
was that all about? I noticed that the newspaper hadn't

offered any comment on her activities. Poor old Sandy. At least they hadn't given her the boot.

By now the taxi had pulled up outside of my house, forcing me to abandon the newspaper. I had to get out and pay the driver, who retrieved my suitcase from the back but drew the line at carting my baggage up the steps to the front door. I watched him turn his vehicle around at the end of the lane, then gathered up my chattels and began the ascent.

I was happy to be home. *O, Little Town of Ashburton, how still we see thee lie*, straight off the slip road from the A38, wedged between the dual carriageway and the Dartmoor foothills. It doesn't have the biscuit-tin prettiness of some Dartmoor villages, no duckpond or thatched cottages. It's an old stannary town, where for centuries tin mined on the moor was assayed and stamped. Shops catering for tourists may have replaced its ancient trades, but it's quirky, with lanes and passages the tourist can easily miss, the ruins of history buried in its stone walls, with green hills rising up behind it and a little river sliding sneakily through its heart. I love it. I never want to live anywhere else.

I'd worried about Kate whilst I was away. I rent the top floor of the house she occupies with Adam. They're expecting their first baby in a few weeks and she's been having a rotten pregnancy, her daily sickness not confining itself to mornings, and with no sign of her nausea abating as the birth approaches.

I dumped my baggage at the foot of the stairs, pausing to extract a parcel from one of my shopping bags, and headed for Kate's kitchen door. She answered my knock, grinning as we hugged. She looked beautiful as ever, but heavy-eyed, as if she wasn't getting enough sleep.

'How was the trip?' she asked, and added mischievously, 'How was Marcia?'

'We managed not to come to blows,' I admitted, 'although she doesn't approve of me at all.' I had, in her words, *wasted* the expensive education that Brian had paid for by setting myself up as *some sort of paid dogsbody* and not pursuing a proper career. Becoming the owner of what she referred to as *a junk shop* had done little to raise my status in her eyes. 'Anyway, never mind me, how are you?'

'I'm not throwing up so much,' she admitted, eagerly unwrapping the gift I had brought her. She held up the spotted Babygro. 'Aw . . . thanks! But this one,' she added, stroking her beachball tummy, 'keeps me awake most nights, kicking.'

'How's Adam managing at the cafe?'

'Chris Brownlow is still helping out. He doesn't go back to college until next month.'

Chris was the son of one of my clients and had taken on working at Sunflowers as a holiday job.

'Cup of tea?' she asked. 'Piece of cake?'

Frankly, I was ravenous. Breakfast at Brian's seemed like a long time ago, but I knew I'd emptied my fridge before I went away and I'd better go shopping. Besides, I wanted to call in on *Old Nick's* before closing time. 'Not just now, thanks.' I squeezed Kate's arm. 'Catch you later.'

As I dumped my bags on the sofa upstairs, I could see the red light of my ancient answerphone flashing. For a moment I thought it might be a call from Daniel. But it wouldn't be. With a sinking feeling inside, I remembered it would never be a call from Daniel again.

I pressed the play button and a loud, slightly raucous voice demanded to know what I'd been up to in the big city. It was Ricky. 'Give us a call when you get back,' he urged, so I settled myself down on the sofa, kicking off my shoes and putting my feet up on the coffee table. The shopping could wait. Within moments, Bill appeared from my bedroom, leapt onto my lap and began an enthusiastic greeting procedure, treading my midriff with his paws and purring like a Geiger-counter, whilst simultaneously headbutting the hand that was holding the phone. He must have missed me. He'd probably been living in my flat the entire time I'd been away, going downstairs only for meals. I smoothed his black head and told him how gorgeous he was.

'Druid Lodge Theatrical Hire,' came a slightly weary voice at the end of the phone.

'Ricky, it's me.'

'Princess, where are you? At the station?'

'No, I got a taxi home.' I ignored his tutting. 'There was one waiting at the station entrance,' I lied, 'I thought I might as well get in it.'

'Expensive journey home,' he sniffed.

Yes, it had been.

'You know we'd have picked you up.'

14

'Well, I'm here now.'

'So come on up! *Maurice* and I would love to see you. You can tell us all about what you got up to in London. D'you see any shows?'

Ricky and Morris are two of my oldest friends and I love 'em dearly, but actually, I'd been fancying a quiet night in. Then I remembered something. 'Do you know anything about this business with Sandy Thomas? The paper said she'd been accused of causing an affray. Something to do with some councillor?'

'You mean Alastair Dunston.'

I knew I could rely on Ricky. 'You know about it?'

'Know about it?' He cracked with laughter. 'Darlin', we were there! It was a fundraising bash for the air-ambulance.'

'When was this?'

'A few weeks back.'

I frowned. How come I hadn't heard about this until now? 'Where was I?'

'Oh, gawd knows! Up to no-bleeding-good, I expect. Look, why don't you come up to the house, let us cook you supper? You can hear all about it and tell us about your trip.'

'Deal,' I agreed without hesitation and disconnected. I glanced at my watch and then at Bill, who'd settled down on my lap, purring, his paws tucked under, his one emerald eye closed in contentment. Anyone would think he was *my* cat. 'Sorry,' I told him, lifting him off my lap. 'But I want to get to the shop before it closes. I'm going to have to get going.'

Sophie and Pat man *Old Nick's* for me in return for the rent-free space they occupy. They have done so since I unexpectedly inherited the shop from a former client, Mr Nickolai, after he just as unexpectedly got himself murdered. It's an arrangement that works well. Neither of them can afford to pay rent. Sophie doesn't sell enough pictures and all Pat's money goes on running a sanctuary for abandoned animals with her sister and brother-in-law. But their being in the shop gives me time to pursue my domestic goddess business, the one that actually earns me some money. Most days, they take it in turns. But that afternoon they were both in the shop, Sophie's dark head bent over a watercolour she was painting and Pat frowning over some jewellery on her worktable. Elizabeth was there too, arranging books on the shelves in alphabetical order. She comes in to offer a hand now and then. As always, she looked cool and elegant in a spotless white blouse, her silvery-blonde hair swept up into an elegant chignon, and made the rest of us look scruffy.

'Nice to see the place is still standing,' I announced as I walked in. 'Hello!'

'That's about all it is,' Sophie complained. 'The till's hardly rung all week.'

'It hasn't been quite that bad,' Elizabeth corrected her with a smile. 'The book exchange is starting to work well.'

'At least it brings people in through the door,' Pat agreed, without looking up from what she was doing. 'Hello Juno.'

I passed her a bag of some unusual beads I'd picked

up from a specialist shop in Covent Garden. I'd bought big, soft paintbrushes for Soph and an Edwardian hair-slide for Elizabeth. They all went through the you-shouldn't-have-but-I'm-glad-you-did routine and after recounting my adventures in London I had a brief and rather depressing look at the sales ledger.

Sophie tickled the palm of her hand experimentally with a new paintbrush. 'At least Christmas is coming.'

I shuddered. 'It's only October.'

'Now you're a shopkeeper, Juno, you've got to start thinking of these things early.' Pat held up what looked like a pumpkin earring. 'I'm making these for Hallowe'en.'

'Exactly, I've got you and Soph to think about these things. It doesn't make any difference to me. Antiques are the same whatever time of year it is.' I had to admit that in the run-up to last Christmas they'd made the shop look fabulous. If only *Old Nick's* was on North Street or East Street, instead of stuck down narrow and dingy Shadow Lane, it might have made a difference.

'These things take time to build,' Elizabeth observed. 'There's no point in getting despondent.'

'No. Grit and determination is what it takes.' I thumped the counter with my fist in mock resolution and announced I was going to the loo.

Nick's old bathroom is on a landing halfway up the stairs, part of the old flat above the shop and, together with his kitchen, comprised the staff facilities. I was just about to come out again, having done what I needed, when I heard Sophie say, 'Are we going to tell her?'

17

'Let sleeping dogs lie, that's what I say,' Pat responded. 'Juno's going to find out about it soon enough. Why upset her before we have to?' I pulled the bathroom door to softly and listened.

Sophie sounded angry. 'What the hell's he done it for?'

'He needs a proper phone signal and broadband to be able to work.' This was Elizabeth's voice. 'He's got nothing up at that farmhouse.' They were talking about Daniel, my all too briefly loved-and-lost lover. He'd inherited a farmhouse up on Halsanger Common, a few miles out of town. Practically a ruin, it lacked even the most basic of facilities and he was living in a caravan whilst it was being rebuilt. 'I don't suppose he's renting an office just for fun.' Elizabeth retained some contact with Daniel through the doctor's surgery where she worked as a part-time receptionist and where he was a patient.

'But does he have to rent one around the corner?' Sophie demanded. 'So near to here?'

'I imagine finance has something to do with it and there probably wasn't a lot of choice.'

'You don't think he's done it deliberate, like?' Pat asked. 'To be near Juno?'

'In order to torment himself, you mean?' Elizabeth asked mildly.

'He's the one who broke it off,' Sophie objected. 'He can torment himself all he likes, but I don't want him tormenting Juno.'

Pat grunted. 'I don't know why he broke it off in

18

any case. I know she gets up to some daft things, damn dangerous some of 'em, but what's the point in worrying?'

'Don't forget he lost his first wife in tragic circumstances.'

'Well, I know,' Pat conceded, 'and that's all very sad. But, be honest, any one of us could get killed any day, just crossing the street.'

Elizabeth gave a soft laugh. 'True, but Juno does have a tendency to throw herself into the traffic.'

'You sound as if you're defending him,' Sophie accused her.

'I think I understand why he broke with Juno,' she responded calmly, 'but I still think he's wrong.'

I decided it was time to stop lurking on the landing and came down into the shop.

'So where is it, then?' I asked as the three of them turned to look at me. 'This office that Daniel has rented?'

Sophie threw Pat an agonised glance.

'It's around the corner on East Street,' Elizabeth responded before either of them could speak, 'above the beauty therapist.'

'At least he won't have to go far to get his nails done.'

No one laughed. Sophie's eyes glistened dangerously. 'Don't look so tragic,' I told her. 'It's all right. Really.' I smiled but couldn't contain the sigh escaping from my chest. 'I can't control what he does so . . .' I shrugged, 'it makes no difference to me.'

This was a lie. During our short relationship, Daniel had worked away a lot, so I was used to long periods of not having him around. And if he stayed up in his lonely caravan, out of my way, perhaps I would stand some chance of forgetting him. But if he was renting an office in town, we were almost certain to run into each other. And that would be a different thing altogether. Suddenly, I wished I'd gone sailing with Brian after all.

CHAPTER TWO

Ricky and Morris's place is practically my second home. An imposing Georgian residence set in lovely grounds it sits high on a hill overlooking Ashburton. I've stayed there a lot. As well as being home to Ricky and Morris, it houses several thousand theatrical costumes, which they hire to groups all over the country. During the time I'd been away, *Oklahoma!* had been returned, and they'd sent out *Half a Sixpence*. The leaves might be only just on the turn, but they were already gearing themselves up for the pantomime season. I try to help them out with the packing and unpacking when I can, but these days, I don't have much spare time.

'So, what's all this about Sandy Thomas?' I'd kept them entertained, telling them about the shows I'd seen in London during the creamy fish pie and minted peas. Now that we'd arrived at the plum crumble, I reckoned it was their turn.

'Well, there's not a great deal to tell,' Ricky admitted, making me feel he'd got me there under false pretences.

Morris shook his bald head. 'It was all over very quickly. I don't think anyone realised what was going on.'

Ricky grinned. 'Not until the champagne started flying.'

'Can we start at the beginning?' I asked. 'What was Sandy doing there? Was she covering the event for the paper?'

He shrugged his shoulders. 'S'pose.'

'It was quite early on in the evening,' Morris explained. 'People were still arriving. Everyone was just standing around in the ballroom, glasses in hand . . .'

'Mingling,' Ricky interrupted, putting a cigarette to his lips.

'The waiters were bringing trays of canapés round, then there was the sound of breaking glass,' Morris went on. 'One of the waiters had dropped a tray.'

'He'd got in the way of Sandy, waving her arms about.' Ricky drew on his fag, leaning back in his chair, draping one long arm over the back. 'She looked a bit rough, to be honest.'

Morris frowned. 'I don't think she could have been there officially.'

'Anyway, she was giving it large,' Ricky went on, 'screaming abuse at this Alastair Dunston chap, and then she threw her glass of Buck's Fizz in his face.'

'But you don't know what it was about?'

He shrugged. 'She called him a lying bastard.'

'No.' Morris corrected, holding up a finger. 'She

called him a *conniving* bastard. She called him a *lying* pig. I got the impression,' he added with a coy smile, 'that she and Dunston had been involved.'

'His missus didn't look very happy about it,' Ricky grinned, obviously enjoying the memory, 'neither did he, standing there, face all dripping with orange.'

'What happened to Sandy?' I asked

'She was escorted from the premises by hotel staff.'

'But the police weren't called?'

'No, although technically,' Morris added, thoughtfully polishing his gold-rimmed specs, 'I suppose it was an assault.'

'Fascinating. Do we know anything about this Councillor Dunston?'

He frowned. 'Isn't he behind that new development they want to build at Woodland? There's been a lot of fuss about it in the paper. Lots of objections. Perhaps Sandy's been covering that.'

'But that wasn't why she threw a glass of pop in his gob,' Ricky chuckled. 'You should've seen her face. They'd been shagging, I'd lay good money on it.' He took another drag on his cigarette, blowing a smoke ring that hovered like a halo above his silver hair. 'But whatever they'd been up to, I reckon it's over now.'

I frowned. 'I don't think it's over for Sandy. In the paper she was accused of stalking him, of harassing his family. She's not allowed within a hundred yards of his house.'

'Yeh, well, hell hath no fury like a woman scorned. Perhaps he'd tried to give her the elbow and she wasn't having any. Perhaps she can't leave it alone.' He jabbed his cigarette in my direction. 'Why don't you turn the tables on her, ring her up and ask her all about it?'

I smiled, but shook my head. I couldn't do that. A woman scorned, that was what I was. Daniel had accused me of taking stupid risks, recklessly endangering my life. He wasn't prepared to wait around whilst I got myself killed, he told me, so he put an end to our relationship, almost before it had begun. For the first time since I had known Sandy Thomas, I felt sorry for her.

The following Saturday morning I drew up at No. 4, Daison Cottages, the house that Elizabeth shares with fifteen-year-old schoolboy, Oliver Knollys. She poses as his aunt. I know that they're not really related because, some time ago, I was responsible for putting them together. Elizabeth was homeless, anxious to leave behind a past that had become too interesting, and sleeping in her car. Olly had been secretly living alone since the death of his nan, terrified the social services would find out and take him into care. Sharing the house together seemed to be the perfect solution for them both, and so far, it had worked out well. No one questioned that Elizabeth wasn't the long-lost relative she claimed to be and she and Olly got on well, drawn together by a love of music and a genial acceptance by them both that they made up the rules as they went along.

Not much had happened in the intervening week. I got back into my working rhythm, soon felt like I hadn't been away. I managed to catch up with Our Janet before

24

she departed for the wilds of Heck-as-Like, met her over a coffee to discuss her mother's welfare. Maisie still refused to consider leaving her cottage in Ashburton to live in a care home near her daughter and we both wondered how long she would be able to carry on alone, even with help from me and the care agency Janet employed to look in on her every day. But at ninety-six, Maisie was still going strong. Cussedness can carry you an awfully long way.

For the first few days I couldn't stop wondering if I'd bump into Daniel in Ashburton. Each time I had to pass the beauty therapist's, usually on the opposite side of the road, I found I couldn't drag my eyes from the upper-floor window, where I knew his office was, in case I might catch sight of him. I didn't, but I did spot Sandy Thomas, hurrying along Sun Street, head down, shoulders hunched, as if she didn't want anyone to notice her. A couple of people laughed as she went by. *Now you know what if feels like*, I told her silently, remembering the unwelcome attention her newspaper articles had focused on me. But it was only the thought of a moment. I felt sorry for her really.

I'd been invited up to Daison Cottages that Saturday morning to view Olly's latest gadget, but when I arrived, Elizabeth was alone in the kitchen. 'He's gone up to the woods to retrieve it,' she explained as she filled the kettle. 'He'll be back in a minute.'

Toby, her pale and spindly Siamese cat, was dreaming on top of the stove. I stroked his ears gently then sat down at the kitchen table. 'What is it this time?'

'A wildlife camera-trap.'

'One of those things you see photographers using on the telly?' I asked. 'They strap 'em to trees and leave them in the hope that some rare animal might wander by?'

Elizabeth nodded. 'The camera is set off by movement.'

I grinned. 'Don't tell me, Olly wants to be a wildlife photographer.'

'That is the latest,' she admitted with a smile.

'Aren't those cameras expensive?'

'Actually no, this one was quite reasonable. He found it on the Internet. When badgers started digging up our potatoes, he decided he'd like to record their night-time activities. He started off filming them in the garden, but their sett is up in the wood there.'

I gazed out of the window. Daison Cottages had originally been built as council houses for agricultural workers, four in a row, with the road in front of them and open country all around. Behind the houses, fields swept up to a wood on top of the hill, which was where the badgers hung out.

'But I'm restricting filming nights to Fridays and Saturdays,' Elizabeth went on. 'Olly hasn't got time to go up there and retrieve the camera on school mornings, and he spends ages poring over the results.'

'The badgers don't mind being film stars then?'

'Not at all. But Olly needs to buckle down, he's got GCSEs this year, and these badgers are a great distraction.'

'Perhaps he'll get fed up of them.' In the past he'd been fixated with a drone, but he didn't seem to fly it much these days. He clattered in through the back door at that moment, looking as if he'd just got up, one half of his shirt hanging down over his trousers and his hair standing up in spikes. Was it my imagination, or was he a little taller than when I'd last seen him? Something was different. Was his fair hair a little darker, greasier? At fifteen, were teenage hormones finally starting to kick in?

'Hello Juno!' he grinned. 'Nice holiday?' He was clutching the camera, its case patterned in camouflage colours, a green webbing strap attached. He flipped the camera open and used his thumbnail to flip out a memory card. 'We'll watch it on the laptop.' He pulled it across the table towards him, opened the lid and keyed in his password as Elizabeth delivered mugs of coffee and sat down. Olly inserted the memory card into the laptop and an image flashed up on the screen.

'The camera's set to night-time,' he explained, 'that's why it's in black and white.'

We were looking at a picture of the woodland floor and the entrance to the badger's sett, a black hole in a sloping bank stamped to bare earth by the passage of snouts and paws, fallen leaves in patterns of grey scattered over the ground. Immediately in front of the camera was a pool of white light, the surrounding woodland fading into darkness. Olly had fixed the camera low down on a tree trunk to get the best view of the sett entrance. In the bottom right-hand corner of the screen the time was recorded in glowing numerals, seconds ticking away as a tiny moth danced, ghostly white, in front of the lens. Olly grinned. 'That's what started the camera off. It's triggered by movement, see.'

At 8.47 and 16 seconds the previous evening the first badger's snout emerged, his eyes shining, two bright reflecting discs. He came out cautiously at first, then sat and scratched his flank, raking at his fur with fearsome hind claws. Another badger emerged from the sett behind him, trundling like a little tank, snuffling at the ground around him. I could hear him grunting. I hadn't realised the camera recorded sound too. Then the two of them started rolling around, play-fighting. 'This is great footage, Oll',' I told him as a third badger emerged. Then they all vanished like magic, in the blinking of an eye. We were staring once again at the empty forest floor. 'What happened then?'

'Timer went. See, movement is what starts the camera filming, but you can set it to film for however long you want. This is set at a minute. Then it stops. That's why it looks as if they've vanished.'

'Until another movement starts it off again?'

'Yeh, that's right. It blinks once a minute. Look at the timer. See, it's 9.14 now.'

'But what's started the camera off this time? I can't see anything.'

'Sometimes the wind will start it off, if trees and stuff are moving about in front of the camera.' He grinned. 'A spider did it once, dangling down in front of the lens.'

'Look,' Elizabeth pointed at a tiny bright spot, travelling from left to right. 'See that little eye? It's a mouse or a shrew moving along the ground there.'

The camera blinked again. The mouse had dis-appeared and another badger stood between the trees, his broad white face stripes glowing in the dark. 'I didn't see him come out.'

'That bank's full of holes.' Olly explained, 'he could have come out anywhere.' We watched as the badger came right up to the camera, his blunt nose in close-up as he sniffed the lens. Then he turned and disappeared. Badgers kept appearing at intervals, a minute's footage at a time, snuffling, snorting, scratching, tumbling and playing, until, frankly, I began to find them a bit boring. I cast a glance at Elizabeth, who gave me a wry smile. Olly, meanwhile, was transfixed. 'More coffee?' Elizabeth mouthed at me, and I nodded. By now, the timer on the screen was showing two minutes to midnight. Then something scared the badgers, sending them scurrying down into the safety of their sett.

Elizabeth frowned. 'What was that?' After a few moments came the shrill *yip* of a tawny owl, but that was not what had frightened them away. We stared at the screen, patiently waiting for something to appear. Nothing moved. The wind stirred, fluttering leaves. Then came a noise like heavy breathing, almost like sobbing, the crashing and snapping of twigs as something rushed through woodland undergrowth. Deer, perhaps? The noise came again, a tortured drawing in of breath, like a runner who has reached his last gasp and can run no further. No deer made that noise. This was not something, this was someone. The sound was very close to the camera now, but whoever was making it was out of sight. It came again, tortured breath, desperate, heaving. Elizabeth frowned. 'That sounds like a woman.'

The camera blinked. Something pale, out of focus, stood close-up against the lens. The time showed one minute past midnight. Still the noise, that tortured gasping. Whoever it was had stopped in front of the tree, unaware of the camera strapped to it, desperate for breath.

The paleness in front of the lens resolved itself into a shape as it moved away. It was a leg, a woman's calf and ankle, a foot in a low-heeled sandal. Not a shoe for running in, for running alone in a wood at midnight. As she lurched away from the camera, almost stumbling on the uneven ground, we saw the whole figure: the back of a woman, her dress grey in night-time colour, her hair glowing silvery white. Just for a moment. But as she turned to look behind her, the camera blinked. We didn't see her face. We were staring at nothing, an empty space between the trees where she'd been standing. It was 12.05. Something else was in front of the camera now: a man's shoe, a trainer, the gathered cuff of dark jogging trousers. It moved away and we glimpsed a hooded figure following the woman through the trees. The camera blinked again. We waited tensely for whatever was coming next. For a moment, nothing. Then the crashing sound again, the sound of running, closer now, the woman doubling back on herself. Nothing to see except a white moth dancing against the dark. Then a scream quite close, a sickening thwacking noise that came, once, twice, three times. It was 12.09. The camera blinked. Now something was obscuring the lens, a silver cloud of wire-like strands that the bright light shone through.

'What's that?' Olly breathed, his voice barely a whisper.

'It's hair,' I whispered back. 'I think it's that woman's hair.'

'Then she must be lying . . .'

She must be lying on the ground, her face turned away from us. We watched in horror as the cloud of hair gradually slid out of sight of the camera, as her body was dragged away. We could hear a man's heavy breathing as he grunted and muttered, struggled with the effort of dragging her weight. The camera blinked. It was 12.12.

Then it was morning. We were gazing at the woodland floor in daytime colours, in brown and green and gold. We could hear birdsong, see the flickering movements of birds in the undergrowth. Then Olly's innocent face as he grinned into the camera before he took it down from the tree.

'Run it back,' Elizabeth said urgently. 'Run it back to when we first hear that woman. It's around midnight.'

We watched again as the scene unfolded. 'It's murder, isn't it?' Olly's voice trembled, his pointed little face white with shock. 'We're watching a murder.'

Elizabeth reached for her phone. 'We've certainly witnessed an assault.'

'Olly, when you went to fetch the camera, you didn't notice anything?' I asked, 'Any sign that anyone had been there?'

'Well, the ground was a bit scuffed up, but I thought that was the badgers.'

Elizabeth was speaking into the phone, asking for police and ambulance.

'You stay here with Elizabeth, wait for the police,' I told him. 'I'm going up there.'

He sprang to his feet. 'I'm coming with you.'

'Look, there's a chance that woman may still be alive. She could be lying there, needing our help. But if . . . if she's not . . . the police won't want too many people treading about up there.'

'But you don't know where the badgers are,' he protested, 'the tree where the camera was.'

'All right, you can show me. Then, you come back here. The police will need you to show them the way.'

As we left, Elizabeth was still patiently explaining what we'd witnessed to the emergency services.

In the bright, golden light of a sunny morning it was difficult to believe what had happened during the night, what had unfolded in shades of grey on the screen like some old horror movie. The daylight world, the world of colour, was warm and kind, alive with birdsong. Olly and I hurried up the hill, reached the edge of the wood and halted, hungry for breath. Beneath the canopy of birch and oak, hazel and holly grew, and a tangle of bramble and blackthorn. The badgers' sett was not far in, set in a steep bank, the earth around the dark entrance mounded with bare soil where the badgers had dug.

'I strapped the camera to that one.' Olly pointed to a birch a few yards away. 'You can see, low down on the trunk, where I cleared the ivy away.'

He made a step towards it but I grabbed his arm. 'Don't go any closer. That's where she was lying, there might be evidence.'

We looked around. There was no sign of the woman. 'Where d'you think she . . . I mean where did he . . . ?' Olly's voice tailed off.

'I don't know.' The only thing we did know was that she had been dragged away from the camera, out of sight of the lens. I yelled a hello, my eyes scanning the leafy jigsaw of the woodland floor for any movement. We listened, ears straining for a response. A jay, hunting among the oaks for acorns, shrieked in alarm, and we saw the flash of its white rump, the shimmer of its blue wings as it flew off. Otherwise, silence. But if the woman had been lying in the wood all night, hurt and unable to move, she might not have the strength to call out. She might be dying somewhere close by, hidden, whilst we searched for her and couldn't find her. A few yards off I made out a clump of crushed and broken ferns. They might have been flattened by something heavy being dragged over them, something like a body. I looked at Olly. 'I want you to go back now.'

'I should stay here with you,' he protested, 'in case that bloke is still about.'

'I think he's long gone.' A siren sounded in the distance. 'That'll be the police or the ambulance. Go on, Oll.' They'll need you to show them the way.'

This time he didn't argue, just nodded and hared off in the direction of home. I followed the trail of broken ferns down a slope into a clearing, stopped and looked

33

around. The wood was obviously being managed, trees pollarded or selectively cut down, sawn logs lying in tidy piles. But there was no sign of the woman. Dark ruffles of fungus had grown like frills around the foot of an oak, one piece broken off, showing the bright yellow flesh within. Had some animal taken a bite from it, or had something broken it off in passing, unnoticed in the night, something dragged along the ground?

I might not have attached any significance to a mound of broken branches heaped nearby, if I hadn't been searching. I drew close to it and crouched, peering through the network of twigs and concealing foliage. I could see something pale lying in there, something too still. Something dead. Holding my breath, I lifted a branch.

I was staring at a piece of the woman's dress, pale blue, not grey as it had looked on the night-camera, but, smeared with the green sap of broken plants and scattered with fragments of leaf. I flung the branch aside and tried to drag another out of the way. It was tangled and I was forced to shake it free. I didn't want to disturb things but I could see the back of the woman's head, her hair short and wavy, blonde not silver, except where it was clotted dark with blood. I stood up and moved around, trying to see her face. I crouched and stared into dead, doll-like eyes. Her cheek was pressed against the ground, half hidden among the leaf litter. But I could see enough to recognise her. A wave of sadness washed through me. It was Sandy Thomas.

CHAPTER THREE

'I messed it up, didn't I, when I went back to get the camera? I trod all over where she'd been lying, where that bloke had stood.' Olly's eyes were swimming with unshed tears and his chin trembled.

Detective Inspector Ford smiled. 'You haven't messed up anything, Olly,' he reassured him. 'If it wasn't for you and your camera, we'd never have known this dreadful crime had taken place.' The inspector had viewed the film in grim silence and now the woods were crawling with police.

'It's a pity *you* felt it necessary to disturb the body, though, Miss Browne.' Detective Sergeant Christine deVille, aka Cruella, was on her usual sparkling form. She doesn't like me, and if there's any possibility she can land me in trouble with her boss, she'll give it her best shot. Today she was looking particularly striking, in a violet blouse that suited her pale skin and dark hair and matched exactly her strange-coloured eyes.

The body, I thought sadly, that's what Sandy was now. I'll never forget her eyes looking up at me, dead, robbed of all expression, of life. I stared across the table into Cruella's icy violets. 'I thought there was a chance she might still be alive. You can't tell from the film. It sounds like a vicious attack, but we couldn't be sure she was dead.'

Her little mouth twisted. 'It would have been better to wait for the professionals.'

The inspector shot her a look from beneath his heavy eyebrows but made no comment.

'Did any of you know the victim?' he asked.

'I knew her,' I said. 'She'd written about me in the newspaper. She was always asking questions about what I was up to.' I didn't add that I'd found her a complete pain in the arse. 'I didn't know her well, but if I saw her in town, we'd sometimes stop for a chat.'

The inspector sighed. 'I wonder what she was doing alone in those woods at that time of night.'

'I saw her up there once,' Olly said.

We all turned to look at him.

'When was this?' Elizabeth asked.

'One morning, couple of weeks back, must have been a Saturday, when I was getting the camera. It was early and she was out jogging.'

The inspector frowned. 'Jogging?'

Olly nodded. 'There's a track that goes through that bit of wood, goes round in a loop like, meets up with the road. I've seen people running on it before.'

'And you're sure it was her?'

'Oh yes. She was going really slowly, puffing and blowing. I remember thinking that she wasn't very fit.' He grinned and then looked around at us, stricken with guilt. 'Sorry.'

'No, that's very interesting, Olly. Sergeant,' he added to Cruella. 'Get some people up there to search that track. It's possible our victim went that way last night.'

'Sir.' She stood up and went outside, talking into her radio. As she did so, there was a tap on the back door and the burly figure of Detective Constable Dean Collins slipped into the room.

'Any sign of the murder weapon?' the inspector asked.

'No sir, but there's a lot of sawn logs lying about. The medical examiner thinks it's likely to have been one of those. And we've found a car abandoned about a mile up the back road, on the far side of the woods. It's unlocked, key still in the ignition. I ran a check and it's registered to the victim.'

'Well, at least we know how she got there. Forensics on it?'

'Yes sir, and her handbag was in the car. No phone, unfortunately. But there's a bill with her address on. It's possible she was on her way home. She doesn't live far from here.'

'Right. Then that's our next port of call.' The inspector rose heavily to his feet and held up the camera's memory card. 'I'm going to have to keep this, Olly,' he told him. 'And no more night-time filming in the wood for now, all right? It's a crime scene. The badgers will just have to get along without you.'

Olly nodded solemnly, still pale with shock.

'And no one is to know of the existence of this film.' His stern gaze swept us all. 'Absolutely no one must find out about this for the time being. It's our secret. D'you understand?'

We all nodded.

'D'you understand, Olly?' he repeated.

'I can keep a secret,' he responded.

I can vouch for that. Olly can keep a secret. He has a whacking great big one buried in his back garden, as a matter of fact.

'C'mon, Collins. Take statements, Sergeant,' he added as Cruella slipped back into the kitchen. Dean gave me a sly wink as he followed him out of the door. Cruella sat down at the table, favoured me with a thin smile and sharpened her pencil.

Dean Collins and I are friends. I'm godmother to his daughter, Alice. She's just over a year old and is soon to be blessed with a brother or sister. Dean's wife, Gemma, is a few weeks ahead of Kate in the pregnancy department, and I realised, as I laid eyes on her husband that morning, the birth must be imminent. All these babies. When I was in London, I'd managed to catch up with an old university friend of mine, Jade, who as well as enjoying a successful career as a financial analyst and marrying a property developer, already has two children, boys seven and five. What about me, she'd asked politely, wasn't it time I got on with it? Didn't I feel the old biological clock ticking away? Well, no, quite frankly. There's obviously something the matter with me. It's not that I don't like babies. How can you not like babies? I'm as happy to cuddle a baby as the next woman. But whenever I hand it back to its mother, I am not seized with the longing to possess one of my own. As I say, there's probably something wrong with me. Anyway, I didn't feel Dean's wink that morning had been appropriate in the circumstances, and so I told him on the phone, later that evening.

'You didn't phone me to tell me off about winking,' he answered in flat northern vowels. He was still at the police station; I could tell by the buzz going on in the background.

'No, of course not. I wanted to know how Gemma's coming along. It's not long now, is it?'

'She's fine thanks, but you didn't phone me about that, either.' He dropped his voice. 'You want to know if I can tell you anything about the murder of Sandy Thomas.'

How well he knows me. 'And can you?'

'You saw the film,' he said bluntly. 'We haven't got much more to go on. Forensics are going over the car and her body is with the pathologist. So, it's a waiting game at the moment, till we get the results.'

'Suspects?'

'Well, the bloke in the film seems likely, but we can't identify him at present.'

I ignored this attempt at sarcasm. I'd realised during the day just how little I knew about Sandy. I'd certainly no idea where she lived. She lived alone, Dean told me, in a rented cottage about a mile up the road from the place where her car was abandoned. 'Did she have any family?'

'One sister in Pontypridd. And she was divorced, no children. Her ex-husband's a local builder. He's coming to do the formal ID in the morning. And before you ask, he has an alibi for last night.'

'Collins!' a voice yelled in the distance.

'Look, I've got to go, Juno,' he said abruptly, and disconnected. Duty had called.

What was Sandy doing up in those woods? I kept thinking about what Olly had said, about Sandy jogging in the early mornings. It was difficult to imagine her in jogging clothes. She was always a bit overweight, perhaps she was trying to get fit, to shift some flab. But she wasn't there to jog that night. If Dean was right and she was on her way home, why stop in such a lonely spot? Why stop at all? But she had. She'd got out of her car, leaving the door open, the keys in the ignition. She'd got out in a hurry. Was her killer in the car with her? Had she fled into the wood, a place she knew because she jogged there, a place she thought she might hide, lose her attacker? She'd managed to escape him for a while, to run until she couldn't run any further. I remembered the terrified sobbing of her breath as she rested for a moment, minutes before she was killed, and I felt a shiver run through me, of horror, of pity and sadness. Poor Sandy.

Her ex-husband had an alibi. It seemed he was not

the man who had followed her through that wood and brutally battered her to death. But what about Alastair Dunston, the councillor she'd publicly insulted, thrown a drink over in front of his wife, the man who'd accused her of stalking him and his family, did he have an alibi for last night?

CHAPTER FOUR

I got through most of Monday without mishap. It's always a busy day for me and I often don't make it back to the shop until closing time. But I like to pop in, even if Sophie or Pat have already cashed up and gone home. There's always the vague hope I might have sold something, made some money. I hadn't, of course, except for a pound on the book exchange. We sell second-hand paperback fiction. If someone buys a book stamped with *Old Nick's* inside the cover, they can return it and buy their next book half price. It's beginning to become quite popular. It allows me to keep reselling the same books until they fall apart and has the added advantage of bringing people into the shop who might not otherwise come. Of course, it doesn't make much money, but it's better than nothing when there's precious little else rattling around in the till.

During my week in London, Marcia had asked the question I've been asked so many times by different people. Why, as I know so little about antiques, as I'd never wanted to own an antique shop in the first place, as it had been willed to me by Old Nick, apparently out of spite, as the place was doing nothing but costing me money, did I persist in hanging on to it? Why didn't I just sell it and have done? And the answer is that I still don't know. Because it's a challenge, because I've got something to prove to Old Nick, even though he's dead, or to his family, none of whom I'm ever likely to lay eyes on again? To myself? I have no idea. Perhaps I'm like Maisie. Just put it down to cussedness.

I decided I'd ring Dean Collins from the shop.

'Of course we're talking to Alastair Dunston,' he responded in answer to my question. 'And,' he added, knowing what my next question would be, 'he has the perfect alibi for that night. He was at a Rotary Club dinner with sixty people.'

'And were he and Sandy having an affair?'

'He says not. He says she was sent by her newspaper to cover a few council meetings and started coming on to him. He agreed to an interview about his new housing development, which took place over a drink, and that was all there was to it. He said that anything else was entirely in her head.'

'Do we believe him?' Whilst Sandy was a little overweight, she was blonde and attractive. It's true, I didn't know her well. She could be determined in following up a story, but as for becoming so obsessed with the damn man that she started stalking him, I couldn't see it somehow. She seemed too down to earth, too sensible. On the other hand, she had thrown a drink over him in a public place, which seemed to indicate a fairly intense level of emotional involvement.

'We're not just taking his word for it,' Dean went on, 'but trouble is . . .' he gave a deep sigh, 'we haven't found her phone. It's not in her bag or her car, or at her place of work. So far, we haven't turned it up at her cottage.'

'You think the killer took it?'

'Perhaps. It's possible she was just in the wrong place at the wrong time.'

'You mean, her murder was random? Her killer was a stranger?'

Dean sniffed. 'Some nutter.'

'You don't think he was in the car with her?'

'There's no evidence of that.'

'Then she must have stopped for him. In a wood, on a lonely road, at that time of night?'

'He could have tricked her into it, stood by the road, flagged her down, pretended there was some emergency.'

'I don't think many women would stop in those circumstances.'

He chuckled down the phone. 'I bet you would.'

I ignored this because it was true. 'But she might have stopped if she knew him.'

'There were skid marks on the road, as if her car had come to a sudden stop, as if she'd had to brake suddenly. There's also a second set of marks going across the road at right angles to it.'

'Another car blocking her way?'

'Looks like it. Unfortunately, the tyre marks aren't clear enough to give us the make of vehicle.' Dean sighed. 'We've been trying to spot her car on camera, but so far, no success. Trouble is, there's too many little back roads and lanes round here, too many ways you can cut through. It's like a labyrinth. And none of these minor roads have got any CCTV on 'em.'

I should hope not, I added silently, although in this case, I could see one would have been useful. Poor Sandy, I couldn't help wondering what she'd already been through before she wandered within range of Olly's camera.

Dean seemed to read my thoughts. 'She wasn't raped. Sex doesn't appear to have been a motive for her murder. And it's clear from the film that, whoever her killer was, he's not the right height or build for Dunston.'

'He could have ordered a hitman.'

Dean made a derisive noise, perilously close to a snort. 'Let's not stray too far into fantasy, eh? Alastair Dunston is just a local councillor, not some high-up politician with too much to lose.'

'What about the ex-husband? You said he's got an alibi.'

'Yeh, though it doesn't entirely put him in the clear. He was in The Bay Horse till eleven, he says, drinking with mates. Well, that bit checks out. But one of these mates got so drunk that Thomas and another friend had to help him get home, walked him back to his place. This took them till about eleven fifteen. But then the other friend left. Now we know from the film that Sandy was killed 12.09. According to Thomas, he stayed with his drunken mate until gone one o'clock. The problem is, this mate was too drunk to remember anything about the night before, doesn't even remember leaving the pub, let alone anything after that.'

'So, it would've been possible for Thomas to have slipped up the hill and murdered Sandy.'

'Yeh, just one problem,' Dean interrupted. 'The bloke in the film isn't him either. You can tell by looking. Phil Thomas is just a whippersnapper of a bloke. And neither he nor Dunston take the same size shoes as the killer. He left footprints in the mud.'

'And that's all we've got to go on?'

'So far. And I hope I need hardly remind you,' he added, a little self-righteously, 'that this conversation never took place.'

'Of course not, Detective Constable Collins,' I assured him. 'Mum's the word.'

I didn't go straight home as it turned out. After I'd locked up the shop, I nipped down to the Co-op to get something for supper. As I came out with my bag of shopping, a dog started barking across the street, a whippet, silver-grey, tied up outside the Spar opposite. It was Lottie, Daniel's dog. She was barking for my attention, her tail lashing from side to side. Constrained by her lead from rushing towards me, she was dancing up and down on her tippy-toes, her whole body quivering in welcome.

'Oh, Lottie,' I whispered sadly. She'd belonged to

Daniel's dead wife, Claire, but had adored me from our first meeting. The feeling was mutual. I wanted to run across the street, crouch down and give her a big hug. But I couldn't because coming out of the shop was the tall, dark-haired figure of Daniel Thorncroft, the man who had ripped a chunk out of my heart.

He didn't see me. 'What are you making such a fuss about?' he asked as he stooped to release her. The warmth, the laughter in his voice was like a punch in my chest. 'Keep still, you silly creature, I'm trying to untie you.'

I stepped back into the shop and watched as he disentangled Lottie's lead and strode up North Street. He had a long stride. He turned to cross over King's Bridge, seemingly oblivious of Lottie's reluctance to keep to heel. She kept looking back, staring longingly in my direction. For a moment he frowned, but he couldn't see me, hiding inside the shop doorway. He gave her a gentle tug as they turned the corner and disappeared.

I hurried back the way I had come, to the nearest place of refuge, *Old Nick's*. After I'd fumbled my way through unlocking the door, I collapsed on a chair inside, letting my bag of shopping drop, the tins rolling out across the floor. I hadn't seen Daniel since the day he had slammed the door on our relationship. I really thought that I had pulled myself together. But one glimpse of his hawkish profile, the sound of his voice, had reduced me to tatters. I let tears roll down my face unchecked, tears of longing but also of rage, of impotent fury, not just at him but at my own weakness, my own stupid reactions. How dare the bloody man do this to me? I don't know how long I sat there but the chimes of St Andrew's Church, striking the hour, brought me to my senses.

I smeared hot tears across my cheeks, got up, sniffing, and went up to the bathroom. The mirror over the sink showed me a woebegone face and drowned lashes, my flushed cheeks clashing horribly with the riot of red hair. I couldn't show anyone a face like that. I set the cold tap running and bathed my eyes repeatedly. Then I went up to the kitchen and put the kettle on whilst I cooled down. I could really have done with something stronger than tea but there wasn't any alternative.

'You're going to have to do better than this,' I told myself severely. Daniel had accused me of needlessly endangering my life. This was unfair, I don't intentionally meddle in murder investigations, I just seem to get sucked in. In frustration I abandoned the tea and threw it down the sink. Perhaps I've been stupid in the past, I reflected as I plodded down the stairs, got needlessly involved, but I had learnt my lesson. I retrieved a can of sweetcorn that had rolled across the floor under Sophie's worktable and returned it to my shopping bag. I was horrified and saddened by the murder of Sandy Thomas, but it wasn't my job to find her killer. I didn't have anything to go on, anyway. But whatever happened, I was not going to fall apart when I next laid eyes on Daniel Thorncroft. 'Go up and punch him,' I told myself as I set off down Shadow Lane. That was a much better idea.

CHAPTER FIVE

Next morning, after I'd walked the dogs, I had Maisie's shopping to see to, so it wasn't until the afternoon that I was able to put into action my plan to visit a certain shop in the nearby town of Moretonhampstead. I have decided that if the customers won't come to me, I shall have to go to them. *Tigerlily,* the establishment to which I drove my little Van Blanc, had recently opened, standing in the middle of a row of shops, handily near to a tea room. I'd noticed it on my last visit to the town, pausing for a look in the window. It's a pretty shop, filled with painted and stencilled furniture: old chests of drawers, dressers, dressing tables and the like, painted with flowery swags, birds and butterflies by the shop's enthusiastic young owner. But the shop still looked unfinished to my eye, needed dressing up. And as I told the slightly sceptical Hester as she stopped sanding down an old sideboard to attend to me, the pretty dressing-table set, cut-glass scent bottles and powder bowls that I unwrapped from my basket, not to mention the enamel-backed hand mirror, compact and hairbrush, would decorate the surfaces and would certainly appeal to those customers who liked her furniture. She thoughtfully spread open a white lace fan I had brought as she considered, and we came down to the question of *how much*.

'Fact is,' she told me bluntly, 'I don't have a lot of cash.'

Fact is, I could have told her, neither do I. But I didn't want to lug the stuff back home again, so after a bout of genteel haggling, we settled on a price that suited us both and I came away well pleased with the afternoon's venture, the slightly guilty feeling of having stolen sweets from a toddler ameliorated by a glimpse of the price tag on a chest of drawers.

When I'd set out it had been a fine day, the high blue sky clotted here and there with big dollops of mashed-potato cloud. But as I headed home, not taking the most direct or straightforward route but the one which appealed to me most that afternoon, it seemed the clouds had massed together, sunk low towards the horizon and turned an ominous grey. I passed Beetor Cross, a weathered granite monument that stands by the roadside and marked the ancient trackway before the road was built. It disappeared in the nineteenth century, to be discovered some years later, doing duty as a gatepost. This happened quite a lot back then, reverence for ancient standing stones and archaeological artefacts not being what it is today, the missing stones from a Bronze

Age hut circle recently found built into the wall of a Victorian pigsty.

Just beyond the cross I came to a junction called The Watching Place. You can take your pick from the stories about how it got its name. The signpost points to Postbridge in one direction, Chagford in the other, and down Long Lane to the lovely village of Manaton. According to local folklore, the spot was either the site of a gallows, or the place where highwaymen watched for the approach of travellers, or the site of a plague-stricken house. I headed for Postbridge, from where I could meander my way to Ashburton.

It pleased me to take my time, trundling along in my little Van Blanc. The moor opened up on either side of the road, the low, windswept grasses fading to bronze, bracken fronds turning crispy with rust, the twisted thorn trees crouched ready for autumn storms that were yet to buffet them. It took my mind off other things. Like Sandy Thomas and Daniel.

Suddenly I stamped on the brake, the van screeching to a halt on the gritty verge, and I turned my head to make sure I'd seen what I thought I'd seen. Sure enough, just a few yards off the road, two men were putting a dog up into a tree. It was hanging by its jaws from a branch too high up for it to have reached on its own, its body dangling several feet in the air. As I slammed the door of the van, I heard it making an unearthly noise, the closest thing I've heard to a dog yodelling.

'What are you doing to that dog?' I yelled, marching towards them across the grass.

The two men turned to look at me, both young, barely more than boys. They could have been brothers, their fair hair almost white. They were cocky with it. 'It's a game.' The taller of the two gave me a knowing smile. 'He loves it.'

'Doesn't look like it to me.'

He reached up and supported the dog's body from underneath, allowing it to let go of the branch and drop down to earth. It was a sturdy Staffordshire bull terrier type with a blunt muzzle and broad chest. As it landed on the ground it bounced excitedly around the two boys, barking.

'See?' the boy grinned as the dog leapt around him. 'He loves it. He wants to get back up.' He seemed anxious to reassure me. The other boy stared at me in silence, his dark eyes hostile.

Sure enough, the dog kept jumping up in a futile attempt to reach the branch above its head, and when the boys lifted it a second time, gripped it in his jaws and shook the branch with ferocious glee, a shower of twigs and leaves raining down.

I stood and watched for several minutes. Each time the boys lifted the dog down from the branch, it was raring to get back up there again. It seemed deeply wrong to me, but there didn't seem to be any cruelty involved, other than to the tree. After a while, the boys got fed up of my watching and took the dog off for a walk across the moor, turning round once to see if I was still there.

I drove home but I wasn't happy. Once they've got a grip of something, bull terriers are bred to hang on. Pat has a Staffordshire, Samdog, and there's nothing he loves more than a game of tug-of-war. It seemed what the boys were doing was just a variation on the same game. The dog wasn't hurt, or being bullied. He seemed to love it and yet I still felt troubled.

When I got back to the shop, I phoned the RSPCA and reported what I'd seen. I thought they might not take me seriously, but the man on the phone was keen to hear the details. 'For the dog, it is just a game,' he agreed, 'and he probably was enjoying it. But it's a game that's used in training dogs to fight and that's illegal.'

'You mean training dogs to fight each other?' I asked in horror.

'There's a lot of it goes on, I'm afraid. Big money involved.'

How could I have been so stupid as not to realise what was going on? 'I should have put a stop to it,' I said bitterly.

'I doubt there's much you could have done. You've already done the best thing, by reporting it to us.'

'But if I'd phoned you straight away . . .'

'They would have scarpered before we got there. But if you should ever come across anything like it again, phone us, or the police. Like I say, dogfighting is against the law. It's a cruel practice and it needs stamping out.'

Too right it does. I told Pat about it as I closed up the shop. She listened, her mouth gaping in horror, her knitting needles shocked into stillness. 'There's some evil buggers about,' she scowled, shaking her head. 'Cockfighting, that's what used to go on here in

Ashburton, and bull-baiting, years ago. They were a bloodthirsty lot, back in them days.'

'Still are, it seems.' I couldn't stop thinking about that poor dog and what might happen to him.

'Here, I didn't tell you,' Pat said, brightening up as she thrust her knitting needles through her ball of wool and put her knitting away. 'We got a new helper up the farm. Nice lad. Eduardo his name is. He comes from Spain.'

'How did you get hold of him?' I didn't think that Pat's sister and brother-in-law could afford to employ anyone, much as they needed the help.

'We don't have to pay him nothing. He works for bed and board, see, 'cos he wants to learn about working with animals. It's all part of a scheme on the Internet. You have to advertise yourself on this website, and that puts you in touch with people who want to come and work for you. Sue set it all up. You have, like, online interviews.'

'What's it called, this scheme?'

'Work Around the World, or something like that. Lots of foreign students do it. Most of 'em just want a working holiday. Eduardo wants to improve his English, he says, although he speaks it pretty good already. We got another boy coming next week, an' all.' She frowned. 'He's coming from Slovenia or somewhere like that.'

'Have you got room for two of them?' The original Honeysuckle Farm had been pulled down years ago, the spacious eighteenth-century farmhouse replaced by a hideous and not-so-spacious bungalow.

'Oh, Eduardo's sleeping in our old caravan up the end of the field. He's got everything he needs. He comes down to us for meals or when he wants a bit of company. The new lad will be sharing with him.' She grinned. 'Let's hope they get along.'

'Sounds as if they'll have to. Anyway, you get off home, Pat. I'll lock up.'

'Okay.' She slipped a turquoise jacket on over her orange striped jumper and plum-coloured trousers. For someone who combines colours so beautifully when she knits or makes jewellery, she has a blind spot about her own wardrobe.

'That is a ghastly combination,' I told her frankly.

She laughed. 'Well, it's only me, isn't it?' She turned to go and then almost spun around on her heels as she remembered something. 'Oooh, I forgot! Some bloke phoned for you from the *Dartmoor Gazette*. I wrote his name and number down. It's on the counter there.'

My heart sank. This could only be about Sandy Thomas. Why else would anyone from the *Gazette* want to talk to me? The police had kept my name out of it, announcing that her body had been found by a member of the public but not specifying who. Olly's involvement and the existence of the film footage had also been kept secret. I knew he and Elizabeth would never have said anything, so how had the information leaked? Unless it was someone within the police, and that seemed unlikely. Well, I wasn't going to phone him back and if he contacted me again, I'd deny all knowledge.

But as I was locking the shop door a few minutes

later, someone called my name. I looked up to see a man walking towards me down Shadow Lane. I didn't know him. He looked about fifty, thin and slightly stooping, with floppy grey hair. He wore jeans and a leather jacket. He smiled. 'It is Juno Browne, isn't it?'

'It is,' I answered guardedly. I was sure we hadn't met.

'Guy Mitchell,' he introduced himself. 'I phoned earlier, left a message with one of your colleagues. Could I have a word?'

'You're from the *Dartmoor Gazette*.' I recognised the name now. He didn't just work for the newspaper. He was its editor.

'Most people call me Mitch.' He extended a friendly hand.

I didn't take it. 'Look, I've got nothing to say.'

He frowned. 'You don't know what I want to talk about yet.'

'This is about Sandy, presumably?' I sighed. 'Look, I don't know anything about her death.'

He seemed puzzled. 'Well, no, why would you?' Either he knew nothing about my discovery of her body or he was making a good job of pretending that he didn't. He scratched his head. 'Look, Miss Browne, I just want a few minutes of your time. We want . . . all of us at the *Gazette* . . . we want to find out what happened to Sandy. It's nothing to do with anything I'm planning to print, I promise you.'

I hesitated. I'm not sure I believe in reporters' promises. 'Okay,' I agreed reluctantly, 'but it'll cost you a pint.'

* * *

56

Actually, it cost him a glass of Chardonnay. The Old Exeter Inn on West Street can lay claim to being one of the oldest pubs in the country, a tavern having stood on its site since the twelfth century. It's a place of low ceilings and small, oak-panelled rooms, dim little corners for dining, which a canny management lights atmospherically with candles. Sir Walter Raleigh got arrested here and sent to the Tower and it's not difficult to imagine that in some shadowy corner he might still be hanging about. Sweep aside a curtain just off the bottom of the stairs, and you find yourself in a small room of dark oak panelling known as The Confessional. It's within easy reach of the bar, but a great place for a chat when you don't want to be disturbed.

'I'm really sorry about Sandy,' I said.

Mitch placed a glass of wine on the table in front of me. 'We're all devastated at the paper.'

He sounded genuinely upset. I realised it must be difficult for him. Sandy's murder was major news but, so far, the newspaper's coverage of her death had been very restrained. Sandy was a colleague, presumably a friend. They were treating her death with respect.

He smiled sadly. 'Poor Sandy. She could be a bit of a handful at times, but I had a lot of time for her, as a matter of fact. When she first came to the newspaper, we put her in charge of the small ads. She had no journalistic training, I don't really think she'd had much of an education, but she was determined, you know, to break into the journalistic side. She was putting herself through an Open University course. And I could see she had a nose for a story. So, I'd give her the odd little thing, now and again. And she was coming along all right.'

'Was she working on a story when she died?' I asked.

He shook his head. 'After that business with Alastair Dunston, I confined her to the office for a bit. We're a small, independent newspaper and I could do without her getting us sued.'

'Do you know if she and Dunston were involved?'

He shrugged. 'The police asked the same thing, but the truth is, if they were, then none of us at the *Gazette* knew anything about it. And Sandy wasn't exactly what you'd call discreet.'

I took a sip of wine. There was a tapestry hanging on the oak panelling opposite me, depicting Sir Walter laying down his cloak for Queen Elizabeth. It was pretty hideous but there was a lot of work in it. I wondered how much Guy Mitchell really knew. 'Aren't the police getting anywhere?' I asked, trying to sound casual. I already knew from Dean they didn't have much to go on.

'They came into the office and searched her desk, took away her laptop. Her phone is missing, they couldn't find that.' He paused and shot me a sharp look. 'After the police had gone, we found this.' He pulled a notebook from his pocket and laid it on the table. 'At least, Evie found it, she shared a desk with Sandy.'

I stared at a dog-eared, spiral-bound notepad, its tatty red cover doodled on in biro. 'Is this Sandy's notebook?'

'Evie had borrowed it to scribble a phone number on and forgot she still had it.'

'Shouldn't you give it to the police?'

'Oh, I intend to,' he assured me. 'But first I wanted to ask you if you could throw any light on this.' He flipped open the pad at a page and slid it towards me. 'See, that's the phone number Evie took down. That's her writing there. She says she took that call on the Friday morning, the day before Sandy was murdered.' He flipped back a page and pointed with a forefinger. 'So, this must have been written before then. This is Sandy's writing.'

I stared. A message was written on the page in thick pencil and ringed around heavily for emphasis: *Ask Juno Browne.*

'Well, did she?' Mitch asked. 'Did she ask you?'

I frowned, completely at a loss. 'Ask me *what*?'

'I was hoping you could tell me.'

'No. She didn't ask me anything. I haven't spoken to her since before I went to London. I've been away for ten days. The only time I've seen her since is when I spotted her walking down Sun Street, but we didn't speak. She was in a hurry. I don't even think she saw me.' I stared for a moment at her handwriting, the heavy, emphatic rings around my name. 'If Sandy wanted to ask me something, I've no idea what it was.'

Mitch sighed. 'Pity.'

'You were hoping it might be a clue to her murder.'

He nodded. 'It's probably nothing, of course.'

'How old is this writing anyway? Couldn't it have been written months ago?'

He pointed to some telephone numbers written above my name. 'These are all connected with a story that went out in the previous week's issue. She wrote your name afterwards.'

Someone in the corridor outside spoke suddenly. 'Let's see if there's a table free in here,' and the heavy curtain at the doorway was flung back.

Detective Sergeant Christine deVille had been smiling at whoever she was with, but at the sight of me her expression froze, to be replaced by one of deep suspicion, her dark brows snapping together, her small mouth tightening. I could see what it looked like. Ashburton's amateur sleuth, who had information about Sandy Thomas's murder that the police wanted to keep secret, locked in private conversation with the editor of the local newspaper: it didn't look good.

'Excuse me, just a moment,' she said to someone over her shoulder, and then to me, 'Miss Browne, could I have a word with you?'

I followed her into the hall, and then through a door into the privacy of the ladies' loo.

'If you've been talking to Guy Mitchell about the case . . .' she began in a fierce whisper.

'Of course I haven't,' I responded, 'He doesn't know that I know anything about it.'

Her dark eyebrows disappeared into her fringe. 'So, you just happened to bump into each other?' she asked scathingly.

'No.' I explained what Mitch had told me about finding Sandy's notebook. And about my name being scribbled in it. 'But I don't know what she wanted to ask me; she never got the chance.'

Cruella chewed this over for a few moments, her little mouth working like a furious rodent whilst she glared. 'If you have breathed one word about this investigation . . .'

I held up my hands in surrender. 'I haven't, I swear.'

She slammed her way out of the ladies without further comment. I caught up with her in The Confessional where she was staring at the relevant page on the notepad. Mitch looked at me and shrugged. 'I'm taking this,' she informed him, 'it's evidence.'

I cursed inwardly. I wanted to take a closer look at that notebook, at those names and numbers, and now I'd lost my chance.

'You should have handed it in to us as soon as you found it,' she told him.

'I was on my way to the station,' Mitch responded mildly.

Cruella glowered again for good measure, and exited through the curtain like the wicked witch in a pantomime.

Mitch laughed. 'She's a charmer, isn't she?'

'She has her moments.' I didn't see who she'd come in with, but whoever it was, she was now explaining in a fierce whisper that there had been a change of plan. If they'd been intending to spend a cosy evening having a drink, it seemed that the discovery of the notebook had ruined all that. I'd have felt sorry for her if I could have got over the desire to wrap my fingers around her throat and throttle her; if she hadn't been the person who'd filled Daniel in on so many little details about things I'd been up to, things that I'd tried to keep secret.

In other circumstances I might have stuck my head

around that curtain to get a sly look at her companion, but right now I was far more interested in Sandy, in what it was she wanted to ask me. If she wanted to talk to me, why hadn't she tried to get in touch? I must ask Pat and Sophie if she'd come into the shop whilst I was away, or if she'd left any phone messages that they'd forgotten to tell me about.

I took another sip of wine. 'Did you know Sandy's husband?'

He shook his head. 'They'd separated before she came to work at the *Gazette*. I got the impression their parting was amicable enough.'

'No motive there, then?'

He gave a bitter smile. 'Not that I know of. We've all been racking our brains, trying to think if there was anything she could have been working on that could have got her into trouble but, like I said, I'd confined her to barracks.'

'What about Alastair Dunston? You say you don't think they were having an affair, but there must have been some reason she ended up throwing drink over him.'

He shook his head. 'She was supposed to be reporting on what was said at the meetings about this new development he's building at Woodland.'

'Yet he accused her of stalking him, of going to his house.'

'If she did, I don't know why.'

'There's been some controversy about this development, hasn't there?'

He smiled. 'Just a bit. For a start, the old girl who owned the land it's being built on left it in trust for nature conservation. Her son managed to contest that, get a ruling overturned. Then he sells the land to Dunston to build houses on.' He stopped to sip his pint, shaking his head in amusement. He gave me a questioning look. 'You know that every county council has to build so many new homes each year? There's a government quota it has to fulfil.'

I nodded.

'Did you know that Devon has already exceeded its annual quota?'

'It doesn't need any more houses?'

'It needs *affordable* houses, but that's something different.' He shot me a sideways glance. 'There's a public meeting with Dunston about the development in Woodland on Thursday of this week. It could be interesting.'

I couldn't get to sleep that night. What was it that Sandy had wanted to ask me? I hadn't spoken to her in weeks. What did she want to know? I tried to recall every conversation we'd ever had but I couldn't come up with anything remotely likely. But whatever it was, I told myself in an attempt to think rationally, there was no reason to suppose it had anything to do with her death. Yet she'd pencilled heavy dark rings around my name. *Ask Juno Browne.* If Sandy had been able to ask me what she wanted, if I'd been able to answer her, perhaps she might not now be lying in the cold, dark confines of a mortuary drawer. That heavily pencilled message was likely to haunt me to my grave.

I turned over, punched the pillow a few times and closed my eyes. Bill, asleep on the duvet, didn't stir. My own sleep had been elusive since I'd caught sight of Daniel. *I'm sorry, Miss Browne with an 'e'*, those had been his last words to me. *Miss Browne with an 'e'*, it used to drive me mad when he first started calling me that. I found it really irritating. He almost never called me Juno, always Miss Browne or simply Miss B. I'd love to hear him call me that now.

CHAPTER SIX

I was out shopping for Maisie next morning when the rain started, a sudden, violent shower that drove everyone scurrying for the nearest shelter. I ducked into Sunflowers and blagged a free cup of coffee from Adam. He was standing in the window, bearded and burly like an out-of-sorts pirate, his arms folded, glumly watching the rain slanting down in needles and bouncing up off the cobbled street. There were no customers in the cafe at that moment so he was happy to oblige. We talked about Kate and her pregnancy. I don't seem to get much chance to chat to him these days, even though we live in the same house.

Coffee arrived as a couple rushed in from outside, sheltering from the downpour, breathless and laughing, their hair flattened by the rain. Across the street a leaf-clogged drain had filled up and a large puddle was beginning to form. Adam got up to see what the couple wanted, and I sipped my coffee in silence, watching the leaves floating on the surface of the puddle and waiting for the rain to stop. I made my escape when the sun came out briefly, but it started again with a vengeance as I lugged the shopping back to Maisie's and I was sopping wet by the time I reached the door of Brook Cottage. I stopped in the porch, shaking the rain from my hair, slipping out of my wet shoes, and squelching into her kitchen in soggy socks.

'You look a right mess,' she informed me frankly, glancing up from the paper she was reading.

'I wasn't dressed for the weather,' I admitted.

'You'd better towel that lot off,' she added, nodding towards my dripping curls.

'Thanks.' I grabbed a towel hanging from a hook on the back door and rubbed my head vigorously whilst Jacko, Maisie's terrier, carried out an in-depth inspection of my wet socks.

'I just been reading about that reporter woman getting murdered,' Maisie told me, shaking her head. 'S'dreadful!'

'It is.' I agreed. 'Poor Sandy.' I cut short rubbing with the towel, it smelt suspiciously of Jacko, and hung it back on its hook on the door.

Maisie scowled. 'Did you know her, then?'

'Not really.' I didn't want to say too much, knowing anything I did say was likely to be held in evidence against me at the next church coffee morning. I began to unpack her shopping.

'It said in here last week,' she went on, pointing at the paper, 'that she threw a drink in that Dunston fella's face.' She was sucking a throat sweet. Apart from the slight aroma of eucalyptus, I could hear it clacking against her dentures as she spoke. She gave a cackle of laughter. 'I'd like to have seen that.'

I turned to look at her, a bottle of lemon squash in my hand. 'Why?' I asked, shutting it in a cupboard. 'Don't you like him?'

'On the council, isn't he?' she responded, as if that explained her antipathy. 'Feathering his own nest,' she added in disgust. 'They all are, that lot.'

I gathered they weren't the lot she'd voted for. I put her cheese away in the fridge. 'I'm afraid I haven't been paying them much attention.'

'He came to our church meeting once, him and his stuck-up wife, smarming up to people,' she continued in a spirit of Christian charity, 'but he don't cut no ice with me.'

Very few people cut ice with Maisie. 'Cheap as chips,' she snorted.

'Is he from a local family, d'you know?'

She shook her head. I could see through her thin curls to her scalp. Extreme old age or years and years of too much perming lotion, I wondered?

'I don't know where the Dunstons come from. They was living round Plymouth way one time. I know they made all their money out of quarrying. Back in his dad's day, that would have been.'

'Well, he seems to be doing all right now. Alastair

Dunston's a property developer. He's behind that new development in Woodland.'

'Woodland!' Maisie gave a derisive snort. 'What's the point of building houses there? Middle of nowhere. They ain't got no shops.'

'It's only a mile or two up the road. They can shop in Ashburton, or Newton, if they need to. Besides, so many people get their shopping delivered these days, being in the middle of nowhere doesn't matter so much.' I know people need somewhere to live, but the depressing fact was that major development on the edge of Newton Abbot meant it was creeping closer to Ashburton all the time. If more development was allowed at Woodland, it wouldn't be many years before we were all joined up.

'There used to be a nice old pub at Woodland,' Maisie remembered, 'but it closed down.'

'Opened up again, now,' I told her. 'New owners. In fact, it's a very nice restaurant. Talking of food, what d'you want for your lunch?'

'I'm not hungry.'

'You've got to have something.'

'All right,' she sighed, as if doing me an immense favour, 'I'll have a ham sandwich.'

'Great.' My culinary skills don't extend far but I can manage a sandwich. 'Have you given any more thought to having those ready meals delivered?' I asked as I began buttering bread. 'Janet left you the brochure, have you looked at it?'

'Not really. I don't fancy it.'

I picked up the brochure and thrust it under her

nose. 'Have a look. Pick out a few things you like the look of. We've only got to ring up and order and they'll deliver. I'll phone them, if you like. You ought to give them a try.' Maisie tutted and began leafing through the pages. She paused over a photograph of a suet pudding and custard. 'That looks nice,' I said encouragingly, although the custard was so yellow that I suspected the photographer had poured paint in it. 'And what about that chicken casserole?'

'All right, I'll give it a go,' she agreed grudgingly. 'It'll shut you and Our Janet up at any rate.'

When I got back to *Old Nick's*, Pat was telling Sophie all about the new arrival from the Work Around the World scheme, who'd turned up unexpectedly ahead of schedule the night before. 'His name's Dalek. Would you believe it? Dalek is a proper boy's name in Slovakia.'

'He can manage the stairs, then?'

'We haven't got any stairs,' Pat frowned, my joke going completely over her head, 'he's sharing the caravan with Eduardo.'

Sophie stifled a giggle.

'He seems a very nice lad,' she went on, 'although he don't speak much English. Not like Eduardo.'

'Well, he can only get better. By the way, whilst I was in London, Sandy Thomas didn't come in, did she, asking to speak to me?' I didn't think it was likely. If she had, and they'd forgotten it, I was sure the fact of her being brutally murdered would have brought it back to mind.

Pat shook her head solemnly but Sophie frowned

for a moment, pushing her specs up the bridge of her nose. 'No,' she said, as the bell on the shop door jangled. 'Definitely not.'

It took me a moment to recognise the Wicked Witch of the West. I always think of her in a pointy hat with her face painted green, as she was when I first met her at a fancy-dress party. The slightly ruddy complexion of the imposing woman standing in the doorway, dressed in a tweed cape and felt hat, took me a second or two to process, by which time, Lady Margaret Westershall had already swept into the shop and stood before me at the counter, a ponderous white bulldog padding in her wake.

'Juno, I need your help,' she declared, 'the police are absolutely useless.' She looked tearful, which was not like Lady Margaret who generally has little time for sentiment.

'What's the matter?' I asked, grabbing her a chair.

'It's Florence.' She sat down heavily with something like a sob. 'She's been kidnapped.'

CHAPTER SEVEN

Florence was Lady Margaret's bulldog. Sophie had painted her portrait, a proud mum with her three puppies. Wesley, the white one currently flopped on the floor in the shop, panting, was the only puppy Margaret had kept.

'She just disappeared,' she told us as we gathered around. 'One minute she was out in the front garden and the next she was gone. The police keep asking me if I'm sure she hasn't just run off, but Florence wouldn't run off. She likes her home comforts too much. Someone's taken her. I know they have!' She snapped open the clasp of an ancient crocodile handbag, flipped out a tiny handkerchief and forcefully blew her nose.

'Would she go off with someone?' I asked. 'Willingly, I mean?'

She shook her head. 'She's friendly with strangers but

she wouldn't let anyone take her away. She's not like Wesley.' She glanced down at the dog sitting by her feet and grunted. 'He's anyone's for a sausage.'

The mention of sausage made him look up optimistically. Wesley was cute; although out of puppyhood, he was still young enough to look appealing. He hadn't yet developed that adult bulldog look of having been hit in the face with a shovel. 'Have the police done anything?'

'They sent a young man to see me, a Specialist Dog Theft Officer.' She rolled her eyes in exasperation as she pronounced the title. 'Now that dog theft is officially a crime, they've appointed someone to deal with it. But they've only one officer to cover the whole of the area, and he looks about fifteen. He was a nice boy but . . .' she broke off, flapping a hand dismissively. 'He poked about the front garden for a bit. He told me I shouldn't have left her alone in the front garden. Her own garden! He told me to fit a bell on the front gate so that I know when anyone's coming in. Well, I will, of course but . . . he kept asking if Florence had been microchipped.' She shook her head impatiently. 'Well, of course she has! Then he put me on to the dog rescue group – they're a group of volunteers – who asked exactly the same thing. Make sure the microchip paperwork is up to date, they said, so that I can prove she's mine.' She sniffed into the handkerchief. 'Well, I can prove she's mine, all right, but first I have to find her! I've posted flyers all over the place. The whole village is on the lookout for her. I'm offering a reward,' she added defiantly. 'I know the police warned me not to, but I don't care. I'll do anything to get her back. I've sent her details to the council dog warden and the local animal shelters. The dog rescue group have put her photograph on their lost dog website. They say they're going to advertise on all their social media platforms. But do you know what they told me? On average, forty-five dogs are stolen every week . . .' she paused, her chin trembling, 'and only twenty per cent are ever reunited with their owners. She's been gone four days now,' she said, dissolving into tears. 'Wesley misses her. I miss her . . .'

Pat slid out of her chair, mouthing quietly that she would make a cup of tea and slipped upstairs to the kitchen.

'I'm sure she'll turn up.' Sophie's attempt at comfort lacked conviction and Lady Margaret shook her head, sobbing.

'D'you know what my worst fear is?' she asked, wiping her eyes. 'I'm afraid poor Florrie will end up on one of these dreadful puppy farms, that someone will try to breed from her. Bulldog mums must always have a vet in attendance when they're giving birth, you know, because their hips are so narrow, and the puppies' heads are so big. And if they don't have someone there who *knows* . . . they can die.'

Sophie patted her arm ineffectually. Wesley who had been observing her distress with a frown that looked like mounting concern, began licking her hand, which seemed to have a more soothing effect. 'Oh dear, I am sorry!' She smiled weakly as she smoothed his head. 'You girls must think I'm such an old fool!'

'Not at all.' Dog theft was a heartless crime. I could imagine how broken-hearted I'd be if any of the Tribe went missing. I'd be out of my mind with worry. 'Was Wesley in the garden when Florence disappeared?'

'No.' She gazed down at him with a mixture of fondness and exasperation. 'He was snoring his head off in the conservatory. But I haven't left him on his own since, not at home or in the car. I won't take the risk. He comes with me everywhere.'

'How much does a bulldog cost?' I asked.

'A boy puppy will set you back about two thousand.'

Sophie's eyes rounded with shock. 'Two thousand!' she echoed.

Lady Margaret shrugged. 'More for a girl, of course. Three thousand easily.'

'No wonder they're a target for thieves.'

Pat chose this moment to come in with the tea. 'It's disgusting,' she declared, handing the mugs round. 'Can't flipping give 'em away at the rescue centres.'

Sophie frowned. 'What, bulldogs?'

'No, dogs in general. Nor cats. I mean, if somebody wants a dog, why can't they get one from a rescue . . . ?'

I thought I'd better cut in before she started on her well-rehearsed rant about how fancy dog-breeders were responsible for the crisis with homeless dogs. It wouldn't go down well with Lady Margaret at the moment, who was in enough of a state as it was.

'What would you like me to do?'

'I've got photos of Florence from when I painted her portrait,' Sophie volunteered quickly.

'I'll post them on Facebook.'

'Thank you, my dear.' Lady Margaret smiled. 'If you could just come around and have a look, Juno,' she added, turning to me, 'at the scene of the crime, as it were, that would be a start. You're so clever with these things.'

'I don't know about that,' I responded doubtfully. I looked at my watch. It was a bit late in the day for looking at anything. 'I'll come first thing in the morning, after I've walked the Tribe.'

This and the reviving effect of a cup of tea seemed to cheer her up. She patted my arm as she stood up to leave. 'I knew that I could rely on you. I knew when I first met you that you were a good 'un.'

I don't know about that either. I don't imagine Ricky will think I'm a good 'un when I phone him later to tell him I won't be coming to help pack costumes tomorrow morning, after all.

The village of Lustleigh, where Lady Margaret has lived for the past sixty years, has to be one of the loveliest in Devon. I parked outside of The Cleave, the old pub that rubs shoulders with the ancient church of St John, opposite the thatched Primrose Tea Room, its walls painted to match its name, and a gallery selling local arts and crafts. There's only one other shop in the village, for food and other essentials, which also acts as post office, and that, apart from a Saxon cross standing on the little green, would appear to be that. Unless you know differently. I followed the little path across the green, past the tiny Gospel Hall and around a secretive little corner to a shallow brook, where rushing water echoes as it passes beneath a stone railway bridge, one of the few remnants of the line which, before Mr Beeching got at it, brought a dozen trains a day through Lustleigh.

The path carries on between fine detached houses on one side and a glorious cricket ground on the other, a long, open field edged by mature trees. It's easy to imagine players in traditional white, hear the thwack of leather on willow during lazy, sunny afternoons. Further along the path stands Wreyland Manor, a medieval building with a stone arch fronting its overhanging porch, its solid white walls pierced by mullioned windows and shaded by a deep thatch.

But I wasn't going as far as the manor that morning. I stopped by the cricket ground outside a large Victorian house set back from the path on a high bank, its garden sloping down to a little wooden gate that bore the legend, Cleave View. This was Lady Margaret's place.

She must have been keeping watch for me, for no sooner had I laid a hand on the gate than the front door opened and Wesley pounded down the path with that jaunty rolling gait that bulldogs have, and Lady Margaret was waving and hallooing from the doorstep. She was dressed in an old tweed skirt and sweater. On her ample bosom bounced a rope of chunky beads in butterscotch amber that I'd have cheerfully killed for.

'So good of you to come!' she cried when Wesley's rapturous greeting allowed me to get in through the gate.

'You've got a fine view of the cricket ground,' I told

her as I climbed the path that wound its way up the bank between low-growing shrubs.

'That's why Peter bought the place.' She stood back to let me inside the house. 'Wesley, for goodness' sake, get out from under Juno's feet!' She led me into the conservatory at the back. It seemed she lived alone, and despite the title, had no servants apart from a cleaning lady who came twice a week. She was related to the Westershalls of Moorworthy House only by marriage, and would probably have described herself as comfortable, rather than wealthy. As we passed through the living room, I stopped to admire Sophie's portrait of Florence and her three pups, in pride of place above the mantlepiece.

'I wonder where my Florrie is now,' Lady Margaret sighed sadly. 'I just hope she's all right.'

'She's worth a lot of money,' I reminded her. 'I'm sure whoever has taken her will be treating her well. The last thing they will want to do is damage their asset.' In truth, I wasn't sure about this at all. I'd spent the previous evening doing some research on the Internet and found information I certainly didn't intend to share with Lady Margaret. Type the words *dog theft* into any search engine and you'll discover horror stories of animals stolen for puppy farming, dogfighting, or worse, scientific experimentation. I hoped and prayed none of these would be accurate in Florence's case.

'I don't care how well they are treating her,' she declared. 'If I ever get my hands on whoever has stolen her, I'm going to bloody murder them.'

The conservatory doors opened out on to the back garden, which was mostly laid to lawn and offered fine views of Lustleigh Cleave, the wooded hillside that looks down over the village. 'You told me that Wesley was here in the conservatory when Florence was taken. Where were you?'

'I was in the living room, on the damned phone, talking to the secretary of the Motor Neurone Society about the arrangements for our dinner in a couple of weeks.' It was motor neurone disease that had cruelly taken her husband Peter two years ago, and the society was a charity for which she volunteered, working tirelessly to organise fundraising events.

We wandered out into the garden. It was large, but bordered by the gardens of other properties on all sides. A thick laurel hedge separated it from its nearest neighbour and a stone wall from the garden behind it. 'Could she have got out this way?' I pointed. 'Through that hedge?'

'No, my dear, there's a solid fence behind that hedge. And anyway, Florrie would never have attempted to get into that garden. Charlie lives there and he doesn't take kindly to intruders.'

'Charlie?'

'He's a Rottweiler.'

'So, she couldn't have got out that way, and more importantly, no one could have got in?'

'No. She must have been in the front garden.'

'What if someone like the postman opened the garden gate and left it open, would she go out?'

'She might toddle along the path for a bit, but she wouldn't go far. She likes to sit by the gate and watch people go by. In the summer there are so many visitors on the path to Wreyland Manor. She loves it when people stop to say hello to her. Not everyone does, you know,' she added solemnly. 'Some people don't like bulldogs because they think they are ugly, or fierce. But she's so friendly. It's a horrible thought, that someone just took her. I know I'm a snob, thinking this way, but one tends to assume that the sort of people who visit here, who come to enjoy the beauty of Lustleigh and the countryside, aren't the kind of people who would steal someone's dog.'

I doubted very much that this was an opportunist theft, that someone walking by simply took a fancy to Florence. She'd been targeted. I was still considering the garden. There was no way to drive a vehicle in. 'Where do you park your car?' I asked.

'I've got a garage around the corner. I have to walk from there. It's a damned nuisance when you've got a lot of shopping, I can tell you.'

I asked her to show me, and we walked out through the front gate, Wesley snuffling his way ahead of us, snorting at weeds. We walked along the Wreyland path until we reached the point where it crossed a long tarmac road edged by the gardens of some fairly grand houses. Whoever took Florence must have walked her all along the path on to this road, where they must have had a vehicle waiting. It was a walk of several hundred yards and they'd been lucky not to bump into any neighbours who might have questioned what they were doing. I wondered if they'd had a lead with them.

'How much does Florence weigh?' I asked.

Margaret gave a crack of laughter. 'You think they might have carried her?' She gave it a moment's thought. 'She must weigh a good fifty pounds.'

Fifty pounds of reluctant bulldog? Not an easy carry.

We walked back the way we had come, arriving at the little wooden gate to the front garden. I noticed a plastic cable-tie threaded around the gatepost. 'How long has this been here?'

'I don't know. I suppose some children put it there. I keep meaning to cut it off.'

'Did you show it to the police?'

'No.' She frowned. 'Is it significant?'

I smiled. 'Probably not.'

She eyed me suspiciously. 'But you think it could be?'

'It could be a kind of chalk mark. Some people think that if you find a chalk mark on your gate or on the pavement outside your house, it's been left as a message for thieves. The mark identifies the property as a place where there's something worth stealing.'

Lady Margaret was nodding. 'I've heard that. They used to say that Gypsies did it. They would come back later and rob the place.'

'Someone told me recently that cable-ties had taken over from chalk.' That someone was Dean Collins. Apparently, in a recent spate of burgled houses cable-ties around the gatepost had been a common feature. This could mean that Florence was targeted by someone scouting properties looking for likely pets to steal, leaving a message for those who'd follow with the right dog-handling skills and the right vehicle.

We went back into the house, where Margaret made coffee. Wesley flopped down on the floor by my feet. Bulldogs have a very particular way of lying, flat on their tummies with their hind legs straight out behind them. I don't know of any other breed that does it.

I picked up a photo in a silver frame of a young man in uniform. 'Is this Peter?' I asked.

'Yes,' she called back from the kitchen. She came into the room then. 'He was the best of the Westershalls, you know – the rest were a rotten lot. Bad 'uns, every one of 'em.'

They certainly were. I'd helped to put some of them in prison, including her god-daughter, the spoilt and entitled Emma. Margaret didn't seem to hold this against me. In fact, we'd agreed that if anyone could benefit from several months having her head shoved down a prison toilet, it was Emma.

'I met Peter at a dog show.' Margaret brought in the coffee pot. 'He loved bulldogs. He was trying to breed out some of the health problems – they suffer terribly with their breathing, you know, which is why they snore so – and they're not long-lived. He wanted to breed them back to the way they used to be in the eighteenth century. You see engravings of dogs bull-baiting back then and they were quite different-looking, not such a squashed muzzle. But back then – in Peter's day, I mean – people weren't interested so much in welfare, only in preserving

81

the characteristics of the breed.' She sighed. 'Of course, it's all big business nowadays.'

'Has Florence had puppies before?' I asked.

She shook her head. 'No. I thought it would be good for her to have babies once but I've no interest in breeding pups for profit.'

'So, when you sold Wesley's two sisters, how did you advertise them for sale? Internet or in the newspaper?'

'No need,' she responded, shrugging. 'I told the breeder Peter had got Florence from and she already had a waiting list as long as your arm.'

'No one came to the house to see them?'

'Of course, the eventual purchasers of the puppies came. No responsible dog owner would buy a puppy without seeing it with its mother – and what's more,' she added forcefully, 'I wouldn't sell a pup to anyone who tried.'

'But other than those two? No strangers?'

She frowned as if struggling to remember, her hand idly fidgeting with her beads. 'This was over a year ago. No, wait, there was a woman who came just in case either of the sales fell through. But I'm pretty sure she got fixed up elsewhere.'

'And no one else in the village has had a dog taken?'

'Not that I know of.'

'And no one's seen anyone suspicious hanging around?'

Lady Margaret sighed, reaching in her sleeve for a handkerchief. 'It's pretty hopeless, isn't it?'

'Not at all,' I assured her, lying. 'You said you'd offered a reward.'

'Here,' she picked up a flyer from a pile on the sideboard and handed it to me. There was a photograph of Florence, taken in the garden, with a heading in block letters above 'MISSING' and then a description of her below: *Florence, pedigree English bulldog, three years old, fawn colour with white markings on forelegs, face and chest, missing from Cleave View, Lustleigh. Much missed. Substantial reward for information leading to her recovery. No questions asked.* 'I've posted these up around the village.'

'Well, this could be an inducement to someone,' I said. 'Can I take some? I'll put them in the shop, give a few out among Ashburton's doggy community. You never know, someone may have heard something.'

Lady Margaret thrust a sheaf in my direction. 'Please do.' She stifled a yawn. I could see by the dark smudges beneath her eyes that she wasn't sleeping.

'I'll go,' I said. 'You and Wesley could do with a nap.' Wesley had got a head start, in fact, and was already snoring, his head down on the rug.

'Tell me,' Lady Margaret asked as she showed me to the door, 'how is that young policeman, the one who got shot at Moorworthy House? Is he all right now?'

'Dean Collins? He's so all right he's going to be a father again in a week or two.'

'Well, that's good news. Peter and I couldn't have children, you know,' she added reflectively. 'Peter would have liked them, but it didn't worry me too much.' She smiled and patted my arm confidingly. 'I'd rather have dogs.'

CHAPTER EIGHT

The church hall was packed that evening for the public meeting. Woodland is a community of a bare two hundred souls and most of them had crammed themselves inside. The little hamlet consists of a farmhouse, a few houses clustering around the church and occasional properties scattered up the hill that leads to The Rising Sun pub. That's all there is to it. It's peaceful and green, surrounded by fields, and the subject of the meeting, a proposed new residential development of thirty houses halfway up the hill, with all its accompanying traffic, was certain to make an impact on the Woodland inhabitants, shattering their countryside quiet. The company behind this proposed development belonged to one Alastair Dunston.

With a few minutes to spare, I slid into one of the last remaining seats, next, as it turned out, to Guy Mitchell from the *Dartmoor Gazette*.

'Any news on Sandy?' he asked softly, a moment before I could ask him the same question. I shook my head.

'Are you for or against this development?' I asked, raising my voice slightly against the background hubbub. The atmosphere was already highly charged, like the dawn before a battle.

'I'm just here to report on what's said,' he answered, grinning, 'on both sides. I'm strictly neutral.'

I didn't believe that.

'And you?' he asked.

Truth to tell, I'd really come to the meeting to get a look at Alastair Dunston, Sandy's putative lover and unwilling recipient of her Buck's Fizz. On the subject of the proposed development, I was almost certainly against, unless Dunston could persuade me otherwise, which I doubted. Mitch was looking around him at the people crowding in at the back of the hall. I was lucky to have got a seat, by now it was standing room only. He gave me a nudge. 'That man back there in the denim jacket, see him?'

I turned for a sneaky glance. Standing by the door was a slim man, probably in his forties, of average height, with short brown hair. 'What about him?'

'That's Phil Thomas,' Mitch responded from the corner of his mouth.

'Sandy's ex?'

'Mm. Do you think he cares passionately about what goes on in Woodland?'

'He might, I suppose.' But I thought it was more

likely that he was there for the same reason as me, to take a look at Alastair Dunston.

Dunston himself appeared at that moment, through a doorway at the back of the hall, along with two other suits, one male, one female. They sat at a table facing the people in the hall, Dunston in the middle. 'Good evening, ladies and gentleman,' he said and a hush fell over the meeting, 'thank you all very much for coming.' He introduced his colleagues, who had instantly forgettable names and positions within his organisation. All eyes were focused on the man himself.

It was the first time I'd laid eyes on him and I have to admit that his photograph in the newspaper didn't do him justice. He was of average height with well-cut grey hair and the kind of tan you don't get from living in Devon unless you spend all your time toiling in the fields and he didn't look the toiling type: expensive suit, white shirt, dark tie and a glimpse of gold cufflinks. His smile was charming and confident and I could see what Sandy might have found attractive in him. But Dean was right, he hadn't the correct build to have been the man following her in the woods. It didn't mean he hadn't had her killed, though. The woman on his left – blonde ponytail, blue suit and manicured talons any bird of prey would be proud of – clicked something on her open laptop and behind their heads an artist's impression of the proposed development appeared on a white screen.

Bracken Combe was written in curling green script above a coloured sketch of detached modern houses, their steeply gabled roofs, shuttered windows and stable doors obviously intended to give them a countrified appearance. *An exclusive development of superior, luxury properties, comprising unique, architect-designed houses completed to exacting specifications, convenient for transport links and with uninterrupted views of the surrounding countryside.*

'This is Phase One of our development,' Dunston began with a note of pride, as his bloody-clawed companion clicked her way through a variety of sketches showing the properties from front, back and side elevations, including their double garages, outside dining spaces, patios with hot tubs and in two cases, swimming pools. 'All of the properties run on clean energy and, I think you will agree, have been designed to blend sympathetically into the rural environment.'

'Bollocks!' called a voice from just behind me, and everyone laughed, including Dunston who obviously wasn't fazed.

'Phase Two of the development,' he continued smoothly as another artist's sketch appeared above his head, 'comprises—'

'Excuse me!' a voice called out.

Dunston paused, eyebrows slightly raised, as a man stood up at the other end of my row. 'I was hoping to save questions until the end of our presentation,' he smiled, 'but, please, carry on.'

'Why are you building here when your company is sitting on brownfield sites in Plymouth and Exeter? Why can't these properties be built there?'

'There's a great demand from people wishing to

live the country lifestyle, for properties in a more rural environment.'

'Demand?' A woman in the front row spoke up. 'What there's a demand for, what there's a crying need for, is affordable housing for local people.'

There were mutterings of agreement all round, a few people clapped.

'If we could proceed with our presentation,' Dunston continued, smiling, 'you will see that in Phase Two of the development there are properties planned which will fulfil that requirement.'

'No, I'm sorry, I've got your brochure here.' The woman held it up. 'And it's full of words like *prestigious*, and *select*, or *exclusive*. It doesn't say anything about *affordable*. It mentions *cinema rooms* and *home offices*. Well, the people who live round here can't afford houses like that. And it also says there are . . .' she stopped and read from the brochure she was holding *'excellent investment opportunities* . . . what's that supposed to mean?'

'It means they're meant for rich people to buy as second homes,' someone called out in disgust. 'And then rent 'em out to make more money.'

'Air-bloody-bnb!' cried a voice amidst a rumble of disgruntled muttering.

The man beside Dunston, a balding individual with a nasty moustache, spoke in the patronising tone of a teacher explaining something very difficult to a class of backward children. 'We obviously can't tell people what to do with their homes once they've bought them.'

'You could refuse to sell them as second homes,' the woman pointed out.

'That's actually very difficult to enforce.' He shook his head sadly. 'There's nothing to stop the people *we* sell them to, from selling them to whoever they like.'

'Bollocks!' repeated the person behind me.

'If we could move on,' Dunston continued, 'as I've been trying to explain, Phase Two of the development comprises three-bedroomed houses and four more compact, starter homes.'

'Rabbit hutches!'

I was fast falling in love with the person behind me. I turned to look into a pair of wicked blue eyes beneath the brim of a battered fishing hat, belonging to an old man with a fuzzy white beard. He was obviously enjoying himself.

'And I suppose they get built last, do they, these starter homes?' a voice asked.

'If they ever get built at all!' There were mutterings of agreement all around.

Another woman rose to her feet, her voice trembling with emotion. 'My husband and I moved here three years ago. I know that makes us incomers in the eyes of a lot of people here – but we bought the old Long Barn. It was a derelict when we bought it. We've spent our life savings doing it up . . .'

'And a lovely job you've made of it,' a man in the crowd assured her.

'Thank you. We've turned the two outbuildings into holiday cottages, as income for our retirement. We're just getting going. We've had our first holidaymakers staying this year, and we've got bookings for next. We're just across the road from where you're planning to build. We advertise Long Barn as being surrounded by beautiful countryside, as having uninterrupted views of the fields and woods. If your building goes ahead as planned, the visitors next year will be looking at a building site, and after that, at a lot of new houses. Well, who's going to come on holiday to look at that? You'll ruin us. You'll ruin us before we've even got started.'

'I think you're worrying unnecessarily,' Dunston assured her smoothly. 'I'm sorry if you'll be inconvenienced whilst the houses are being built – there's no way around that, unfortunately,' he conceded, spreading his hands in a conciliatory gesture, 'but once they are built, I promise you, you won't be looking at an eyesore. You will see that this is an extremely attractive development—'

'How are you building it at all?' a man demanded angrily as he stood up. 'I own a smallholding, up the hill from where you're going to build. For the last three years I've been trying to get permission to turn an existing barn on my land into a house so that I can live there with my family, so that we can be there to look after our animals. At the moment, I have to drive three miles every day, there and back from Ashburton. But the council tells me that I can't build one house for my family to live in because it would create excess traffic and put a strain on the existing infrastructure. So how are you getting away with building thirty houses a few yards down the hill?'

'I'm afraid I don't know why you've been refused permission,' Dunston told him. 'You'll have to go back to the council, keep trying.'

'But you're on the council, aren't you?'

'It's who you know, mate!' someone called out.

'Funny handshakes!' cried the old man behind me.

There was a ripple of applause around the room, which Nasty Moustache attempted to quiet with a gesture of his spread hands. He looked uncomfortable, as if he thought the mob might turn violent. Dunston, though, had kept his cool. 'Yes, the man with his hand raised at the back there!' he pointed, grabbing an opportunity to move on.

'I understand this land was originally set aside for nature conservation.'

My heart missed a beat. There was no mistaking that voice: Daniel must have come late to the meeting. I didn't trust myself to turn around to look at him. I lowered my head and clasped my hands together in my lap. Mitch frowned at me. 'Are you okay?' he whispered. I didn't speak, just nodded.

'It was decided that the land is of no great environmental significance,' Dunston answered, 'and that there is sufficient land for conservation set aside close by.'

'The only way such a conclusion could have been reached,' Daniel responded, 'is if the necessary wildlife survey has been carried out. In which case, where is the report?' The room had gone very quiet, possibly because his voice carried a natural authority that Dunston's lacked.

'The report is pending,' Dunston responded evenly.

'But it will be available for public scrutiny when it is complete?'

'Of course.'

'In order to facilitate access to your building site,' Daniel went on, 'it will be necessary to rip up close to a mile of ancient hedgerow.'

Nasty Moustache lost his patience. 'There are trees all around!'

'There is woodland on either side,' Daniel responded evenly, 'but the hedgerow is an essential corridor for wildlife linking the two. If you break that link, your development may as well be an airport runway. Wildlife will not be able to cross it.'

'So, you think that a few bunny rabbits are more important than homes and jobs?' Nasty demanded.

'It's not the bunny rabbits,' Daniel answered with unruffled calm. 'It's the dormice, voles and other small mammals that are an essential part of the food chain, as well as reptiles and nesting birds. Also, Phase Two of this development will require the destruction of a barn which has housed generations of barn owls whose habitat is already severely threatened.'

'We intend to build barn owl nesting boxes on the gable end of the properties in that location,' Dunston responded.

'Really? It doesn't say that in your brochure.'

'It'll be in the report.'

'Which is pending?'

I didn't need to turn around. I could see Daniel's sardonic smile, hear it in his voice.

'It is.'

'Then I shall be most interested to read it. And see what other solutions your company has to offer for the environmental damage this development is certain to cause.'

Dunston seemed to have temporarily mislaid his smile. 'Shall we move on?' he enquired, among general muttering. 'Are there any other questions?'

The meeting carried on for another hour, with very few people seemingly in favour of the development. Arguments became increasingly heated, although most of what was said was a repetition of what had been said before, and inevitably, the debate began going around in circles. Mitch leant over and whispered, 'So, who's the tall guy at the back, the environmentalist guy?'

'How should I know?' I asked.

'Because when he was speaking you were the only person in the entire hall who didn't turn around to look at him.' He grinned and I smiled reluctantly.

'His name is Daniel Thorncroft,' I admitted. 'He runs a company called Rewilding UK. They're involved in environmental projects.'

'I'd like to get a quote from him when this is all over.'

I shrugged. 'Fill your boots.'

He gave me a shrewd, sideways glance. 'Fancy a drink after, a quick nip up to The Rising Sun?'

I looked at my watch. It was still early. 'Why not?'

The meeting began to break up. I dared a peep behind me to look at those standing at the back of the hall. Daniel had disappeared. He must have seen me, sitting

93

down the front. I'm too tall and have too much red hair not to be recognisable from the back. I was probably the reason he'd left so abruptly. Mitch slipped out of his seat. 'He might still be outside. I'll see if I can catch him.'

I nodded. I'd catch him up once Daniel had gone. Phil Thomas had also disappeared. I looked for him on the way out but couldn't see him. I realised he couldn't have been the man following Sandy on Olly's film, for the same reason as Alastair Dunston: both of them were too short, too slight in build. But Sandy's killer could have been in the pay of either of them, and I would have liked a few words with Phil Thomas.

The old chap in the seat behind me was also getting up to leave, supported by a younger woman I took to be his daughter. 'You don't think much of this development, then?' I asked, smiling at him. He didn't answer, just smiled back and nodded.

'Oh, Dad don't know what the meeting's about,' his daughter told me as she guided him out. 'He just likes to come along and heckle. Don't you, Dad, you like to shout things?' She lowered her voice. 'It's ever so embarrassing. He does it in church.'

I made my way out into the fresh air. There were little knots of people hanging around by the exit, still discussing what had gone on, but there seemed to be some kind of disturbance out in the road, where several cars were parked. The female with the red talons was screaming something into her phone whilst Alastair Dunston stood staring at a dark blue Mercedes which, presumably, was his. Nasty Moustache was shouting about something being a bloody disgrace whilst Dunston stood silent, his tan blanched white, a pulse of fury beating in his cheek. I wondered if someone had let his tyres down, but it was worse than that. Red paint had been poured over his shiny blue bonnet. It lay like a puddle of blood, thick and viscous enough for someone to have scrawled a word in it, in letters that stayed starkly visible as the thick paint congealed. Just one word it was. *Murderer*.

CHAPTER NINE

By the time I arrived on the scene Guy Mitchell was already taking pictures on his mobile phone and it was clear he'd forgotten all about a drink at The Rising Sun. He was no longer reporting for his newspaper on a boring old planning meeting; he had a story to run. I could just imagine the headline: *Local Councillor Branded Killer. Accusation Scrawled in Blood on Car.* I looked around. There was no sign of Daniel, he'd already disappeared. The other person who'd disappeared was Phil Thomas.

'They caught him red-handed, then?' Ricky grinned as I was telling him and Morris about it next day. I thought I'd better put in some time in the costume department after having let them down the day before. We were doing alterations for *Cinderella*.

'Not exactly. He'd worn gloves, but he did have paint on his shoes. Dean said he didn't seem concerned about

96

getting caught. When the police questioned him at home he came straight out and admitted it. They've charged him with criminal damage, but Dean thinks Phil Thomas did it just to put the frighteners on Dunston.' I'd got all this information in an early morning phone call. I have to make good use of Dean whilst I can. Once Gemma's given birth and he goes on paternity leave he's going to be as much use to me as the cloth cabbage I was trying to sew on an ugly sister's hat. And it won't be any use asking Cruella.

'So,' Morris paused in the act of trying to thread a needle, temporarily relaxing his squint, his glasses perched on top of his bald head. 'Phil Thomas must believe that Dunston murdered Sandy, then. Seriously.'

'That's what I asked Dean. He says that maybe it's just payback for Dunston having had an affair with Sandy, which Thomas claims he knows he did, whatever Dunston might say.'

'But he and Sandy were divorced before that, surely?'

Ricky gave a cackle of laughter. 'Doesn't stop him getting jealous about it, does it? Maybe poor old Phil didn't want a divorce. Maybe he still loved her.'

I shrugged. 'He certainly seems to hate Dunston.'

'But how did the police know it was Phil who damaged the car?' Morris asked. 'It could have been anyone at that meeting.'

Ricky rolled his eyes. 'He'd written *murderer*. Do wake up, Maurice!'

'Dunston spotted him at the meeting,' I told him. 'He saw him slip out early.'

Ricky shook out the skirts of a ballgown he was trimming. 'He was suspect number one.'

'So, Dunston recognised him,' Morris resumed his squinting attempt at the needle.

'I wouldn't have thought they'd have moved in the same circles, would you?'

'Why not?' Ricky objected. 'They were shagging the same woman.'

'At different times. And even if two men were . . . shagging the same woman,' Morris added, colouring slightly, 'it doesn't mean they'd know each other.'

'There could be an older enmity between them, you mean?' I asked. Morris nodded, finally threading his needle the moment before I was forced to tear it from his hands and thread it for him. He returned his specs to his nose. 'Well, whatever the cause of his actions,' I went on, 'Dean says the police are keeping a weather eye on Thomas, and on Dunston. Neither of them is in the clear yet with regard to Sandy's murder.' I wanted to talk to Phil Thomas, ask a few questions myself. But I didn't know where he lived and Dean was unlikely to tell me. 'But he did tell me that the police have found no trace of Dunston's DNA in Sandy's car, although there is plenty of Thomas's. But it used to be his car,' I added, 'before the divorce. There are still some of his old tools in the boot.'

'So, no reason why his DNA shouldn't be in the car?' Ricky asked.

'Exactly.'

We all lapsed into silence then, concentrating on our work.

'How's old Mag-bags anyway?' Ricky demanded after a few minutes. He can never stay quiet for long.

I couldn't help laughing. 'Can you possibly be referring to Lady Margaret Westershall?'

He and Morris had known her for years, performing at fundraising concerts for various of her charities.

'Yeh, old Mag-bags!'

'She's desperately worried about her dog.'

Morris glanced up over his specs. 'No news?'

'Not so far.'

Ricky grunted. 'I don't know why anyone would steal an animal that's so bloomin' ugly.'

I told him what she was worth and he let out a low whistle. 'Besides,' I added in Florence's defence, 'she's very affectionate. Lady Margaret's terrified about what might happen to her. And I'm worried about Margaret. She doesn't look well. I don't think she's sleeping.'

Morris shook his head sadly. 'She's always had a weak heart.'

'Really? I didn't know that.' Now I was even more worried.

I put in the rest of the day with Ricky and Morris but made it back to the shop by closing time. Pat was just closing up. Pumpkin earrings were selling like hot cakes, she told me with a grin, she was going to have to make some more. Sophie had sold a painting of a donkey and I'd sold an oak candle box and a set of cigarette cards. Not a bad day at all.

'How's your new boy making out?' I asked Pat. 'Dalek?'

She grimaced. 'He's a lazy toerag, if you ask me. Don't like getting his hands dirty.'

'He's not really in the right place then, is he, at an animal sanctuary?'

'That's what I said to Sue. Why come and work with animals if you're 'fraid of a bit of muck? Anyway, from what we can work out, he didn't want to come. His dad sent him, sent him to find out what a day's work was like. But he don't get on with it, not like Eduardo. He spends half his time gabbling away on his phone to his girlfriend back in Slovenia – or Slovakia – I can't never remember which one it is.' She shook her head in disapproval. 'I don't think he's going to last long.'

I laughed. 'Doesn't sound as if he's going to be any loss.'

'Well, no, he's eating us out of house and home. I think Ken will send him packing if he doesn't start buckling down.' She shrugged on her coat. 'I'll be off, then. Bye, Juno.'

After she'd gone, I sat for a few minutes, squaring up the money in the till drawer and gloomily contemplating what I was going to do with the long evening stretching ahead of me. I was just reaching for my jacket when the shop phone rang.

'Oh, there you are!' cried a voice as I picked up. 'I've been trying to reach you all day!'

It was Lady Margaret, breathless and agitated. 'I must have tried your mobile a dozen times.'

I shoved my hand in my pocket and realised my phone was probably still where I'd left it that morning, charging up on the table at home.

'I'm sorry,' I began, but Margaret carried on. 'I found the dreadful thing on my doormat when I got up to let Wesley out first thing this morning. Someone must have slipped it under my door during the night.'

'Found what?' I asked as she drew breath.

'This terrible letter. It's a ransom demand,' she answered, breaking into a sob. 'For Florence.'

CHAPTER TEN

'You haven't shown this to the police?' I asked an hour later as I sat staring at the sheet of white paper which lay on Lady Margaret's dining table, radiating menace.

'No, of course not. You can see what it says.'

The message was clear and unequivocal. 'If you want your dog back, bring five thousand pounds in a white carrier bag to SX543631 tomorrow night at 9 p.m. Come alone. Any sign of the police and we'll cut your dog's head off.'

'I don't care about the money,' Margaret declared. 'I just want to get Florence back.'

'You don't think perhaps you should show this to the police?' I suggested.

'No! No! I dare not take the risk. You've read what they say in the letter.' Her pale blue eyes were swimming with tears. 'You will help me, won't you, Juno dear?'

'Of course I'll help you. But are you sure?' I didn't point out that by giving in to the kidnapper's demands she would only be encouraging more kidnappings.

Margaret wasn't stupid, she'd worked that out for herself. 'I've already drawn the money out,' she told me defiantly.

I frowned at the message. In time-honoured fashion, the ransom demand had been written with letters cut from a newspaper and glued on to the paper. It must have taken ages. It would have been quicker and simpler to have printed it. Done for dramatic effect, I suppose. Just like using a map reference instead of naming the place. It was all calculated to pile the pressure on poor Margaret. And there was no guarantee that the message had really come from the kidnappers. It might have been a heartless prank by some bastard who'd seen one of her flyers about Florence being missing. 'This map reference,' I asked, pointing, 'do you know where it is?'

'I looked it up, of course.' She unfolded an OS map that had been lying on the table and spread it out. 'It's here, I marked it with a cross. It's the village of Shaugh Prior but,' her voice began to tremble, 'the letter doesn't say where in the village I'm to take this bag of money.'

Shaugh Prior, that name was ringing bells for some reason. I frowned. 'You don't have a larger-scale map?'

She thought for a moment. 'There might be a box of them in the loft.'

I spent half an hour scrabbling around among the dust and cobwebs, aiming a torch beam into all the boxes I could find, some of them intriguingly filled with objects wrapped in newspaper. If I hadn't been on a mission to find the map, I'd have loved a nosy into them. But I found the map we wanted, dropped it down through the hatch to Margaret and a puzzled-looking Wesley, and descended the somewhat rickety loft ladder.

'You deserve a drink,' she announced, as we arrived back downstairs and spread the new map open on the table. I didn't argue, just pulled a few cobwebs from my hair as she poured me a very large gin. We found Shaugh Prior again, a village on the western edge of Dartmoor, not far from Plymouth. I traced a dark line with my finger, the old railway line that used to link Plymouth to Tavistock. It was closed down years ago, it's a cycle path now, Drake's Trail, they call it. I tapped my finger on a black spot just outside the village. 'Here,' I told her. 'It'll be here they want us to take the money I'll bet.'

Lady Margaret frowned. 'But what is it?'

'It's the old railway tunnel. It was blocked off when the railway closed, but it's reopened now, it's part of the cycle path.'

'Why would they want us to meet them there?'

'Because it's dark,' I said in disgust. It was all part of the theatrics, intended to scare us. And it was working on me. I'd never visited Shaugh Prior Tunnel but as I stared at the map, I remembered with a sinking heart what it was that made the name so memorable.

Large gin or no large gin, I was determined to drive home that night, despite an offer of a bed from Margaret. The poor old girl didn't really want to be left on her own. The wait for next evening would be agony for her but she didn't possess a computer, and there were things I needed to find out before we met up with Florence's kidnappers. They had told her in the letter that she must meet them alone. Well, that wasn't going to happen. There was no way I was going to allow an elderly lady with a heart problem to toddle into a dark tunnel clutching a bag full of money to meet potentially violent criminals. After a long argument, she agreed that I should be the one to go. But only if I promised on my life that I wouldn't ring the police in the meantime. 'And that includes your friend, Dean Collins,' she warned me.

Shaugh Prior Tunnel, I'd remembered, was a favourite haunt of some of Cordelia's friends.

Cordelia, the cousin who had brought me up, sadly no longer with us, was deeply disapproved of by Brian's wife, Marcia, even though the two of them had never met. As he was posted abroad through much of my childhood, it was Cordelia with whom I spent my holidays from boarding school. She was an astrologer by profession and owned a little New Age shop in the nearby town of Totnes. This alone was enough, in Marcia's eyes, to condemn her as a totally unsuitable person to be responsible for bringing up a young girl, and was undoubtedly the cause of my *wayward preference for the company of extremely odd people*.

I wondered if she'd have included Lady Margaret Westershall in that category. Cordelia was a wise and funny lady and for someone who guided her life by the stars, remarkably down to earth. Unlike many others in her profession, she made no claim to be psychic, interpreted charts strictly according to 'the rules' of astrology and resolutely refused to adopt a silly name or a fake mystic persona. Some of her friends, on the other hand, were self-consciously weird. There was Norman – Nutty Norman as he was known on the quiet – who used to hang around at night in paranormal hotspots, sensing the vibes. He went with a group of equally batty friends, complete with infra-red cameras and equipment for detecting sudden drops in temperature or other indications of ghostly manifestation. Berry Pomeroy Castle was a favourite haunt of theirs, as was Shaugh Prior Tunnel. I don't know what Norman and his friends smoked during these long dark vigils, but I remember tales of encounters with spectral apparitions, of hearing ghostly voices and footsteps and experiencing strange vibrations. More often than not, they simply sensed 'a presence'.

What my laptop told me, once I'd got home and fired it up, was that the 'presence' in Shaugh Prior Tunnel was 'an aggressive and hostile spirit encountered by many paranormal investigators and believed to be the ghost of an old railway worker'. Apparently, he pushes people. Well, if that's the worst he can do, I don't think he's much to worry about.

Far more worrying was the fact that the kidnappers, waiting in the darkness of the tunnel, would get a clear view of me coming along the cycle path towards them, which, from what I could gather from a website, was a wide and level path with woods on either side. The tunnel is three hundred metres long and curves in the middle, from where it is impossible to see light from either end. There are dim lights set at knee height for the benefit of cyclists and walkers during the daytime, but these are switched out at precisely nine o'clock – the time arranged by the kidnappers for our rendezvous.

I'd arranged to pick up Margaret with the money in plenty of time the following evening. She insisted she would come with me as far as the cycle path and refused to consider leaving Wesley at home. 'What if this is just a trick to lure me out of the house so that thieves can break in and steal him?' She had a point, I suppose, and at least he'd be company for his anxious mum whilst I was in the tunnel rescuing Florence.

There was only one other point that bothered her. 'I don't possess a plain white carrier bag,' she told me. 'Do you suppose a Waitrose one will do?'

CHAPTER ELEVEN

I drove, in Lady Margaret's car. She was too agitated to drive. We parked at Shaugh Bridge. Around us, the wooded walks, so pretty in the daylight, were darkening into shadow. There was still some light in the sky, a golden smear left by a sinking sun. There seemed to be no other vehicles parked and no one else about.

We'd arrived much too early. We waited in the car as the minutes dragged by. To pass the time I told Margaret about Sandy, not about Olly's film of course, but her involvement with Alastair Dunston, and how Phil, her ex, had written the word 'murderer' on his car.

'Threw her drink over him, did she?' Despite her highly anxious state, Margaret smiled. 'I should like to have seen that.' She sounded like Maisie.

'Do you know him, then?'

'Oh, I've met him, come across him at charity do's and so on.'

'What's he like?'

'Charming,' she said, then added, 'too bloody charming.'

I checked my watch. It was almost nine.

I tried to persuade Margaret to stay in the car, but she was determined to come with me until we were in sight of the tunnel and so, she assured me, was Wesley. We trod the lonely cycle path together, in silence save for Wesley's panting. His white shape glowed, luminous in the dimness under the trees, as well as the white carrier bag I'd brought, containing the ridiculous amount of cash. The other thing I carried was a fairly chunky torch, heavy enough to act as a weapon if need be. I was feeling nervous myself, edgy. Innocent nocturnal sounds, the rustling in the branches made by birds as they settled into their night-time roosts, took on an ominous quality.

The tunnel came into view, its gaping black mouth carved into a wall of rock. I tried to ignore its resemblance to the open maw of some giant beast waiting for its dinner. I glanced at Margaret. She was breathing heavily and slowing down almost to a stop. I reached for her arm. 'Are you all right?'

She paused, stretching out to rest her hand on the fence next to her. 'I just need a moment,' she breathed, putting her other hand on her chest. The stress was getting to her, but she managed a smile. 'I have my tablets in my bag, if I need them.'

'You should go back to the car. Wait for me there.'

She shook her head. 'Wesley and I are staying right here,' she responded, taking in a deep breath, 'and if you're not back out in ten minutes, I'm calling the police – it's what I should have done in the first place.'

Ten minutes, I thought to myself, might be a bit late. I could be lying dead in that tunnel long before that.

'You will be careful, won't you, my dear?' she asked anxiously.

'You can depend upon it,' I told her. She gave me a hug. 'Take this.' She handed me an old leather glove. 'It's for Florence,' she explained. I bent down and patted Wesley. 'Look after your mum,' I told him, but he was occupied sniffing a nettle.

As I approached the entrance of the tunnel, I could see that up to about head height its stone walls were painted white. Helpful, whilst the lights were on, as they were now. Set low into the walls the dim bulbs spread a sheen of silver over puddles on the tunnel floor, but did not cast much light above. There was no sign of anyone. The only sound was the echoing drip of water, and the steady thumping of my heart. I walked slowly, turning once to look back the way I'd come, at the tunnel mouth I'd left behind. The grey of dying twilight was just visible. Lady Margaret had sensibly tucked herself out of sight.

I thought I heard a footstep in the darkness ahead of me and stopped, ears straining. 'Hello?' My voice echoed around empty walls. Then silence. My imagination was getting the better of me. The wind whistled along the tunnel, a shrill moan like the ghost of an ancient locomotive. I was scared enough, I could have done without the atmospherics. I sensed cold air coming from my right. There was a break in the tunnel wall, a barred metal gate blocking off what I guessed was once an old railwayman's refuge, a place where he could step out of the way of oncoming trains. It could also be a place where someone watching for me could hide and wait. I flicked on my torch and shone it through the barred gate. There was nothing moving in the darkness. I couldn't see anyone. Perhaps there was no one here at all, this whole thing was a hoax. I flicked off the torch and kept walking.

I could only have travelled about a hundred yards but I felt as if I'd been in this damned tunnel for hours. I looked back, but the dim shape of its mouth was lost in blackness, the only light now the feeble glow from low-level lamps set into the walls. I felt a prickle of fear between my shoulder blades, a definite feeling that I was not alone. I wondered if I might be about to receive a phantom push. The tunnel began to curve, I must have reached the middle. As if on cue, the lights went out.

There's darkness, and then again, there's darkness. It was as if someone had thrown a black velvet shroud over my head, enfolding and smothering. I was completely blind. Blind panic is what I felt. For a moment I struggled to flip on the torch, my gasping breath loud in my ears. It lit up the tunnel, a wavering light in my shaking hand and then a voice yelled. 'Kill that light!'

I killed it. The voice echoed. 'Stand still!' it commanded. 'Stay right where you are!'

I did as I was told, stayed blind, rooted to the spot.

111

Could the owner of the voice see me, somehow, see me in this blackness, this sightless dark? Then from far down the tunnel, I discerned a dim blob, a nebulous glow, slowly getting brighter as it came towards me. I couldn't make out what it was at first, it seemed to be floating in the darkness like a luminous jellyfish bobbing in the black depths of the ocean. As it drifted closer it gradually resolved itself into a gigantic pink head, lit up from within, a clown's carnival mask with rosy painted cheeks and smiling lips, a tiny pointed hat balanced on its bald, bulbous crown. It sat on the shoulders of the person wearing it, a giant pink balloon completely concealing the head of the man inside. He was dressed in black so that the great glowing head seemed bodyless. It stopped a few feet in front of me. The light from the mask was so bright, I squinted. I could feel heat coming off it.

'You're not the woman who owns the dog,' the voice was disguised, muffled, with a strange buzz as if a bee were talking. Something about it was oddly familiar. It was not the voice that had shouted at me before. There was more than one of them then.

I stared at the smiling pink face. 'She sent me instead.' It was just as well. Margaret would have had a heart attack by now. I might have one myself, my heart was pounding like a jackhammer.

'That wasn't the deal.'

I shrugged, tried to look braver than I felt. 'D'you want the money or not?'

'Show it to me.'

I lifted the carrier bag.

'Show me,' the voice insisted, and I opened the bag up. The great pink head nodded. I could dimly make out the head of the wearer, a dark blob inside.

He reached out and I took a step back, thrusting the bag behind me. 'Not so fast, Big Head. Where's the dog? Where's Florence? You don't get this until you hand her over.'

'She's here.'

'Where? Show me.'

A light flicked on in his hand and he pointed. Further down the wall of the tunnel I could see another barred gate, and slumped on the floor beneath it was Florence, tethered to one of the bars, her head hung low in misery. 'Florence!' I shouted. At the sound of her name, she swung her head in my direction. I made a move towards her, but Big Head stepped in front of me. 'Money first.'

I shoved the bag at him and he caught it, pulling out a bundle of notes and flicking through them to satisfy himself they were real. The big head nodded in satisfaction, and from within it came a weird, buzzing laugh. Then the light of his great head went out. We were in blackness again. An almighty shunt in my chest sent me sprawling backward and I landed on my arse on the wet floor, cursing as my torch rolled away. Footsteps ran off down the tunnel, joined after a few moments by a second pair. I groped in my pocket for my phone, fumbling for its buttons. Its blue light showed me where my torch was lying and Florence, still tied to the gate of the refuge. Of the kidnappers there was no sign.

I pocketed my phone, flicked on the torch and went to

greet the dog. In the white torchlight she looked grubby. There were no marks of injury on her but her whole body was trembling. I kept repeating her name gently, and that seemed to reassure her, but as I drew nearer, she began to lick her chops nervously. She didn't know me. I dropped Lady Margaret's leather glove in front of her and gave her time to sniff. She stood up, her rear end began to wag as she recognised her owner's scent, and she took the glove gently in her mouth. 'That's right, Florence, you hold on to that,' I recommended, smoothing her head. I struggled to undo the knots that tied up her lead. 'Let's get out of here.' She trotted placidly beside me, the glove held in her mouth, as we followed the light of my torch back to the mouth of the tunnel and into the open air.

It was fully dark by now. I couldn't see Margaret on the path ahead and called out to her. What if she'd collapsed, what if all the strain had been too much? Then Wesley barked, and after a few moments they both came hurrying into view, Wesley in the lead. Relief flooded through me. 'Oh Florrie! My Florrie!' Margaret cried. Wesley barked and she let his lead drop and he thundered towards us to greet his long-lost mum.

'She's all right,' I called as Margaret hurried after him. 'They haven't hurt her.'

'My Florence,' she crooned, stooping down to hug her bodily. Florence wriggled in her embrace and licked her face whilst Wesley capered ecstatically around them both. I found it all a bit emotional.

'I'm afraid they took the money,' I said, swallowing the lump in my throat.

'I don't care about that.' She clung to Florence, tears of joy streaming down her cheeks. 'I never thought I'd see my little Florrie again.'

'Perhaps we should get going,' I suggested after a few more moments. I couldn't be sure the kidnappers weren't still hanging around somewhere. I helped Margaret back on to her feet and she gathered up the dogs' leads. 'I'm sorry, my dear. I haven't even asked you if you're all right. They weren't violent?'

'No,' I assured her, 'just profoundly scary.' I didn't mention the shove that sent me sprawling. After all, that could have been the ghost.

Florence ate a hearty supper, then flopped down to sleep in her basket, apparently exhausted. Wesley snuggled up next to her and kept washing her face. 'I'm taking her to the vet first thing in the morning,' Lady Margaret declared, 'get her checked over.'

I gave her the details of my experience in the tunnel over a double brandy. She listened in horror but was still adamant about not going to the police. 'I don't care about the money,' she repeated. 'It's worth twice that to get Florrie back.'

I understood how she felt but I still resented the fact that the kidnappers got away with it. The more I thought about it, the more stupid I realised they'd been. They'd indulged in all the dramatics of the huge clown's head and the pasted letter, but had chosen to arrange the handover in a tunnel. If we had involved the police, it would have been an easy place to trap them. I hoped I could persuade Margaret to talk to the police eventually. I couldn't give them a description of the man who'd taken the money, but that ransom note was evidence. It might contain fingerprints or other traces that could identify the kidnappers. If they struck again.

In the light of morning, Lady M might be more open to persuasion. But not tonight. For tonight I'd had enough. I was going back to Ashburton, to my own bed, to sleep, perchance to have nightmares about a giant clown's floating head.

CHAPTER TWELVE

'Bleedin' hell, Juno!' Ricky protested, glaring at me across the table. 'What d'you want to do a stupid thing like that for?'

'Well, I could hardly let Margaret go on her own.'

'You should've made her call the police.'

'She was frightened. They threatened to kill her dog. If anything had gone wrong—'

'Sod the dog! If anything had gone wrong, *you* could have been killed.'

I hesitated a moment. I'd popped in for coffee and a chat on Monday evening and was beginning to wish I hadn't. 'Well, it didn't,' I responded weakly.

'We're only thinking of you, Juno,' Morris added, gazing at me reproachfully.

'I know,' I relented, reaching out to give his hand a

squeeze. 'And I did try to persuade her to call the police, but she wouldn't.'

Ricky scowled. 'I'm surprised at Mag-bags, giving into blackmail. She's usually a feisty old bird.'

'But the dogs are her weak spot,' Morris pointed out. 'They're like her children.'

'And perhaps more importantly,' I added, 'Florence is her one remaining connection to Peter. He bought her for Margaret as a puppy.'

Morris nodded sadly. 'And she's all right now?'

'Florence? I think so.' Margaret had called me earlier. 'The vet checked her over this morning and she's okay physically. But she refuses to go near the garden gate.'

'Can dogs suffer from PTSD?' Ricky asked.

I shrugged. 'Why not? But look, the reason I told you about all this was that I thought you might know where someone would get a mask like that. You've never made one for anyone locally, for a show?'

'This giant clown's head?' Ricky frowned. 'No, we haven't. And I can't think of any shows where a prop like that might be needed.'

'Some show about a circus?' Morris suggested, getting up from the table to fill the kettle. '*Barnum*? *The Greatest Showman*?'

Ricky nodded. 'That's a point, but we've never costumed either of those shows.'

'But we could ask around,' Morris said. 'Find out if anyone has done either of them locally.'

'This head,' I told them. 'It reminded me of something from a carnival. You know, those torchlit

118

carnival processions? They make lanterns out of canes and some kind of see-through material – it looks almost like tissue paper – and they light them up from the inside, giant lanterns. That's the sort of thing it was.'

'But you said the man was wearing it?'

'Yes, it was sitting on his shoulders, his head was inside. I couldn't see his face.'

'So, how was it lit up?'

'It must have been battery-controlled. And he had some kind of switch.'

Ricky puffed out his cheeks. 'Trouble is, if it was for a carnival, it could have been made by anyone. People tend to make their own stuff for carnivals, at least in the villages around here. It's a community event.'

'So, you don't know of any hire companies that specialise in carnival costumes?' I asked.

'Often it's a school art department that gets involved in making that sort of thing,' Morris put in. 'The school here in Ashburton made them for the carnival last time.' He nodded at Ricky. 'We could give Sally Frost a ring. She's on the carnival committee.'

'Ask her if she knows anyone who made a clown's head lantern?' Ricky sounded sceptical.

Morris shrugged. 'It's worth a phone call.'

I'd realised overnight what the clown's voice had reminded me of. 'What do you call that thing that the Punch and Judy man puts in his mouth to make Punch's voice?'

'A swozzle?' Ricky shrugged. 'Easy enough to get hold of. You can buy one in a joke shop.'

119

I sighed. No hope that the man wearing the clown's head must be a Punch and Judy man, then.

'So, supposing you find the person who made the mask, and that leads you to Florence's kidnappers,' Ricky asked, 'what are you going to do? Demand her money back?'

'I don't know,' I admitted. 'I'm just worried that now they've tried it once – and who's to know whether this is the first time – they'll try it again.'

Morris shook his head, agitated. 'There seems to be so much of this dog theft going on.'

'There was a woman on the local TV news recently, said she lost both her dogs when they went out for a walk. They ran on ahead of her and that was the last she saw of them. She thought the thieves might have called them with one of those silent dog whistles.'

'It's the daft prices people pay for 'em these days,' Ricky grunted, 'it just encourages thieves.'

'That's true,' I admitted, 'but it's not just pedigrees that are the problem. Any old mutt is priceless to its owner, and that's what these bastards are banking on.'

The Bay Horse was where Phil Thomas came to drink with friends. It's a traditional-style pub with real ale, a fine pie and pizza menu and a great big screen for showing important football matches – well, important to people who like football – and that Tuesday night there was a match on. I arrived at half-time, just as they were dishing out free roast potatoes.

It was packed inside but as I squeezed my way

120

through the noisy crowd, I caught sight of Phil Thomas, a drained pint glass on the bar in front of him, obviously awaiting his chance to get it refilled. He glanced up as I arrived at the bar next to him, stared for a moment from shrewd blue eyes and then began nodding slowly as if the sight of me confirmed some long-held suspicion. 'I wondered how long it would be before you turned up.' I must have looked taken aback because he added. 'You are Juno Browne, aren't you?'

'Yes, but I don't think we've met.'

'You want to talk about Sandra.' He smiled grimly. 'She must have been a real thorn in your side, I reckon.'

'I didn't always like what she wrote about me,' I admitted, 'but I am very sorry that she's dead. I would like to talk to you.' I nodded towards his pint glass. 'Can I get that?'

He seemed to be assessing me with a stare, then decided to abandon waiting for his pint and jerked his head in the direction of the beer garden at the back of the pub. 'Let's go outside. We can hear ourselves think out there.'

The beer garden was empty apart from the usual smokers huddled by the door, and we fought our way through the cloud of cigarette smoke and sat down at a rustic picnic table. 'Look, I really am sorry about what happened to Sandy. Do you mind if I ask you some questions?'

He shrugged, picking up a beer mat, flipping it over. 'It's what you're here for, isn't it?'

'Yes, but you don't have to answer them.'

He smiled sadly. 'Sandra was a big fan of yours, she'd have been disappointed if you didn't show an interest in what happened to her.'

'I want to know who killed her. And why.'

'So do I.' His shoulders heaved in a sigh and he looked sad. 'I still can't believe it.'

'A few days before she died,' I began slowly, 'she wrote a note in her notepad at the newspaper office, indicating that she wanted to ask me something. But she didn't get the chance. You don't know what it was?'

He shook his head. 'No idea. I hadn't seen her for a couple of weeks. And anyway, she didn't talk to me about her work much.' He was quiet for a moment, staring at the surface of the table.

'Do you really think that Dunston was responsible?' I asked.

He looked up. 'Do I think he killed Sandra?' He grunted. 'No, I don't think he'd have the balls. As for whether he's responsible . . .' He shrugged.

'You wrote "murderer" on his car.'

'I just wanted to get back at the bastard for the way he treated her.' He leant across the table towards me. 'I know everyone thinks that Sandra was thick-skinned, but she was sensitive in some ways. And he humiliated her.'

'How long were you married?' I asked.

'Seventeen years,' he responded thoughtfully. 'We were childhood sweethearts, back in Wales. We grew up together, lived in the same street, went to the same school, got married too young. When the firm I was working for closed down, we moved here. I set myself up as a builder, self-employed. There was plenty of work, I thought we'd settle down and start a family, but Sandra – 'she was always Sandra, there was none of this Sandy then – had other ideas. She got this bee in her bonnet about becoming a journalist. Well, she was already too old to start in that game, and so I told her, but she wanted to go to night school, started this Open University course. Then she got a job with the *Gazette*. I mean, it's only a tinpot local rag but she was over the moon, thought it was just the first rung of the ladder of her career, if you know what I mean, instead of a seat in the last-chance saloon.' He shook his head bitterly. 'It was Sandra who wanted the divorce.' A sour smile tugged at the corners of his mouth. 'I could see I would never be enough for her. Truth is, I suppose, we'd outgrown one another. And I didn't want to hold her back.' He shrugged and looked away. 'She told me I would always be her best friend.'

'And you think she was having an affair with Dunston?'

'I know she was.' He looked back at me, tapped the table with a forefinger. 'She bloody told me she was.'

That seemed odd to me. She hadn't confided in any of her colleagues that she was having an affair with a married man. It seemed a strange thing to confide to your ex-husband.

As if he read my thoughts, he went on, 'It was funny, really, how it came about – that she told me, I mean. You see, after she and I broke up, I met Laura.' He grinned, and for a moment looked like a shy adolescent. 'I wasn't looking to get involved with anyone – after Sandra I thought I'd had enough – but Laura and I hit it off straight away and it wasn't long before we started thinking about moving in together. I didn't want Sandra to find out about it the hard way, about me and Laura, so I told her. That's when she confessed to me about Dunston, that the two of them had been having an affair. She said she'd been wanting to tell me for ages. I told her not to be such a fool. A man like Dunston's not going to leave his wife for a woman like Sandra. But she reckoned she was big enough and old enough to know what she was doing.'

'You said he humiliated her.'

He nodded slowly. 'They were supposed to be spending the night together in some posh hotel up on the moor. They arrived separately. Well, Sandra sees him standing in the reception hall, but he's talking to a couple who turned out to be friends of him and his wife. He'd bumped into them, not knowing they were going to be there. So instead of steering clear and waiting until he's alone, the silly cow goes up to him and practically throws her arms around him. He gives her a right telling-off, tells his friends that he hardly knows her, that she's just some journalist who's been stalking him. Tells her to get lost. And she does. She drives home in tears. He rings her later to explain what happened, but then suggests they have a cooling-off period.'

'Seeing his wife's friends scared him off?'

He nodded. 'After that, he kept giving her the cold shoulder but she'd really fallen for him, she didn't want to let go.'

'D'you know if she was stalking him?'

He paused to think about it. 'She was a difficult woman to shake off once she had the bit between her teeth. But he used her, that bastard.' His fingers tapped the table again, drumming out suppressed anger. 'And then to take her to court like that, pretend he'd never had an affair with her, and after she was dead, poor woman, to tell the police and the paper that he hardly knew her, that she'd been nothing more than a nuisance to him . . .'

'Is that why you threw paint over his car?'

He grinned. 'I'll end up paying God-knows-what for the damage, but it was worth it.' Loud cheering came from within the pub at that moment. Someone had scored a goal. 'Sounds like they're into the second half.' Phil looked towards the door. 'Now if you don't mind, that's enough questions. I'm going to grab that other pint.'

I thought about it all, later, sitting in my flat with Bill for company. Would Alastair Dunston really have killed Sandy, or had her killed, because she had embarrassed him in front of friends, thrown drink over him in front of his wife? Would he have gone as far as murder to protect his reputation, his career, his marriage? I thought about what Phil had said, about him and Sandy marrying too young. Cordelia always insisted that marrying young was a bad idea astrologically. We don't really become adult enough for marriage until the age of twenty-eight or nine, she insisted, when the planet Saturn completes its first cycle, returns to the place it was on the day we were born, bringing with it the requisite wisdom and maturity. It's called the First Saturn Return, she told me. Well, if that's the case, I missed the boat when I had mine a couple of years ago, and I haven't noticed Saturn bringing me anything at all except for a broken-down antique shop. But then Saturn is not known for being the fun guy of the zodiac. Perhaps I'll have to wait now until it comes around for a second time, when I'm fifty-six. 'Or I might just cut my throat now,' I told a contentedly purring Bill. 'Save myself the wait.'

CHAPTER THIRTEEN

The shop was pleasantly full when I popped in the following afternoon, but not with customers. Pat, Sophie and Elizabeth were all there, Ricky and Morris, who'd come in to bring some new items for their vintage clothes rail, and Lady Margaret with the two bulldogs.

Which meant that by the time I arrived, they'd all been given a florid account of my encounter with Clown Head in Shaugh Prior Tunnel. I'd felt forced to tell Ricky and Morris about it because I wanted to ask them about the mask, but all I'd told the girls in the shop was that Margaret had got her dog back when an anonymous individual had responded to her offer of the reward. Sophie and Pat were indignant that I hadn't told them the true story. Elizabeth just gave me an ironic look, a kind of *doing- this-sort-of-thing- is-why-Daniel-broke-off-with-you* look.

'Is everything all right?' I asked Margaret, bending to pat them as the two dogs snuffled a friendly greeting. 'Is Florence okay?'

'Absolutely fine,' she assured me. 'But look, you wouldn't let me pay you for what you did the other night and I wanted to find a way to thank you . . .' I opened my mouth to say that I didn't need thanking but she held up a hand to silence me. 'No, Juno, shut up a minute! Let me say my bit.'

'Yes, shut up, a minute!' Ricky repeated, eyes twinkling.

'And you can belt up too,' Margaret reproved him. 'You wouldn't let me pay you,' she went on to me, 'and so I suddenly thought of all the stuff up in the loft. There's boxes and boxes of it, mostly Peter's mother's stuff. It's not my kind of thing at all, but I thought it might be worth something – you know, there might be the odd thing worth selling – and you might like to have it. You're welcome to it all. I just brought a few boxes over to start you off.'

It was only then I noticed three sturdy cardboard cartons piled on the counter. 'I could sell it for you on commission—' I began.

'No!' she held up her hand again. 'I want *you* to have the money. Iris, Peter's mother, used to collect pottery, hideous most of it, but there might be something that's worth a few pounds. And as I say, you're welcome to anything that's up in that loft, if you care to come and clear it out. I don't want to have to lug it all along the path to the car and your back's younger than mine.'

'But there might be something really valuable in there,' I protested.

'Good. I hope there is. And if there is, for goodness' sake put it in a proper auction. I don't want to know anything about what it fetches.' Margaret rose to her feet, ignoring my attempts to thank her, and gathered up her dogs' leads. 'I'll leave you to rummage through those. I'm off to the pet shop to see if they sell those tracker collars.' Morris bustled to open the door for her, and she swept out.

There was a moment's stunned silence and then Ricky rubbed his hands together gleefully. 'Let's have a look at what the old girl's given you.' He reached out for one of the boxes, but I slapped his hand away.

'Mine!' I told him and hastily opened up the flaps.

The first object I unwrapped from its newspaper packing was a ceramic fish, in glossy shades of blue and green. I placed him on the table on his tummy. He was about a foot long, with a sinuous curve to his body, his head slightly raised up, supported on his lion-like gills, his rubbery lips gaping open.

Pat wrinkled her nose. 'What an ugly thing! What's it for?'

'I think it's a spoon warmer.' I picked it up, turned it over and read the maker's mark incised on the bottom. 'And it's not ugly,' I told her with a smile. 'It's beautiful.'

Sometimes, not being a success in the short term means becoming a greater success in the long term. The Della

Robbia Pottery of Birkenhead opened in 1894 but closed its doors in 1906. During that short time, it mass-produced hand-thrown ceramics, inspired by the works of a fifteenth-century Florentine artist and became part of the Arts and Crafts movement. Its short life has made some of the items it produced rare, and all extremely collectable. Lady Margaret's mother-in-law, Iris, had obviously been a collector. I surveyed the contents of the boxes that I'd brought home to unwrap: the plates, the vases, the wall-plaques, the fish-spoon rest. Some of them I found garish. I'm not keen on religious artefacts myself, so the plaques with cherubs or Madonnas in raised relief didn't appeal to me, even though they could be worth anything from £50 to £100 each. But the vases and plates, with their incised flowers and foliage in shades of cream, yellow and green, I thought were lovely.

I looked on the Internet but valuing them was difficult. Similar pieces to the ones now standing on my kitchen table fetched anything between £400 and £1500. A two-handled baluster jug decorated with foliage and stylised fish had sold on the Internet recently for £600. A lot depended on the artist who had decorated the piece. Cassandra Ann Walker, or Cassandia as she was sometimes known, was the most famous artistic influence at Della Robbia. A plate she had decorated, with incised tulips and ivy leaves, had just sold for £1367. I leant over and picked up the phone.

'I've just been trying to value the collection of Della Robbia you've given me,' I said when Lady Margaret picked up.

'Della what? I thought it was majolica. Hideous stuff.'

'Well, the point is, this could add up to quite a valuable collection. It's very kind of you to give it to me but I don't feel comfortable in accepting—'

'Now look here, Juno,' Lady Margaret cut in impatiently. 'It's of no value to me whatsoever, compared with getting my precious Florrie back. You won't let me thank you any other way and if you try to have this conversation again,' she added forcefully, 'you and I are going to fall out.'

'Right,' I blinked, slightly taken aback. 'As long as you're sure.'

'Absolutely,' she declared.

'Well, thank you very much,' I responded weakly.

'My pleasure, my dear,' she assured me, and put the phone down.

I puffed my cheeks out in a sigh. I knew I shouldn't have caved in so weakly. Let's see how well these things sell at auction, I decided. She might change her mind if they sell for megabucks. 'I tried,' I told Bill, who had woken up from his resting place on the kitchen chair.

He stretched, yawning to show white fangs and a delicate curl of pink tongue, and surveyed the assembled pottery with interest.

'And if you even think about leaping up on to this table,' I warned him, 'you'll end up as a pair of furry slippers.'

CHAPTER FOURTEEN

Next day I packed the boxes of Della Robbia and took them around to Rendells, the auction house on the edge of Ashburton. They wouldn't be holding their next antique and fine art sale for a few weeks, but I reckoned the stuff would be safer stored there than at my flat or in the shop. After that I did some shopping for one of my clients, Tom Carter, who'd finally been offered a date for his hip replacement. He'd been on a waiting list for two years, in a lot of pain and hardly able to move. 'You'll be toddling around like a two-year-old in no time,' I told him. A keen fisherman, walker, and a member of the Dartmoor Search and Rescue, his enforced inactivity had been as much a trial to him as the pain. More recently, he'd become friends with Elizabeth, a relationship that the rest of the staff of *Old Nick's* was watching with interest. I reckoned

Tom's replacement hip should ratchet the interest level up a notch or two.

As I was in town and it was getting on for lunchtime, I decided to grab a sandwich in the deli and go round to the shop to eat it. It was Sophie's day off; Pat would be there alone and she'd probably appreciate the company. But when I reached *Old Nick's*, the lights were off inside and the sign on the door said *Closed*. Puzzled, I unlocked and went in. There was a note on the counter from Pat. *Sorry Juno I had to go*, it read in her large, schoolgirl scrawl. *Please phone me*.

I was hanging on for ages before she answered. 'Oh, Juno!' she sounded breathless, almost tearful. 'I'm sorry I had to leave the shop but I had to come home. Sue phoned. The police are here. Dozens of 'em, there are, crawling all over the place.'

'Why?'

'I don't know.' Her voice broke into a wail. 'They won't tell us. But that Cruella woman's here. I think we're going to be arrested.'

'Don't worry Pat,' I told her. 'I'll be there in five.'

It was actually ten, by the time poor little Van Blanc had bounced its way up the deeply rutted lane that led to Honeysuckle Farm. The recent rain had made the track muddy, and my wheels sloshed through the puddles, splashing the sides of the van. I was going to have to get the hose out later. Severe shortage of funds kept the owners from maintaining the track, or replacing the rotting wooden sign that advertises 'Animal Sanctuary'.

Every penny is spent on feed and vet's bills. And although the animals are loved and cared for better than some people's children, the first sight of the farm is not prepossessing.

On this occasion, my view of the place was blocked by three police cars and a riot van, all of which appeared to be empty. A bored-looking police constable wearing a stab vest was standing by the gate. She eyed me suspiciously as I approached, drawing herself up to her full height and trying to look official, until I raised a hand in greeting. I recognised her from the local station. She'd been round to my flat once with one of her colleagues, drinking my tea and asking questions. I forget what they thought I'd been up to at the time. She recognised me as well, almost smiled. Behind her, across the yard, I could see police officers poking around the outbuildings and in the paddock; they were faces I didn't recognise.

'You've come a bit mob-handed, haven't you?' I said to her. 'What's going on?'

'We're conducting a search.' She hesitated, knowing she shouldn't say any more, but she must have been as bored as she looked because she added confidentially, 'We're acting on a tip-off. Some of these officers have come up from Plymouth.'

'What kind of tip-off?'

Primly, she folded her lips. 'I can't say. It was anonymous.'

One of the policemen suddenly shot out from the outbuilding behind her as if propelled by a rocket. He leapt over the fence, rubbing his leg and cursing. He was followed at speed by a large, black-faced sheep sporting impressive headgear. Bam-a-lam the Ram does not take kindly to intruders. Thwarted by the fence he slithered to a halt, stood in majestic stillness for a moment just to make his point, then turned and stalked back the way he had come. Hiding a smile, I turned my attention to the constable. How was I going to blag my way inside?

I could hear Pat's dog, Samdog, barking somewhere. He must be going nuts with all these strangers prowling about. At the end of the orchard stood the old caravan where the two lads were staying. As I watched, two coppers approached it with a crowbar and began to lever the door open.

'I might have information germane to your investigation,' I told the constable grandly, hoping she wouldn't ask for details.

An uncertain frown drew her thinly plucked eyebrows together. 'What?'

'I can't say.' Two can play at that game. 'I need to speak to whoever's in charge.'

She muttered, pressed a button on the radio she carried and raised it to her lips. There was a crackle and a blast of static before a disembodied voice demanded to know what she wanted.

'There's a woman here says she knows something,' she murmured, keeping her eyes fixed on me. After a moment there was a reply, although I couldn't make out what was being said. 'You're to go on up to the house,' she told me, opening the gate to let me through. 'An officer will come out.'

I thanked her sunnily as I passed and followed the path up to the bungalow. By this time the coppers had managed to force open the caravan door. What the hell was going on? I was only halfway up the path before the door of the bungalow opened and another policeman stood observing me. He was tall and fit-looking, his light brown hair cropped short, shirt and tie under his stab vest.

'I understand you might have information,' he said as his eyes travelled over me. 'Who are you?' He wasn't wasting time on any pleasantries. He wasn't local, I didn't recognise him, and he sounded like a Londoner.

'Juno Browne. I'm a friend of Pat Giddings, and Ken and Sue Roach.' I decided not to waste time on pleasantries either. 'And you are?'

'DI Mike Swift, Devon and Cornwall Anti-Slavery Unit.'

Anti-Slavery Unit? I got a sudden vision of underage girls in miniskirts hanging around on street corners or working in nail bars. 'Slavery? Is that what they've been accused of?'

'They haven't been accused of anything yet,' he responded, tight-lipped. 'We're conducting a search, based on a tip-off.'

Suddenly, everything fell into place: this was about the two boys in the caravan. 'Let me guess, this tip-off came from Slovenia?'

'Slovakia.'

'One of them.'

He frowned at me intently, his light eyes narrowing. 'And what do you know about that?'

I sighed. 'Could I come inside, d'you think? I might be able to help sort this nonsense out.'

Without speaking, he stepped aside to let me through the porch. I glanced into the living room. Pat and Sue huddled next to each other on the sofa, miserably holding hands. Ken was sitting silently fidgeting in his armchair, his usually ruddy complexion a thunderous shade of puce. By the fireplace, lording it over them all, stood a uniformed officer and Detective Sergeant Christine deVille. Judging by the smirk on her nasty little mouth, she was enjoying every minute of it, but her smile vanished when she caught sight of me. 'What's she doing here?'

Pat looked up. 'Juno!' she cried, as if the cavalry had suddenly galloped in. But DI Fit-Looking Mike Swift steered me into the kitchen before I could speak.

Cruella followed. 'I might ask the same about you.' I told her. 'You're not in any Anti-Slavery Unit.'

'I'm acting as liaison from the local force,' she responded starchily.

'Liaison?' I repeated, disbelieving. Didn't you need some sort of people-handling skills to do that? 'Come on, Cruella!' I jerked an arm towards the three sitting in the living room. 'You know those people in there. D'you really think all this is necessary?' I didn't mean to call her Cruella. It just slipped out. But from the corner of my eye, I saw the corner of DI Swift's lips twitch in a suppressed smile.

'We have information that two young men are being held here against their will,' he told me. 'And forced to work without payment.'

'Under the Modern Slavery Act of 2015—' Cruella began.

'Oh, shut up!' I really didn't have the patience to listen to her parroting. 'Don't you think you'd be better employed trying to find Sandy Thomas's murderer?' I knew that was a low blow but I didn't care. She stiffened. 'That investigation is ongoing.'

'Yeah,' I nodded. 'Going nowhere. This is all a misunderstanding,' I explained, turning to DI Swift. 'There *are* two young men working here. Eduardo's from Spain, he's been here weeks. He's come here to improve his English and, from what I understand, he likes it here and is planning to stay until Christmas. Dalek, he's from Slov . . . *ak*ia. He's a more recent arrival. He has issues with getting his hands dirty. He doesn't want to be here.'

Cruella pounced. 'So, he *is* being held against his will!'

'No, I don't mean that, and you know I don't,' I snapped, exasperated. 'His father made him come. He spends most of his time on his phone complaining to his girlfriend back home. And she, I imagine, is the source of your information.' Neither of them spoke, but I could tell from the look that passed between them that I was right. 'Haven't you heard of the Work Around the World Scheme?' I asked. 'It allows young people to travel and get work experience in return for bed and board.'

Swift looked blank and shrugged.

'Well, don't you think, if you're part of a unit investigating slavery in this country, that you ought to be aware of it?' Through the kitchen window I could see four more policemen tramping about in the fields. 'This is incredible. You're prepared to launch this whole operation on the strength of a single anonymous phone call from someone living in Slovakia, but you've only got to ask Eduardo and—'

'That's the problem.' Swift cleared his throat. 'He's not here. When did you last see him?'

My turn to look blank. 'I'm sorry?'

'When did you last see Eduardo Ramirez?'

'Well, I haven't actually . . . um, I've never actually seen him,' I admitted, suddenly feeling foolish. 'Pat's told me all about him. About both of them.'

'But you've never met either of them yourself?'

'No.'

'So, you've actually no idea what their working conditions are,' Cruella's face could not conceal her triumph, 'other than what Miss Giddings has told you.'

'Well, that's good enough for me,' I responded weakly, but she'd succeeded in making me feel like an idiot.

'We have information the two young men are being held prisoner in a caravan,' she added. 'It's locked, and Mr Roach claims he hasn't got the key.'

'It's not locked any more because I just saw your men breaking into it,' I told her, returning her glare. 'As for the key, I expect one of the boys has got it. They're the ones who are sleeping in it.'

'Well, we can't ask them. They're missing.'

'Missing?'

'Mr and Mrs Roach say that it's Eduardo's day off,' Swift went on calmly, 'and that he's gone to Exeter for the day. We've tried to contact him on his mobile, but so far, no luck.'

'What about Dalek?'

'According to Mr and Mrs Roach he should be here, working. But he seems to have disappeared as well. We can't find him.'

'He probably made himself scarce when he saw you lot arriving, realised what a lot of shit he's likely to be in.'

DI Swift permitted himself a smile. 'Your account agrees with what Mr and Mrs Roach and Ms Giddings have told us. If we can find the boys and they confirm what you say, then we'll happily leave them all in peace.'

And if you can't find them, I thought to myself, I suppose you're going to start digging up the garden.

Just then there was a knock on the kitchen door and a policeman poked his head inside.

'Well?' DI Swift directed a look at him.

'It looks as if the boys are living in the caravan, sir. It's a bit untidy but it's clean enough and there are two proper beds inside it and a fridge full of milk and beer. Frankly, I've spent holidays in worse.'

'Okay. Thank you, Constable.'

The policeman nodded and took himself off again. A moment later there was a commotion at the front door, and a voice loudly exclaiming in a foreign language that did not sound like Spanish. Two policemen walked into the kitchen, either side of a dark-haired, heavily built young man dressed in a Hawaiian shirt, shorts and flip-flops – not exactly the gear for a hard day's work mucking out the animals.

'Not a word, Ms Browne,' DI Swift warned me in a low voice.

'We found him up at the end of the far field, sir,' one of the constables said, 'hiding in one of the sheds.'

'I say nothing,' the young man announced.

'Well, that's helpful,' Swift muttered.

'No, I say nothing,' he repeated, pointing towards the living room, 'about them. They good people. Good food here. My girlfriend, Katya, *she* say.'

'Just a moment. Can you confirm that your name is Dalek Horváth?'

Dalek gave an emphatic nod and grinned. 'Yes.' He thumped his chest. 'It's me.'

'And you're saying that you have made no complaint against your employers?'

Dalek hesitated a moment, appearing to process the language. 'Yes. I make no complaint. Is Katya.'

'Why were you hiding?'

'Not hiding,' Dalek responded indignantly. 'Resting.'

'Are you here of your own free will?' Cruella demanded.

Dalek frowned, mystified.

'You're here because you want to be here?' Swift spoke slowly and Dalek nodded. That he understood.

'No. I not want to be here. But my ticket home is not before end of month. My father, he tell me if I show face before end of month he give me good kicking.'

Mike Swift cleared his throat. 'I see.'

Now that Dalek had opened up, he was becoming quite talkative. 'My father, he farmer. I do not want be farmer. With pigs. I want be deejay in nightclub.'

'What's that bruise on your leg?' Cruella pointed to a purple crescent shape on his hairy calf. 'Who did that to you?'

Dalek grunted. 'Maureen.'

Cruella's eyes narrowed to violet slits. 'Maureen?'

'Donkey.'

Poor Dalek, it seemed wherever he was, he was likely to get a kicking from someone.

'I do not like donkey, or sheeps, but I stay.' He shrugged. 'It's okay. Food good. But Ashburton is arsehole of world. No nightclubs.'

'Do you know where Eduardo Ramirez is today?' Swift asked, the slightest tremor of laughter in his voice.

'He go to Exeter, see cathedral.' Dalek grinned broadly and thumped his chest. 'On my day off I go to Plymouth. See nightclubs.'

'Try Ramirez's mobile again, will you, Sergeant,' Swift instructed Cruella. 'See if we can raise him.'

Cruella wandered off into the hallway to make her call and a few moments later we could hear her talking to someone. She came back in, still holding the phone. 'He's in Ashburton, sir, just got off the Exeter bus. He's waiting for a lift. ApparentlyMrs Roach promised to fetch him when he returned.'

'Okay, send someone down to pick him up.'

Dalek raised a finger. 'I go too? Get ride in police car?'

Mike Swift smiled. 'Well, that's something most people try to avoid. No,'fraid not, Mr Horváth. Sergeant, stand the men down, there's no need to keep searching. With any luck we'll be out of here within the hour.'

'Sir,' she nodded and went out.

The inspector glanced at me. 'You can go too, Miss Browne.'

I shook my head. 'I'd like to join my friends, if that's okay. Tell them what's going on,' I added pointedly. 'It's time someone did.'

'Of course. I'll have a word,' he said and disappeared into the living room. He closed the door after him so I couldn't hear what was being said.

'I think I'll make some tea,' I told Dalek, who was standing looking as if he didn't know what to do next.

'Good idea,' he nodded, giving me a thumbs up. 'Three sugars.'

Actually, it had been Pat, Ken and Sue who I felt were in need of refreshment; and probably something a lot stronger than tea.

'I'd just like a few words with Mr Ramirez,' I heard Mike Swift say as he came out of the living room, 'then we'll be out of your hair.'

The kettle had scarcely boiled when Cruella reappeared, accompanied by a slim, dark-eyed youth in jeans and a hoodie, who confirmed, in perfect English, that he was Eduardo Ramirez. I made tea, whilst Eduardo gave details of his living and working conditions at Honeysuckle Farm and talked about the various Work Around the World schemes he'd worked at before coming here. He'd been picking fruit in Lincolnshire earlier in the summer, apparently, and helping out at a micro-brewery in Kent. I noticed Mike Swift wrote down details of the website. I handed around the tea to everyone, even Cruella, although I couldn't find the arsenic, then left them to it and took a tray into Pat, Ken and Sue in the living room.

'Thanks for coming up, Juno.' Pat had stopped looking tearful and Ken's face was restored to a less alarming shade of crimson. Sue, a slightly rounder and comelier version of her sister, still seemed agitated.

'I don't think I'd have been much help if they hadn't found Dalek and Eduardo,' I admitted, handing her a mug.

'They don't think we're using slave labour any more, then?' Ken asked gruffly.

'I think they've been straightened out.'

There was a knock on the door and Mike Swift appeared, announcing that he was satisfied that the accounts he had been given were the truth and there would be no charges to answer. He also apologised for the inconvenience.

'So, it was all a misunderstanding, is that what you're saying?' Pat asked him. 'All the fault of that girlfriend of Dalek's.'

He smiled ruefully. 'I'm sure you understand that we have to act on this kind of tip-off. Particularly if it comes from Eastern Europe.' He cleared his throat. 'Miss Browne, could I have a word?'

I accompanied him outside. 'Are your friends all right?' he asked.

'Still a bit rattled but I think they'll live.'

He flicked me a sly glance. 'I know we may appear to have arrived mob-handed but we never know what we might find in these situations.'

'I can imagine.' Why did he care what I thought?

'Anyway, let me give you this.' He handed me his card. 'Just in case.'

'Just in case of what?' I asked.

He smiled and shrugged a little awkwardly. For a moment he looked almost boyish. 'You might think of something.'

I watched him walk off down the path. He had actually turned out to be quite nice. At least he had a sense of humour. Obviously one of the good guys. Just a pity he wasn't Daniel.

CHAPTER FIFTEEN

I was just going to bed when the doorbell rang. I muttered curses as I tramped down the stairs in my slippers, raking a hand through the tangle of my hair before I opened the door. Detective Constable Dean Collins stood on the doorstep, grinning.

'What?' I demanded rudely.

'I hear you've been at it again, making friends and influencing people.'

I groaned. 'You've been talking to Cruella.'

'She told me what had gone on. Can I come in a minute?'

'Sure.' I stood back to let him in. 'Is everything okay?' I asked as we clumped back up to the flat. 'Is Gemma all right?'

He chuckled. 'Ready to pop, bless her. Due any day now.'

'Do you know what flavour you're getting?'

'No, we decided to keep it a surprise.'

'Am I going to be godmother to this one as well?'

Dean checked his stride, looked slightly embarrassed. 'Well, last time, Gem's cousin got a bit upset she wasn't asked so . . .'

I flapped a hand at him. 'Oh, keep the peace, for God's sake!' It didn't bother me. I was sure one godchild was enough. I don't want to spread myself too thin. 'Cup of tea?' I asked, not bothering to stifle my yawn.

'Well, if you're offering.' He followed me into the kitchen and waited until I'd filled the kettle and flipped the switch on before he spoke again. 'You still walking those dogs every morning?'

He knew very well I was. I reached for the teabags. 'Why d'you ask?'

He sat his heavy bulk down at the kitchen table; my chair creaked in protest. 'There's been a lot of dog theft going on around here recently,' then added with heavy emphasis, 'as I'm sure you know.'

I scowled at him. I hadn't told him anything about my involvement with Florence's kidnappers. I'd promised Lady Margaret that I'd keep quiet about the incident. Had someone blabbed to him? Ricky or Morris? Sophie? 'I've read something about it in the papers,' I answered guardedly.

He pulled my slightly battered vintage 1930's biscuit tin towards him, lifted the lid and frowned at the contents before taking out a chocolate digestive. 'This is your last one,' he told me as it disappeared into his gob, 'did you know?'

'I do now.' I plonked his mug of tea down in front of him and sat.

He munched thoughtfully for a few moments and when he spoke, his voice had lost all trace of levity. 'A young woman had her dog stolen today and was seriously assaulted in the process.'

'Oh God, really? Where did this happen, in Ashburton?'

'Not far away. She was on a lonely stretch of road, the dog in the car beside her. She'd noticed a van behind. The driver flashed his lights, sounded his horn, overtook and then pulled in in front of her, so she stopped. A chap gets out of the van, tells her one of her brake lights is smashed. She gets out for a look, goes to the rear of the vehicle and sure enough it is.'

'And she hadn't noticed this before?'

'She told us it was okay when she left home that morning. Anyway, whilst this bloke is keeping her talking, another man gets out of the van and she hears her passenger door open. When she looks, he's taking her dog out of the car. It was one of them titchy things, all hair . . . shiatsu.'

'That's massage, I think you mean a shih-tzu.'

'Right, well it's not my idea of a dog.' He rubbed the bristly hair on his head reflectively. 'Anyway, this fella starts putting it in the back of the van and when she tries to stop him the first man punches her. She tries to put up a fight, but he knocks her out cold. Another driver found her a few minutes later lying in the middle of the road and called an ambulance. There's no sign of the van or the dog. Poor woman's distraught.'

'I bet. Is she badly hurt?'

'Concussion. A few bruises. They're keeping her in hospital overnight, just in case. I don't think she'd have cared too much if they'd just stolen her car. But she's got an autistic kiddie and this dog's his whole world apparently.'

'I don't suppose she got the numberplate of the van?'

'Only a partial, and they're probably false plates. And no real description of the men – average height, average build, dark clothes, dark glasses . . .' he shrugged. 'The reason I'm telling you is, if those are the lengths these characters are prepared to go to just to steal a dog, then I want you to be on your guard, that's all.'

'Thanks.' I took a sip of tea. 'Do you think they smashed her brake light?'

'Probably. It's an old trick used in carjacking. In fact, there doesn't have to be anything wrong with the car, the villains just have to convince the driver that there is, to lure them out of the vehicle. But I've never known it used to steal a dog before.'

'Dogs are big money these days.'

He nodded, staring at me meaningfully and once again I wondered how much he knew about Florence's kidnap. I felt my face growing warm. 'Well, I can't see anyone running off with the Tribe,' I said, 'but thanks for the warning.' I made a mental note to let Becky know. I sipped my tea for a moment. 'Is there any news about Sandy? Any progress in finding her killer?'

Dean pulled down the corners of his mouth. 'You know I'm not allowed to tell you.'

'Well, you could have just said no,' I responded, eyeing him, 'and that would have ended the matter, so I reckon you must have found out something. Alastair Dunston's alibi check out?' Dean frowned but remained mute so I prattled on. 'Mm, rock solid I reckon. He'll have made sure of that. Is he still claiming he wasn't having an affair with Sandy? Phil Thomas says—'

He leant forward suddenly. 'You've been talking to Phil Thomas?'

I laughed. I knew he'd bite on that. 'I bumped into him in a pub.'

'Yeah, like hell,' he muttered derisively.

'Phil says he knows Dunston and Sandy were having an affair because Sandy told him. I wondered if Phil might have killed Sandy out of jealousy because he still carried a torch for her, even after they'd split up, but he's got a new woman in his life now, Laura, so I guess . . .' I stopped and frowned. 'Doesn't she confirm Phil's alibi?'

Dean shook his head. 'Laura wasn't with him and his mates at the pub that night. She confirms what time he came home. But she can't account for that time when Phil's drunken mate was out cold, giving him the opportunity to slip up to the woods and murder Sandy. No one can.'

I sighed. Phil didn't seem like a murderer to me. 'Motive?'

'The point is,' Dean went on, 'Phil's not the man caught on Olly's camera. And nor is Dunston, who, by the way – and you'd better keep this under your hat – admitted to his affair with Sandy under further questioning. He wanted to keep it from his wife, he said. Mind you,' he went on, staring into my empty biscuit tin and sniffing in disgust, 'she must be a bit bloomin' thick if she hasn't cottoned on by now.' He picked up the tin and emptied the remaining crumbs into his palm and then snaffled them with his lips in much the way Wesley might have done.

'Oh my God, are you hungry?' I asked in disgust. 'D'you want toast or something?'

He brushed his palms together. 'No. Just tidying up.'

'And was she stalking him? Sandy, I mean.'

'He caught her hiding in his garden taking pictures on her phone, so she was either desperate to get a sighting of lover-boy or she thought he was up to something.'

I'd like to think it was the latter. 'What? I wonder. You haven't found this phone?'

'No.'

'Pity.'

'We've been checking into his history, but Dunston seems to be an upright citizen, pillar of the community, no shady past, no dodgy dealings that we can discover. No sizeable debts. Not even a parking ticket.'

'So, you've got nothing more to go on?'

'Only one thing. We can't account for Sandy's movements for the two days before she was killed. She was supposed to work on the Saturday and the day before, but she didn't come in. She was killed on the Friday evening but the last anyone heard of her was Friday morning, when she rang in to say she was sick. Thing is, her mate in the office, Evie, called round at

151

her place at lunchtime on Friday to see if she needed anything and couldn't raise her. She thought she might be asleep but then noticed that her car wasn't there.'

'She'd pulled a sickie and gone out?'

'It looks that way,' Dean agreed. 'But where was she, for the last day of her life? What was she up to? That's what I'd like to know.'

I nodded. That's what I'd like to know too. And I wondered why, if she'd been missing from work for two days, Guy Mitchell hadn't mentioned it.

'I didn't know,' he admitted pleasantly when I slipped along to his office lunchtime next day and asked him the question. 'I was out of the office all day on the Friday and didn't know Sandy hadn't come in to work that day until I arrived on Saturday.'

'Evie told you that she had called in sick?'

Mitch gave a wry smile. 'Well, no actually, she didn't mention it. I got the feeling she might have kept quiet about it if I hadn't asked where Sandy was.'

I looked around for Evie but couldn't see her. The office was empty save for one middle-aged man in the corner, working on a computer, typing with two fingers. I recognised him from his photograph in the paper. He wrote about farming.

'It's her day off,' Mitch explained.

'And you assumed Sandy was still unwell on the Saturday?'

He nodded. 'I'd have told her to take the weekend anyway, get over it.'

'Get over what?'

'A migraine, Evie said.'

Migraine can be annihilating, but there's not much anyone can do if you're suffering from one except ride it out. Which made me wonder why Evie had driven over to her house to check up on Sandy during her lunch hour. Was she particularly worried about her for some reason?

'Was Sandy a regular sufferer?'

'She's had 'em before. She was off with one last month.'

'Did Evie tell you that Sandy's car wasn't there when she called around?'

'Not at first. She didn't tell me that until after she'd been questioned by the police.'

It sounded to me as if Evie was trying to cover for Sandy. 'Was she worried Sandy would lose her job if you knew she'd pulled a sickie?'

Mitch laughed. 'I don't think my staff are that frightened of me. I don't exactly put them under pressure. This isn't Fleet Street.' He called out to the feature writer tapping away in the corner. 'Is it, Jim?'

Jim just chuckled and kept typing.

'You said you'd confined her to the office after the business with Dunston. Is it likely she'd have gone off investigating something on her own, used the sickie as an excuse, particularly if she knew you weren't going to come in that day?'

Mitch pulled down the corners of his mouth. 'It's possible.' He shrugged. 'Anything was possible with Sandy.'

'Would Evie know?'

'Well, if she does, she hasn't told me. You'll have to ask her yourself.'

I smiled. 'I intend to.'

It took me a few days to catch up with her, what with one thing and another. One thing being my usual workload and the other being extra hours at the shop as Pat went down with a 'gyppy tummy', which may well have been induced by the stress of the police raid on Honeysuckle Farm. Apparently, the event had had a galvanising effect on Dalek, who suddenly started pulling his weight. This might be put down to guilt at all the trouble his girlfriend had caused, except that he seemed fairly unabashed by the whole incident and didn't really strike me as the guilty type. Perhaps Eduardo had set him straight. He'd realised that he'd landed in a more comfortable situation than many youngsters who join work-away schemes, and didn't want to be sacked in case his father sent him somewhere worse.

I'd promised Sophie a few days off to stay with a friend in Cornwall, so I was pretty much on my own in the shop except when Elizabeth came in. And it was during a long, quiet afternoon that I received a visitor.

I thought she was a customer at first. She spent a long time looking around, picking things up and putting them down again. Because she kept flicking glances in my direction, I began to suspect that she might be a shoplifter. She seemed too well-dressed for that, in a well-cut jacket and carrying an expensive leather bag, but I knew from experience that appearances can be deceptive. She had looped a pashmina around her neck and double knotted it, its ends tucked into the wide shawl collar of her jacket, achieving a look that was casually fashionable. When I try for the same effect, I look as if I'm being strangled by a bundle of washing.

'Can I help you?' I asked.

She shook her head, her bobbed blonde hair swinging. 'Just looking. Is that all right? I'm trying to find a present for a friend.'

'Of course,' I said, and she smiled. As she turned away from me, I had the feeling I'd seen her before. It was not her face, but the way the ends of her long blonde bob rested on the shoulders of that lovely tan jacket, an image that I thought I'd seen before somewhere. She spent a long time flicking through the browser, studying a mounted watercolour of Sophie's, a miniature of toadstools at the foot of an oak tree, before bringing it to the counter. We agreed on how sweet it was, and I wrapped it for her, all the time conscious of the fact that she was watching me. I sensed there was something she wanted to say.

'Was there anything else?' I asked.

'You are Juno Browne, aren't you?' It was more statement than question.

I smiled. 'Last time I looked.'

'I recognise you from the meeting.'

Ah, the meeting at Woodland! Now I got it! That shiny blonde bob had been sitting a few rows in front of me. 'Were you there to object?' I asked.

She gave a wry smile. 'The development doesn't seem to be popular with the locals, does it?'

The locals? She wasn't from around here, then. 'Do you blame them?'

She gave a slight shrug. 'I can see their point of view. But actually, I was there to support my husband.' She added, with a slightly combative glint in her eye, 'I'm Louise Dunston.'

I was ready to explode with curiosity. She hadn't come in just to buy a present for a friend. She wanted something. I indicated a chair by the counter. 'Would you like to sit down?'

'Of course,' she admitted as she sat and placed that expensive bag on the floor, 'it would be more accurate to say that I recognised you from your pictures in the paper.' She brushed the lap of her skirt with highly polished, dark green fingernails that matched her shoes. She didn't look like a *Dartmoor Gazette* reader to me, more likely *The Telegraph,* or *The Times*. And *Vogue*. As if she read my thoughts, she continued, 'After the death of that woman, I was curious to read what she had written. You seem to be a favourite subject of hers.'

That woman. Sandy Thomas. Poor murdered Sandy Thomas. 'Have you come for my autograph?' I asked.

We eyed each other. Her eyes were amber-coloured, but without the warmth.

'Despite what was scrawled on the bonnet of his car, my husband didn't kill her.'

'And why do you need to tell me this?'

She hesitated a moment. 'Because there's something I want you to do for me.'

Now we're coming to it. 'Which is?'

'Unlike the local police, you don't seem to be stupid. You see things they miss.'

I felt almost indignant on behalf of Inspector Ford and Dean Collins, even Cruella. 'I wouldn't describe them as stupid. Pressured and under-resourced, maybe.'

She smiled bitterly. 'The press would just love to pin this murder on my husband and so would the police. Because he's wealthy, and in the public eye. It's the politics of envy. They'd love to make him the scapegoat for their own incompetence, their inability to catch the real killer. They've already interviewed him twice, once under caution—'

I interrupted her. 'You don't think perhaps that's because they believe he might have a motive?'

'Covering up his affair with that woman?' She gave a hollow laugh. 'There wasn't much chance of that, was there, after her little stunt at the charity dinner? Besides,' she added with a slight twist of her mouth, 'she's not his first and I don't flatter myself she'll be his last. You see, I know my husband. And because I know him, I can tell you that he didn't kill Sandy Thomas, or arrange her murder. He couldn't. He hasn't got it in him.'

She made this sound as if this were almost a weakness. I could understand her bitterness. After all, what could an overweight, barely educated woman from the Welsh valleys have to attract Dunston that his elegant, sophisticated wife didn't?

'So, what do you want from me?' I asked.

She sighed, an audible release of tension. 'I am prepared to pay you for any information that you can find that points to the innocence of my husband.'

I hadn't been expecting that. Taken aback, I laughed. 'I'm not a private detective.'

'Perhaps not, but you've solved crimes before.'

'But I'm not someone you can hire.'

She leant forward towards me. 'Look, I am trying to shield my children from the fallout from my husband's cupidity.' There was a note of desperation in her voice. 'God knows that's difficult enough when they can find out about everything and anything on their stupid phones. And if the press and social media get behind the idea that Alastair is a suspect . . . well, he's already received some vile messages on Twitter.' Her amber eyes bore into mine. 'You knew Sandy Thomas. Don't you want to know who killed her?'

'Yes of course I do.' But not for the same reasons she did, not just to establish her precious husband's innocence. He might well be guilty, for all I knew. I wanted to know who killed Sandy because I knew her, because she was a woman who tried to make something of herself, because she died alone with no one to help her. Because her last moments were moments of pain and terror and she didn't deserve that. No woman deserves that. And because she was nosy, and talked too much, and because she cared what happened to people and because she had – suddenly I realised the quality that had attracted Alastair Dunston, the quality that his wife seemed to lack – she had warmth.

But Louise Dunston was a mother and I felt for her in her desperation. 'Let me ask you something. Do you think Sandy was stalking your husband?'

She shrugged. 'Well, we found her in our garden. It was so embarrassing. We had company for dinner – colleagues from his building firm that Alastair insisted on inviting, and their ghastly wives – we'd just gone out on the terrace for drinks and there she was, skulking in the shrubbery.'

'Did she offer any explanation for being there?'

'No. She was just snooping, I suppose. Alastair marched her off the premises pretty quickly.' She leant forward again, her voice softening, almost pleading. 'Look, I'll make it worth your while.'

'I'm sorry. I can't. But I promise,' I added, relenting a little, 'if I do come across any evidence, anything at all, I will communicate it to the police.'

She gave an empty laugh. 'Who will conveniently forget it.'

'No, I don't believe that.'

'Then perhaps you're not so clever after all.' She stood up and flipped a business card down on the counter. 'In case you change your mind.' She swept out without another word, leaving the picture she had chosen, wrapped but unpaid for, on the counter.

I unwrapped it and returned it to its place in the browser. I wouldn't mention to Sophie that she'd had a near miss. There is nothing more aggravating than just missing a sale.

The shop bell rang again. This time it was Elizabeth,

toting a carrier bag full of books. 'Donations from Tom,' she announced, 'for the book exchange. Someone gave them to him but he's not really into thrillers.' She began to unload the books onto the counter. 'They're in almost pristine condition.'

'Any donations gratefully received,' I said, smiling. 'How's Olly?'

'He was a bit shaken for a few days, but he seems to be fine now. He's confining his night-time filming activities to the garden for the present.'

'Are the badgers still digging up your potatoes?'

'Yes, but he's trying to distract them by laying trails of peanuts up to the back door.' She laughed. 'Toby is not amused.'

'Something weird just happened.' I told her about my visit from Louise Dunston. She drew up a chair and listened. 'Don't you think it's odd?' I asked her. 'I mean, why ask me to investigate, to dig up evidence to prove her husband's innocent of a murder he hasn't actually been accused of yet? Not officially.'

Elizabeth put her head on one side, fiddling with a gold earring as she considered. 'Perhaps she's not convinced he is innocent. She's hoping you'll find something that will persuade her.'

'Then why not go to a professional private detective? It can't be because of money. She must be loaded.'

'On the other hand, she might be hoping you'll uncover something that proves his guilt.'

'She's out for revenge, you mean, because of his affair with Sandy?'

Elizabeth shrugged. 'Why not? She must have felt humiliated by the public exposure.'

This would make her a far more devious person than I'd suspected. I thought about it for a moment, but it didn't feel right. 'I'm not sure. I believed her when she said that she's trying to protect her children.'

'She can't protect them forever,' she pointed out. 'And if it's their father they need protecting from, why not get rid of him?'

'Well, whatever she's up to, I'm not getting involved in her scheming.' But Elizabeth had made me think. Just how far was Louise Dunston prepared to go to protect her children? She said that her husband didn't have it in him to have Sandy Thomas murdered. But the question was, did she?

I finally caught up with Evie at the end of the next working day. In the *Dartmoor Gazette* office, they told me she had just left but I might catch her in the car park if I hurried. I did a quick sprint, yelling her name across to a young woman just about to get into her car who I hoped might be her. She turned and regarded me with a querying, guarded look as I approached her breathlessly, a slim girl with a sharply pointed face, brown hair drawn back into a ponytail. I didn't need to introduce myself; she knew who I was. I suppose she would, working for the newspaper, but I still find it disconcerting when a complete stranger has the advantage of me. 'I'm in a hurry,' she warned me. 'I'm going out later.'

'I won't keep you long,' I promised. 'I just wondered

about the day Sandy called in sick. You drove over to see her in your lunch hour. Were you worried about her?'

She sighed, leaning her weight against the side of the car. 'I was,' she admitted, nodding sadly. 'She'd been a bit quiet since that business with Alastair Dunston, depressed, you know, not really herself. She wasn't the sort to bunk off with no good reason, either, so I thought she must be really bad, one way or another.'

'But when you got to her place, she wasn't there?'

She shook her head. 'I know the pills she takes for her migraines zonk her out, so when she didn't answer the door, I thought she might be asleep, but when I saw her car wasn't there in her drive . . .'

'You don't know if she was following up a story of her own? Something perhaps she didn't want Mitch to know about?'

Her smooth forehead puckered in a frown 'Like what?'

'I don't know,' I admitted. 'Maybe something she thought he might disapprove of, or feel was a waste of time.'

'She kept it a secret if she was.' She was thoughtful a moment, pursing her lips. 'I've thought about it over and over. I wish there was something I could tell you, but . . .' She trailed off into silence, shaking her head. She glanced at her watch. 'Look, I've got to go.'

'Just one more thing,' I said as she flung her shoulder bag onto the passenger seat of her car and clambered into the driver's seat. 'You don't know why she'd written my name on her pad, you don't know what it was she wanted to ask me?'

''Fraid not.' She smiled as she shook her head. 'It's nice to meet you, though, finally.'

'And you.'

I watched her start up and begin to back out of her parking space. She'd barely completed her turn when she braked and wound down her window. 'Something Alf said to me the other day, I've just remembered. He's the old bloke who cleans our offices in the evening. Sandy often stopped for a chat with him on her way out. Well, I spoke to him last night and we were having the same conversation, you know, wondering what had happened to her, and he said that the last time he saw her he asked her if she was going out for the evening . . .' Evie smiled a little awkwardly. 'I don't suppose this makes any sense, but he said that Sandy told him she was going to see someone about a dog.' She shrugged. 'Perhaps she didn't want to tell Alf what she really meant.' She grinned as she pulled away. 'Perhaps it was a euphemism for something.'

Perhaps, I thought, as I watched her drive away. Or perhaps she meant exactly what she said.

CHAPTER SIXTEEN

I walked straight back to *Old Nick's*. The *Dartmoor Gazette* was delivered free to businesses, which meant we always had a pile of them under the counter in the shop. We kept them for wrapping things up. I grabbed a bundle of the top ones, hoping the issue I was looking for hadn't already been used to pack up a vase or some dinner plates. I was searching for the same issue I'd been reading in the taxi when I came home from my holiday. There had been something in it about a woman having had her dog stolen. I remembered reading it.

I found it after a few minutes. It was a short article about a woman living in the village of Scorriton who had lost her Labradoodle and believed it to have been stolen. There was no reporter's name attached. There was a photograph of the charming, much missed, Buttons, whose owner was offering a reward for his return and there was a phone number for anyone with information. Had Sandy written the article? I could always ring Mitch to find out, but as the dog owner's number was staring at me from the page, I decided to ring that instead. I grabbed the shop phone.

The ease with which I tell lies sometimes horrifies me. Not so much that I tell them, but that they come to mind so readily that I almost believe what I'm saying. I was following up on an article written by my colleague at the *Gazette*, I told the woman who answered the phone, a Mrs Coombes. I was a reporter, a colleague of Sandy Thomas.

'Oh yes, the Welsh girl,' she answered. 'She phoned us when Buttons went missing. That was weeks ago now. Wasn't she the one who got murdered?'

I confirmed that, tragically, she was, and we exchanged expressions of horror and sadness at her untimely death. I decided to press on before she could start asking questions about whether there was news on the killing. 'I take it Buttons hasn't been found yet?' I asked.

'No,' Mrs Coombes answered shortly. 'I reckon he just ran off. Lisa, my daughter is convinced he got stolen – he disappeared when they were out walking, see – but he was only a young dog. I reckon he ran off after a rabbit. Mind you, we've searched all over. It's been weeks since we lost him, but Lisa and her dad still go out looking for him every day. I reckon he ran off and someone found him and took a fancy to him. We bought him for Lisa's birthday.' She tutted. 'Twelve hundred pound that puppy cost.'

'You offered a reward. Did you get any response?'

'Only from some crackpot. Some joker posted a letter under our door, saying they wanted five thousand pounds if we wanted our dog back – the words were made up with letters out of a newspaper. We were supposed to take the money to some place on the moor.'

A bristle of unease prickled up my neck. 'You don't remember where?'

'It didn't say. Some map reference or other. Of course Lisa wanted to go up there and take the money, but we told her it would be a wild goose chase. It was probably a hoax by some idiot who'd read about the dog in the paper. And we weren't going to take a chance with that kind of money.'

Poor Buttons. 'Did you show the letter to the police?'

Mrs Coombes gave a snort of laughter. 'Screwed it up and put it in the fire.'

As she launched into a tirade about what she'd like to do to people who played malicious hoaxes, I interrupted her flow of invective to ask her a question. 'Well, I don't know,' she answered me, puzzled. 'I'll have to go and check. You'll have to hang on.'

About two minutes later she arrived back at the phone, slightly breathless. 'You're right. Someone has tied a cable-tie around our gatepost. I never noticed it before. How did you know it was there?'

I tried to drag my mind away from wondering what fate might have befallen poor Buttons. It was time to come clean. I rang Dean Collins. 'The lady who had her shih-tzu stolen,' I told him as soon as he picked up the phone, 'the one you told me about. Make sure she hasn't received a ransom letter and been too afraid to tell you.'

'What are you on about, woman?' he demanded in the slightly muffled voice of someone whose mouth is full.

I told him all about the conversation I'd just had with Mrs Coombes, the ransom demand that Lady Margaret had received, and my adventure in Shaugh Prior Tunnel with Big Head, the not-at-all-funny clown.

He swallowed noisily. 'Bloody hell, Juno, why didn't you tell me this before?'

'Because I promised Lady Margaret I wouldn't. I'm breaking my promise to her telling you now. But she's not aware of the bigger picture,' I added in my defence.

'And she handed over how much?' I could hear him chomping again.

'Five thousand . . . What on earth are you eating?'

'Pork pie and Eccles cake.'

'At the same time?'

'Doesn't she realise—?'

'That giving into blackmailers only encourages them? Yes, of course she does. So do I, and I don't need a lecture about it. I'm only telling you because if this latest victim does get a letter, then this may be your chance to set up a trap and catch the thieves.'

'Thank you, Miss Marple,' he responded.

'Never call me that again,' I told him coldly, and disconnected.

* * *

167

I strolled home from the shop, the evening sun just dipping behind the hills, melting like butter into low golden clouds, the sky above my head soft and blue. It wouldn't be long now before the clocks turned back, before it would be dark at this time. Autumn had been creeping up on me unawares and I gazed at the yellowing leaves on the trees as if noticing them for the first time. I love the first signs of autumn. Had I really been too preoccupied to observe these first, subtle changes of season? Right now, I had other things on my mind. Suppose Sandy had been following a story about dog theft? It seemed the thieves weren't afraid to use violence, but could this ultimately have led to her death, to her being followed through the wood and murdered? And why hadn't she told anyone what she was up to?

As I opened the front door and stepped into the hall my nose was ravished by the delicate fragrance of coconut, cardamom and a hint of rosewater. Kate was cooking curry.

Up in my flat, Bill was asleep on the back of the sofa in a convenient shaft of low-slanting sun that turned his black fur to a deep ruby colour. He mewed in welcome when I stroked his head, but didn't wake. I wandered into the kitchen and opened my ancient fridge, flipping the little freezer door to see what I might have in the fling-and-ding department that would make me a quick supper. I was too hungry to cook properly, and the aroma of whatever Kate was cooking only added to my torment. I needed a quick fix. I munched on an apple whilst I made up my mind.

I had a choice between two prepacked supermarket meals: vegetable curry or macaroni cheese. Knowing how inferior the curry was likely to be to the delicious concoction being conjured up in the kitchen downstairs, I opted for the macaroni cheese. I slid off the cardboard sleeve, stabbed the film lid more times than was probably necessary and flung it into the microwave. It's a very old one, with a dial for a timer, and getting the timing right is not an exact science. I set it for roughly the right time, found half a bag of salad leaves in the fridge and emptied them onto a plate with the solitary tomato I found rolling about in the bottom of the crisper. Ten minutes later, after waiting the requisite minute for it to stop steaming, I ate my way through the anaemic-looking, gloopy and flavourless mess on my plate, longing for a hunk of crusty bread to make it tolerable, knowing that the sliced brown in the bread bin wasn't going to do the job anything like as well.

I pushed the plate away from me with a sigh. What would cheer me up now, I contemplated, was a nice glass of red wine. But I didn't have any. I flipped the switch on the kettle to make a cup of tea. As it boiled, I wandered into the living room and dug in my bag for my phone. I usually check it as soon as I'm in range, but I realised I hadn't looked at it all day; in fact, I hadn't checked it since the night before. Someone had left me a message on voicemail. Last night.

It was Phil Thomas. 'I need to talk to you. Something I didn't mention the other night . . . It was something Sandy told me. It might be important. Look, I can't really talk here . . .' I could hear the rumble of heavy wheels driving past, the shouts of working men, it sounded as if he was on a building site. 'Do you want to meet me in The Bay Horse tomorrow night, about seven? We could talk about it then.'

Tomorrow night, of course, was now tonight. I glanced at the clock. I still had time to make it by seven, just about. I cleaned my teeth, changed my T-shirt and raked my fingers through my curls. I didn't have time for anything else. I didn't know how long Phil Thomas was likely to hang around if I didn't turn up on time. After all, I hadn't responded to his message. I tried his number as I walked along the street, but there was no response. Perhaps The Bay Horse didn't have much of a signal either, although I was pretty sure I'd seen a sign for free wi-fi when I'd been in before.

There was no match on. The pub was quiet when I stepped inside. No sign of Phil at the bar, just a couple of men nursing pints at a table in the corner, a man and a girl behind the bar chatting. I bought my glass of red and then wandered out into the beer garden, in case Phil was waiting out there, but despite the balmy evening the garden was empty. No sign of him.

I found myself a table inside and waited.

After half an hour, it didn't look like he was coming. I tried his phone again, but it went straight to voicemail. I left a message, about who I was and where I was, and perhaps if he wasn't coming, he could message me with whatever he wanted to tell me. Twenty minutes later I'd finished my glass of red and decided I'd had enough of waiting around. I was just about to leave when my phone made the muffled strangled noise it makes when a call comes in. Phil's number displayed itself on the screen.

'Hello Phil,' I said.

'Who is this?' It was a woman's voice, tremulous and tearful.

'Juno Browne,' I responded. 'Who—?'

'You left a message on Phil's phone.' It sounded like an accusation. She'd got the wrong idea, obviously.

'I'm a friend of Sandra's,' I explained, as the quickest way of setting her straight. 'Phil asked me to meet him at the pub tonight. He said he had something to tell me . . .' I remembered his girlfriend's name. 'Are you Laura?'

Whether she was Phil's partner or not, she began sobbing down the phone. 'Are you all right?' I asked stupidly. Plainly, she wasn't. 'Has something happened?'

'Phil had an accident at work,' she sobbed out.

'Is he hurt?'

There was no response but heart-rending sobbing, and I knew the answer was worse than that. 'He's dead,' she managed at last. 'I've just come back from identifying his body . . . they gave me his phone and watch and things and—'

'Oh, Laura, I am so sorry. Listen,' I went on as she continued to whimper like some wounded animal, 'isn't anyone there with you? Are you on your own?'

She took in a ragged breath. 'Just me.'

'Somebody ought to be with you. Are you at home? I could come round if—'

'My sister's coming, but she can't get here for a bit . . . she's trying to find a babysitter.'

'Well, if you'd like me to . . . until your sister arrives?' Someone ought to be holding the poor girl's hand, making her a cup of tea. I might not be good for much, but I could manage that.

'All right,' she sniffed, and gave me the address.

Ten minutes later, I found myself outside a small, modern house in Roborough Lane. The girl who answered the door to my knock was short and slim, with straight brown hair, her face pale with shock, her reddened eyes staring into a bleak reality she could not even have imagined a few hours ago. Her voice, when she spoke, was barely more than a whisper, almost drained of breath. 'Thank you for coming.' She turned away, leaving me to close the door behind me, and sat down in the middle of a battered leather sofa, her arms folded across her chest, as if she was trying to make herself as small as possible, and rocked herself silently.

The place was open-plan, which allowed me to keep an eye on her from the kitchen area whilst I fiddled with making tea. Beyond the sofa and a glass coffee table there wasn't much in the room except for two large beanbags and a wide-screen television. Glass doors opened out on to a small, sloping lawn, and beyond, the hills on the far side of the A38. Not a bad view, if your heart hadn't just been ripped out of your body.

I placed a mug of tea on the table in front of her. 'Laura,' I began as gently as I could, 'you've had a terrible shock. Don't you think you should see a doctor?'

She didn't look at me, just shook her head. 'He can't do anything.'

'Would it help to talk about it?' I asked tentatively. 'Do you know what happened?'

'He fell,' she sniffed, a tear smeared like a glistening snail trail across her cheek. 'He was up high, on scaffolding. Something gave way. Police say they won't know for sure what happened until the accident investigators have finished.'

'Where was this?'

'A site in Plymouth. They were building a block of flats.'

'I see.' What I really wanted to ask her was whether she knew why Phil had tried to contact me last night, if she had any idea what he wanted to talk to me about, but now was not the time. The poor girl was trembling. I found a coat on a hook in the hallway and placed it gently around her shoulders.

'This is Phil's coat.' She sobbed wretchedly and hugged it around her like a magic blanket.

I had no idea how to comfort her, how to lessen her suffering. But when I tried an arm around her shoulders she rolled into me, hiding her face in my shoulder, and wept.

After what seemed like an eternity there was a knock at the door and I answered. Laura's sister looked like a twin, slightly taller and blonder, and as I opened the door she rushed into the room, enfolding Laura in a hug as she burst into a fresh attack of sobbing. I was instantly forgotten, and let myself out, relieved at being able to leave, guilty at wanting to.

173

Instead of walking home, I turned at the end of Roborough Lane into Eastern Road and headed for the police station.

'Hello, here's trouble!' the desk sergeant remarked genially. 'What can I do for you, Miss Browne?'

'I wondered if Dean Collins was about.'

'I'm afraid he's not here at the moment. Detective Sergeant deVille is on duty.'

'In that case, I'll leave it, thanks,' I responded, not daring to speak too loud in case the violet-eyed Medusa emerged from her lair and demanded to know what I wanted.

The desk sergeant chuckled as if he understood. I snuck off home.

The smell of curry still lingered in the hall. Kate was there, just about to rescue the washing from the line before it got dark. I wrested the laundry basket from her grasp and ordered her back inside. She didn't argue. 'Thanks, Juno.'

'Where's Adam?' I asked.

'Still at the cafe, prepping stuff for tomorrow. We've got a big booking for lunch.'

I took the laundry basket into the garden. I stood in the gathering gloom, flipping away moths that were trying to settle on the tea towels, folding and filling the laundry basket until I had worked my way from one end of the line to the other and it was piled high. I could smell the smoke from a nearby bonfire, a proper autumn smell. Someone was burning leaves.

I stared across the shaggy grass. Every now and again

I make attempts to get to grips with this garden, to tame it, to turn it into something productive and useful for Kate and Adam.

I had dug a small herb garden close to the back door where they could easily nip out from the kitchen and grab the herbs they wanted. But the invading brambles from the adjoining field that I had hacked back earlier in the summer were once again clambering over the garden wall, apparently invigorated by their haircut. Blackberries dark as bruises glistened among the thorns. At least Adam would be able to make apple and blackberry pie for the cafe. I toted the laundry inside, pegs rattling inside the peg bag.

Kate was looking a lot better. 'I think I've finally stopped being sick,' she confided, just as Adam let himself in through the front door, obviously knackered.

I left them to their domestic bliss and joined Bill upstairs. It was only a few hours since I'd left him to go and meet Phil Thomas, but it seemed like a lifetime. Unfortunately, it wasn't bedtime yet. I was just contemplating what to do next when the phone rang.

It was Dean Collins. 'Hello Juno. I've got some bad news.'

'Phil Thomas is dead,' I responded.

'Bloody hell! How d'you know that?'

'Because I rang his number and his girlfriend answered. Poor girl had just been to identify his body.'

Dean cleared his throat as if he felt awkward. 'Yes. Well, local force in Plymouth dealt with it, of course. I only just picked up the news on my way home.'

'Do you know what happened?'

'He was up on a scaffolding plank and tripped, according to witnesses. He banged against a guard rail, which gave way.'

'I had a phone call from him last night. He wanted me to meet him this evening. He said he had something to tell me.'

I could almost hear Dean's brain cells banging around in the void. 'You think it wasn't an accident? Look, building sites are dangerous places. Construction is one of the worst industries to work in for fatal accidents. And about fifty per cent of those deaths are the result of falls from high places.'

'They have safety measures in place, don't they? Don't builders on scaffolding wear harnesses?'

'They're supposed to. But you know what it's like, they get overconfident, careless.'

I wasn't convinced Phil Thomas was the careless type. 'What about this guard rail giving way?'

Dean grunted. 'Yeah, well, according to the bloke I spoke to, scaffolding is checked every seven days. This had been checked only two days ago.'

'Then it should have been safe?'

'I'm keeping an open mind on the subject, until we hear from the accident investigators. As I say, building sites are dangerous places.' He paused a moment, as if making up his mind whether or not to speak. 'I'll tell you something that is interesting, though.'

'What?'

'The firm that's putting up this block of flats –

Riverview Developments – it's owned by Dunston Inc.' He paused a moment as if to let this sink in. 'Phil Thomas was working for Alastair Dunston.'

'But that doesn't make sense. After what Phil did to his car, why would Dunston employ him?'

'He almost certainly didn't. At least not directly. Dunston doesn't strike me as the sort to get his hands dirty, I doubt if he goes near the site much. He'll have a project manager to make sure the building is going to plan.'

'So, the project manager would have employed Phil?'

'Probably not. There'd be several tiers of management. You have to go lower down the food chain. They need to bring in a lot of trades for a development like that – brickies, electricians, plasterers. They hire a ganger to deal with recruitment.'

'A ganger?'

'Gangmaster, to give him his correct title. He'll have hired blokes from all around the area. The way these construction sites work, with contracts and subcontracts and self-employed workers, it's unlikely Dunston would have known the identities of the individuals working for him.'

'But Phil would have known he was working for Dunston?'

'That's more likely.'

'But Dunston's the last person he would have wanted to work for.'

Dean grunted. 'Probably offered good money.'

'After what happened to Sandy? He'd have thought it was blood money.'

'You don't know that. Perhaps he couldn't afford to pass it up.' He was quiet for a moment. 'You think he got himself employed there because of Dunston?'

'It's a bit too much of a coincidence, don't you think?'

'No, I don't, and I wish you didn't bloody think either!'

'Well, I like that! You're the one who phoned me.'

He sighed heavily down the phone. 'All right. Look, I know you want to find out who killed Sandy – we all do – but just leave it to the professionals, okay? Promise me you won't go poking around trying to dig up stuff on Dunston?'

This was probably not the time to tell him that Louise Dunston had offered to pay me to do just that. 'Phil wanted to meet me, to tell me something he hadn't mentioned the first time we spoke.'

'Well, you'll just have to accept the fact that now you'll never know.'

I sighed, thinking of Sandy and her pencilled note. 'No, now I'll never know.'

CHAPTER SEVENTEEN

The green lanes of Devon, which spread through our fair county like the veins of a leaf, are not always the easiest things to drive. Pleasant thoroughfares between hedge banks of wild flowers or through glowing green tree tunnels they may be, but many's the incomer, moving down here from some other part of the country, who suddenly finds himself forced to call on driving skills he's not had to use in a lifetime of city driving. Basically, if you can't back your vehicle down two hundred yards of narrow twisting lane and tuck yourself neatly into the nearest narrow passing place, then you're stuffed. Because at some point, most days, you'll meet a car coming from the opposite direction and there won't be room for both vehicles to pass. One of you will have to back. Usually, in this situation, it's me, even though I know that the other vehicle has passed a passing place only twenty yards behind.

I give way because it's quicker than sitting there waiting for the other driver. I can recognise the panic in the eyes of a woman who, however big the four-by-four she uses to drive the kids to school, basically can't use reverse gear, and I do it because it's no skin off my nose. And I haven't got the patience to engage in some pathetic battle of wills with some clot who refuses to move because he thinks if he gives way some precious part of his anatomy is going to drop off.

So, on this particular morning, I was resigned to backing for two hundred yards because I could tell at a glance that the driver facing me in the narrow lane belonged to the latter category. I couldn't see his face too well through the flickering shadows on his sun-flecked windscreen but I could detect the smirk. Something about the dark grey Transporter he drove oozed toxic masculinity. Besides, he had a mate sitting next to him, so I guess he had something to prove.

I was taking the Tribe home after their early morning walk. We'd been for a scramble through the woods. then run after balls in a field that I know isn't used for livestock. I still had all five of them in the back. They'd settled down peacefully as they always do after a lot of panting and scratching. 'Right, you lot, we're going for a ride backwards,' I warned unnecessarily as I put Van Blanc into reverse. I find it easier to turn to see around the winding corners behind me if I first release my seat belt.

Now, I don't mind backing, but I really object to the kind of driver who thinks it's fun to chase me, to ride on my front bumper all the way. Which is exactly what this git was doing. After a hundred yards or so I'd had enough. I slammed on the brakes, forcing him to do likewise, and wound down my window with the intention of sticking my head out and telling the driver exactly what I thought of him. It was only in the moment when both the doors opened and the two men got out, one carrying a crowbar, that I experienced a sudden sense of alarm that made me flick the door locks. Two men, dark overalls, dark glasses, all trace of hair hidden under baseball caps; identical. They could have been twins. Twin robots.

The driver came to my door. 'Open up!' he ordered. As his passenger went round to the rear of the van where the dogs were, it dawned on me, like a bucket of icy water thrown over me, what they were really after.

The first cyborg was jerking my door handle. 'Get out of the van and you won't get hurt.'

'Fuck off!' I recommended, my voice shaky with fright. But before I could wind up the window, he grabbed a handful of the hair on top of my head, making me gasp. I gripped his wrist and he pulled harder so I raked my fingernails across the back of his hand. He cursed but didn't let go. By now the dogs in the back were going wild, jumping at the windows and barking. In the rear-view mirror I could see Dylan's snout pressed against the wire safety-grill, his lips drawn back to reveal fangs as he threatened my attacker, his hot breath on my shoulder. I felt as if my scalp was being ripped off. I aimed a punch through the open window but only caught my assailant a glancing blow. It was enough to send his sunglasses flying but not enough to make him let go. And it was a stupid move because it gave him the chance to grab my arm.

'Help me deal with this bitch,' he yelled to his accomplice, who was trying to lever open the back doors with a crowbar, despite five demented canines snarling and barking from the inside. 'We can get the dogs later.'

Suddenly there were two of them pulling, one with his hand gripping my hair, the other taking hold of my flailing arm. With no seat belt to hold me in place I was gradually being pulled through the open window like a cork being drawn from a bottle. I wished I was fatter. My shoulders wedged painfully for a moment. Robot Two was trying to get his hands under my armpits. I braced my feet against the opposite window, hoping I could thrust backwards and knock him off balance, but it didn't work. I pushed down hard against the window frame, trapping his fingers beneath my body, and he yelped. With my free arm I clung desperately to the steering wheel but by now there was no resisting their combined force. Robot One managed to get his arm around my neck, his elbow under my chin. I felt the deadly pressure and I knew it was all over. If I didn't want to risk strangulation or a broken neck, I would have to let go. I was hauled, kicking and screaming, through the window and dropped onto the gritty road. As the driver released his hold on my neck, I twisted around and bit his hand, my teeth coming together in the webbing between his forefinger and thumb. He roared and dropped me. I rolled, kicking at his legs. But by then the second man had grabbed me by my T-shirt, half-dragging me to my feet. He landed a punch on my temple and the lights went out.

I suppose I should be grateful to my attackers for rolling me into the ditch instead of leaving me on the road and driving over me. I don't know how long I lay there. I didn't see them drive away: one in the Transporter, one in my Van Blanc. I could only have been out for a few seconds. I remember lying on my back, looking up at the blurry leaves of the hedgerow wavering above me and wondering where I was. I had barely crawled out of the ditch, lying groggy on the gritty road, the salt taste of blood on my teeth, when a giant green tractor thingy stopped in front of me and sat chugging in the road. I tried to explain to the kind man who clambered down to help me what had happened.

'They've taken my van,' I whimpered. 'They've taken the dogs.'

As it turned out, they hadn't taken the van very far. We found it down the road, abandoned, its back doors wide open. But all the dogs had gone.

'Tell me their names again?' The police constable had her pen poised, ready to write them down.

'There's Dylan,' I sniffed mournfully, 'he's a long-haired German Shepherd. He's two years old. Then, there's Nookie, she's about five, she's a silver husky. She has blue eyes. There's Boog—'

'Sorry, Boog?'

'Boogaloo Boogie Nights of Bollywood, that's her

pedigree name. She's a boxer. She's won her class at Crufts. Then there's little E.B. . . . oh dear.' I began blubbing again. It was about the third time since the interview started but I couldn't help it. The thought of all the dogs kept setting me off. What was happening to them now? What was I going to tell their families? I'd been trusted with their most beloved possessions and I'd lost them all. All five of them. 'He's a miniature schnauzer and he's an emotional support dog. You know, he goes into care homes. Then there's Schnitzel . . .'

'He's a sausage dog, right?' the constable guessed, grinning, and I nodded.

'Now then, Juno.' Inspector Ford had been silent, listening patiently, his jutting eyebrows knitted in ferocious thought. I'd already given him an account of what happened. 'Is there any chance you could identify these two men who attacked you?'

I shook my head. 'Not really. I managed to get the sunglasses off one but . . . I didn't get a good look at his face. He had very short hair. They both did.'

'And you didn't manage to get the number plate of their van?'

''Fraid not. Well, I was driving backwards, I mean . . . it was a dark grey VW Transporter, tinted windows,' I shrugged. 'It's not a lot to go on, is it?'

'We're out looking for it, don't you worry. This is the second serious assault on a woman. We're going to catch these bastards. Now, it's obvious you were targeted. They didn't just happen on you. When you walk the dogs, do you take the same route every day?'

I shook my head. 'I'm likely to walk them in different places. But when I'm taking them home afterwards, I usually drive along that bit of road, because I always drop them off in the same order. Nookie's family live the furthest away, so I try to drop her off first, so that way I end up back in the centre of town.' I sighed deeply. E. B's mum, Elaine, would be wondering where I was. Why I hadn't brought E.B. home yet.

The inspector smiled. 'Don't despair. We may find they've left some clues behind in your van. It can't have been an easy task, removing five dogs, especially the larger ones.'

'Let's hope they've both been bitten,' the constable added cheerfully, 'and left trails of blood we can match up to some felons on file.'

I smiled at her attempt to cheer me up, but we all knew it wasn't going to be that easy. I rubbed at my temple where I'd been punched. My head was beginning to ache, a dull, insistent throb.

The inspector watched me beneath his frowning brows. 'Are you sure you're well enough to continue?'

'I'm okay.' I wanted to get the interview over, get the police after those bastards as fast as they could. We'd already stopped once. The moment I mentioned that I had scratched and bitten one of the Robots, then everything stopped to wrap my hand in a plastic bag so that later they could scrape skin from under my fingernails.

'Then can we go over the events in Shaugh Prior Tunnel?' he asked.

I'd had to tell him. I gave him all the information

I could, about the ransom note, what happened in the tunnel, even my conversation with the woman who'd had her Labradoodle stolen. Fortunately, he didn't lecture me about how I should have told the police all this sooner. Thank God Cruella wasn't there. I'd have got it hot and strong from her.

'And you're convinced there were two men in the tunnel?'

'More than one, certainly.'

'But you couldn't identify either of them.'

'I didn't see the second man at all, just heard his voice, and the other one, the one in the clown's head, was talking through a swozzle.'

'So, you couldn't say if these two men today were the same men?'

I shook my head. 'It's possible, but I couldn't swear to it. No.'

'Then I think that's enough for now,' he decided, sitting back. 'If I can't persuade you to go to A and E—'

'I'll be fine.' I had a scrape on one cheekbone and down my forearm where I'd made contact with the road, other than that just a headache. I wanted paracetamol and bed. Not that I was ever likely to sleep again.

'If you'll give us the names and addresses of all the relevant dog owners, then we'll see that they're informed about what's happened . . .'

'No, no, I must do that.' After all, the dogs had been in my care. What happened to them was my fault.

'No, I think you'd better leave that to us. A little job

for you, Constable,' he said pleasantly to the woman sitting beside him.

'Of course, sir,' she muttered, looking less than enthusiastic.

There was a sudden yapping noise from the corridor outside. The door burst open and with a busy clicking of claws on the hard floor, in trotted a small black and tan Dachshund.

'Schnitzel!' I cried, amazed. 'Oh, Schnitzel!'

He jumped up on his hind legs, his forepaws resting on my knees, staring at me from shiny dark eyes, his tail wagging. Then he began to lick my hand. I lifted him gently onto my lap and hugged him as hard as I dared.

Dean Collins followed him into the room. 'We found this one, sir,' he said cheerfully to the inspector, 'when we were checking out Miss Browne's van. He must have got away from the others somehow. He was hiding under the hedge.' He grinned. 'As soon as I got a nutty bar out of my pocket, he shot out like a rocket. Sat there begging for it.'

The inspector raised his brows. 'Nutty bars on duty, Constable?' he asked wryly.

I was still cuddling Schnitzel. 'Oh, you clever, clever boy!' I crooned to him. The smallest of the Tribe he was also the naughtiest, the one who went missing, the last to come when called, the one who could hide in the undergrowth or down a rabbit hole. He was also a bugger for nipping ankles when he was in the mood. 'I hope you nipped 'em,' I whispered into his velvety ear. 'I hope you nipped them, good and hard.'

'Well, that's one happy ending, at any rate,' the inspector said. 'You can take this little chap to his owners, Constable.'

Dean dumped my shoulder bag down on the table. The Robots had left it in my van, probably because there wasn't any money in it.

The inspector looked at me and sighed. 'I'm afraid you're not going to get your van back so quickly.'

'That's all right, sir,' Dean told him. 'I'll drive her home.'

'I really don't need you to do this,' I told him, as he dabbed at the graze on my cheekbone with damp cotton wool.

Dean grinned. 'You haven't seen yourself in the mirror yet, have you? Keep still!'

'Have I got a black eye?'

'You will have by the morning.'

'Great.' Actually, at that moment I couldn't give a stuff what I looked like.

My phone started ringing. 'Leave it,' Dean ordered as I made to reach for my bag. It had been pinging every few minutes. I imagined as soon as each of the Tribe's owners received the bad news from the police constable, they were phoning me, demanding to know what had happened. 'They can wait.'

'What about that woman who had her shih-tzu taken?' I asked. 'Do you know if she received a ransom note?'

'Not so far. Unless she's not letting on. But we talked to her about it, and she seemed like a sensible woman. I'm sure she would tell us if she had.'

Kate walked into the kitchen at that moment with two mugs of tea and a packet of paracetamol. It turned out I didn't have any and Dean had knocked on her door. 'Here we are,' she said, staring at me anxiously. 'How are you feeling?'

My head was throbbing and I wanted to lie down. I couldn't believe it was still only lunchtime. It seemed like years since I'd set off with the dogs that morning. At least we'd got Schnitzel back. But I wondered if I'd ever see any of the others. I was in danger of crying again. I reached for the paracetamol to distract myself.

Then the phone in the living room started ringing. Kate volunteered to get it. A moment later I heard her say, 'Oh, hello Morris. No, it's Kate.'

He and Ricky hadn't heard about what had happened surely? Was it already all over the town?

I heard Kate launching into the story. I closed my eyes in despair and two hot tears trickled out beneath my lids and down my cheeks.

'We will get them, Juno,' Dean promised, reaching out to squeeze my fingers.

'Will you?' The statistics said otherwise. And the police had Sandy's murder to solve. If they didn't find them in a day or two, the theft of a few dogs would soon slip down the list of priorities. 'Any news on Sandy?' I asked, wiping the tears away.

'No. But I went round to talk to Laura, you know, Phil Thomas's girlfriend. She told me that Phil had only been working on that site for a few days.'

'Since Sandy's murder, then?'

He nodded. 'That's right. And Laura couldn't understand it. Because she said he had private work lined up for months ahead. In fact, he was in the middle of putting up someone's garage, and plastering someone else's kitchen – you know what builders are like, always got more than one job on the go – so she didn't understand why he'd dropped everything to work for Dunston.'

'Better money?'

'She didn't seem to think so.'

'Was Phil keeping an eye on Dunston, d'you think? Doing some investigating of his own?'

'Possibly. And you can see how he ended up, so don't you try any.'

'But his death was an accident, according to you.'

Dean scowled. 'Just drink your tea,' he recommended.

CHAPTER EIGHTEEN

The rest of the day was misery. I went to bed but couldn't sleep. Exhausted as I was, my body trembled with the impetus to act, to get up and do something to get the dogs back. But what? And I couldn't ignore the ringing of my phone, the calls from heartbroken dog owners phoning to find out what had happened to their pets. They were concerned about me of course, especially Elaine, who I'd known for years – but they were more worried about their dogs. And they were angry. I couldn't blame them. They were upset. I'd let them down and telling them that the police were doing all they could to find their dogs and catch the perpetrators didn't help.

Kate and Adam insisted on inviting me to supper but for once I couldn't summon up much appetite. I sagged at the table, slowly getting through their bottle of red wine, which helped to numb my feelings but didn't turn out to be such a good idea for my head later. Added to that, Ricky and Morris threatened to visit because they were worried about me. I managed to put them off until tomorrow.

Tomorrow. What was I going to do? One thing I wasn't going to do was walk the dogs. There was only Schnitzel left and his mum had wisely decided to confine him to home for a day or two, for her own peace of mind. I needed the van for the cleaning job I was supposed to do in the morning, and I wasn't going to get it back until forensics had finished with it, so I was forced to ring up and cancel. I lay in bed, trying to plan my activities for the rest of the week if I didn't get the van back. I didn't even want to think about the loss of income. With no dogs to walk and my domestic goddess activities limited to what I could accomplish on foot, I could go broke very quickly. But that wasn't really what was on my mind. It was the dogs and what was happening to them. I couldn't stop remembering the terrible things I'd read about on the Internet. Boog and Nookie could end up in some puppy farm, kept in appalling conditions, worn to death giving birth to litter after litter. E.B. could be sold on to new owners who wouldn't realise he was stolen, or wouldn't care. And Dylan? German shepherds like him were often used as bait in the training of fighting dogs. He could be horribly injured or killed. I wept myself ragged but I still couldn't sleep.

I took a couple more paracetamol. Every time I closed my eyes, I kept seeing those two Robots getting out of the Transporter and heading towards me in my van, reliving the sudden sense of dread I'd felt when I realised what they were after. Could those have been the same men in Shaugh Prior Tunnel? Was Clown Head the man I bit? If only I'd got a proper look at him. Even when I knocked the shades off his nose, I'd only got a vague impression of a man's face, of unremarkable features. And how had they known about me, about my walking the Tribe every day? The answer was obvious, of course. I advertised dog walking as part of my domestic goddess services in, among other places, a free magazine that was sent out to all the surrounding villages. But someone had known about Florence, and Buttons, and the woman with the shih-tzu, and the two dogs that had gone missing when their owner took them out for a walk. Someone, somewhere was gathering information about dogs and their owners. Tomorrow, I would go around and see all the Tribe's families, and apologise in person. I'd warn them about ransom notes and check if any of them had found a cable-tie knotted around their gatepost.

The Tribe's owners decided to get together for a Council of War next evening. They invited me so they could hear at first-hand what had happened, and plan a campaign to get their dogs back. It saved me going around to speak to each of them individually, but I admit I felt a bit apprehensive about being confronted by them all at once. The meeting was being held at Elaine and Alan's house, the home of E.B.

They were all assembled when I arrived, sitting in the living room, with the exception of Schnitzel's mum.

She was too nervous to leave him alone at home and she didn't want to bring him because she thought that might upset the others. I think she felt some kind of survivor guilt on his behalf. But Boog's mum and dad, Nookie's mum and her teenage son, and Dylan's dad, were all squashed on to the three-piece suite, whilst Alan and Elaine occupied chairs brought in from the dining room. There was a vacant one, waiting for me. There was a momentary silence when I walked in. I think they were shocked at the sight of me. So far, they hadn't seen my black eye and scraped cheek. I wasn't looking for sympathy but I don't think they had understood the violence of the attack until then. Dylan's dad, Morgan, stood up and apologised to me for the way he'd shouted at me on the phone and asked if I'd like to sit in a more comfortable chair.

No thanks. I knew I looked a sight. Pat had gaped at me as I'd walked in the shop that morning. 'You look awful,' she'd told me without preamble. 'You should be home in bed.'

Sophie had gazed at me, her dark eyes full of concern. 'You have got a black eye,' she added apologetically, 'and you might still be suffering from shock.'

'I've got to do something. I can't just sit at home.'

I'd phoned the Devon Dog Rescue Group. I got the number from Margaret, and I called as soon as I'd filled Sophie and Pat in on what had happened.

So, after I'd told the whole horrible story once again to those assembled in Alan and Elaine's living room, I repeated what Tim, who runs the local branch of Devon

Dog Rescue, had told me on the phone. First of all, he'd taken all of the dogs' details and promised to post them on their website. He'd also stressed the importance of keeping microchip paperwork up to date.

'He's just repeating what that police officer told me yesterday,' Boog's dad, Jim, complained, 'that Dog Theft Officer.'

'Well, Nookie's is up to date,' her mum said. The claim that dogs resemble their owners is a bit fanciful in some cases, but Alex looked strangely like her missing husky, the same silver white hair and arctic blue eyes. Although in Alex's case the eyes were dramatically lined in black eyeliner. 'When we moved house, it was the first thing I did. I made sure I updated Nookie's address before I did the electricity or the phone or anything.'

'That's all very well, but I read about some dogs that had been found with all their microchips removed, so what do you do then?' Jim asked. 'I mean, what are the police doing? That's what I want to know.' He looked around him for support and there were nods of agreement all round. 'Our Boog is worth a lot of money. I mean, I'm not saying your dogs aren't . . .' he added hastily, looking a bit embarrassed, 'but Boog's a champion. She's won her class at Crufts two years running. Her puppies would be worth a fortune.'

His wife, Wendy, began to cry. 'It's just horrible,' she sniffed, drawing a handkerchief from up her sleeve. 'When I come down every morning to make the tea, I can see her through the glass door in the kitchen, wagging her rear end and scratching at the door, so happy when I open it and say good morning to her. And now she's not there. And I opened the door this morning and there was just her empty basket on the floor and that silly squeaky duck she loves to play with. I can't bear it . . .'

Her husband put his arms around her.

'This may sound like an odd question,' I put in before Wendy got any more emotional, 'but have any of you noticed a cable-tie around your gatepost?'

They looked at me as if I was bonkers and there were a few mystified shakes of the head. 'I'm asking because I know of a couple of people whose dogs were stolen, who have noticed them. These thieves are on the lookout all the time. Let's suppose they targeted one of the dogs – say it was Boog – and they've seen me taking her out with the others. Well, it's too good to be true, isn't it? They can snatch five dogs, all pedigrees, in one go. All they have to do is follow me for a bit and work out the best place for a hijack.'

Jim nodded thoughtfully. 'Well, okay, but how does that help us get 'em back?'

'I think we need to adopt a more proactive approach,' Morgan interrupted, clearing his throat. 'We can't just leave it to the police or this dog charity and hope that they get lucky. We must put up some posters, put stuff on social media . . . I know the police warned us not to, but what do people feel about offering a reward?'

'I will.' Alex raised her hand as if she was in school. 'I'll mortgage the house if it'll get my Nookie home safe.'

'Then she wouldn't have anywhere to come back to, Mum,' her son objected.

Morgan smiled. 'Hopefully we won't have to go that far.'

'But the police—' Alan began.

'The police can't stop us.'

I bit my lip. I couldn't say anything. I knew that offering a reward could be dangerous, but paying up had got Florrie back safely, and who was to say it wouldn't do the same again? 'We have to be very careful,' I pointed out. 'The man from the dog rescue group, Tim, warned me about scammers. They contact people who have put up lost dog posters or mention lost pets online. They'll try to get money out of you, telling you they've got your dog when they haven't. They'll try to get you to transfer money from your bank or credit card.'

'But how can you know whether they've really got your dog or not?' Jim asked.

'You can't. Especially if you've given out a lot of information about it. They can use the details to help convince you. Tim says you should ask them to prove they have your dog by sending you a photo of it, with something that shows the date when the picture was taken, like a newspaper.'

'My God,' Morgan laughed bitterly. 'It's like a hostage situation. Proof of life.'

'And if they do send you a photo,' I went on, 'phone the police or the dog rescue group. But whatever you do,' I added, mentally crossing my fingers, 'never go and meet these people with cash.'

'Well, I don't care what anyone says,' Jim said

roundly, 'I'm going to offer a reward. I'll put it in the local paper.'

'The *Gazette* are planning to run the story.' Guy Michell had already called me, anxious to know what had happened. 'I'm sure they'd be very happy to get behind a campaign to get the dogs back.'

'I'm going to keep looking on the Internet.' It was Alex's son who'd piped up. 'Keep a watch on people offering dogs for sale.'

'Excellent idea,' Morgan agreed. 'I'm going to do that too.'

Jim was nodding. 'I think we all should.'

'There is one thing,' I said. 'If anyone receives a ransom demand, they must let everyone know. Including the police.'

'Ransom demand?' Elaine repeated, horrified.

I nodded. 'A note saying pay up or else. It's important not to try to keep it to yourself.'

I felt like a hypocrite, but the thought of elderly Alan and Elaine, or Alex and her young son, creeping down Shaugh Prior Tunnel in the dark with a bagful of money made me feel queasy.

'Juno's right,' Morgan nodded. 'If one of us receives a ransom demand, then we must share it with the others. All our dogs were taken. If the thieves contact one person, we all have a right to know, to decide what the best action is to take.'

There was a lot of agreement and disagreement and discussion about the wording on lost dog posters and the meeting went on late. But although I longed for my bed,

I felt I couldn't leave before it was over. Morgan offered me a lift home, in a car that smelt faintly of Dylan, and I found it hard not to start blubbing again. I'd barely gone to bed when my phone rang. It was Boog's dad, Jim Bailey, apologising for phoning so late. The cable-tie around the gatepost had been his.

The shop bell rang next morning and in walked Becky, her fair hair twisted up in wispy space buns. She ran a mobile dog-grooming parlour and had taken over my dog walking duties when I'd been on holiday. It was Olly who had come up with the name for her business: LaundroMutt. She was wearing her work clothes, splashed dungarees covered with a plastic apron and wellington boots. You can get very wet trying to shampoo an Old English sheepdog. She gaped at my face in horror. 'I hope you gave as good as you got.'

'I did my best.' Unfortunately, my best hadn't been good enough.

'Let's hope they catch these bastards. I'm keeping my van door locked from now on, I can tell you, when I've got a pooch on board.' Becky did her dog-grooming inside her van, mostly parked in a client's driveway or close to their house, but she could still be vulnerable.

'Seriously, though,' she asked, 'are you all right?'

'I'll live.'

She pulled up a chair and sat, resting one welly boot on the opposite knee. 'One of my customers in Buckfastleigh had her dog stolen a while back. A spaniel. Broke her heart. She never got it back.'

'She didn't get a ransom note, I suppose?'

'I don't think so. She offered a reward. She'd have been willing to pay anything. Anyway, I've just given Lolly a wash and brush-up . . .'

'Lolly?'

'He's a poodle. Look, I don't know if this is relevant at all, but her owner told me this weird story and I thought I'd tell you, just in case. A friend of hers, Mary, was on the lookout for a puppy. She wanted a Pomsky.'

'What the hell's a Pomsky?' Pat scowled, looking up from sticking a tiny witch's hat on to the head of a doll.

'It's one of those new designer breeds,' Becky told her, grinning. 'It's a cross between a Pomeranian and a Siberian Husky.'

There was a moment of silence whilst we all considered the logistical problems of a very small dog and very large dog achieving successful union.

Sophie puffed out her cheeks. 'That must be quite difficult.'

Pat just tutted.

'Anyway,' Becky carried on, 'this friend, Mary, finds some puppies advertised online, on a breeder's website. She watches videos of these lovely pups tumbling about with their mummy and selects the one she wants. Then she contacts the breeder and tries to arrange a visit, because obviously she wants to see the pup with its mother before she buys. And it turns out the breeder lives in Ivybridge and Mary's in Torquay – it's no distance, and they arrange a date. Only, the day before she was due to visit . . .' Becky paused as the shop bell jangled and Ricky and Morris came in. After they'd rolled their eyes and exclaimed over the state of my face, I told them to shut up and sit down because Becky was telling us a story. Becky, obligingly, started again. 'So they arrange a date,' she repeated, 'but the day before she was due to visit, this breeder rings her and says that he is coming to Torquay to deliver a puppy and he could easily bring Mary her pup at the same time, and why don't they meet in Sainsbury's car park? Well, at this point, she begins to smell a rat. She tells this man categorically that she is not buying a dog in any car park, and if she can't see the puppy at home with the rest of the litter and their mother then the deal is off.' Becky glanced around to make sure she had all our attention. She had.

'This breeder tries hard to persuade her. He was very plausible and said he only wanted to save her a journey. But she was adamant about sticking to the original appointment, and in the end, he had to agree to her coming to his house and gave her this address in Ivybridge. But when she turns up, he isn't there, just some woman who says she's his wife. He had to go out, she tells her. And there's only one pup. The breeder's wife claims that all the others had already been sold, but Mary didn't think the pups she'd seen online were old enough to have been let go yet. And she thought that this one pup that was left was very small for its age, didn't look like the same pups in the online advert, and frankly, didn't look too well.'

'What about its mother?' I asked. 'Was she there?'

'Yes, she was, but Mary didn't think she looked too

good either. And the animal was uneasy. The impression she had was that the dog didn't really belong to this woman, that the house wasn't its home. There didn't seem to be any doggy paraphernalia around for a start. And when she asked about paperwork, you know, pedigree certificates and proof of vaccinations and so on, the woman said that her husband had all that and as he wasn't around, they could send it to her later. Well, Mary tells her she's not taking the pup without the paperwork and the woman gets quite stroppy and accuses her of wasting her time and eventually says "well, do you want the dog or don't you?" Mary felt terribly sorry for the poor little thing, but she didn't want to take a sickly-looking puppy that was too young to be separated from its mother, so she left without it.'

'Did she report this to anyone?' I asked.

'She reported it to the breeders' association and she rang the RSPCA. And this is the weird thing – they send one of their officers around to the house next day to investigate, and there's no trace of any dogs, just a confused elderly lady who said she didn't know what they were talking about. Obviously not the woman that Mary had met. The old girl let them search the place, but they didn't find anything. In fact, they called Mary later to check she'd given them the right address.'

'So, what's all this got to do with Juno's Tribe getting stolen?' Sophie asked.

'Well, maybe nothing,' Becky answered, 'but stolen dogs are often taken for puppy farms. It's horrible, they turn the bitches into breeding machines. And the people who run these awful places try to sell the pups off as quickly as possible and they don't spend money getting them vaccinated. They don't care about their welfare at all.'

'And they often hack into legitimate breeders' websites,' I added, 'so that the buyer sees pictures of nice, healthy pups being raised at home, when in fact they're buying a poor creature who's been bred and raised in terrible conditions.' Tim from the Devon Dog Rescue Group had told me all this on the phone. I looked at Becky. 'I don't suppose you happen to have this address in Ivybridge?'

She grinned, took a piece of paper from the pocket of her dungarees and put it down on the counter. 'I thought you'd ask.'

But before I could pick the paper up a long arm appeared from over my shoulder and a hand slammed down on top of it. 'Oh, no you don't!' Ricky snatched it up.

'What are you doing?' I asked, turning around to gape at him.

'I know what you'll be getting up to.' He waved the piece of paper at me. 'You'll be wanting to go there, to this address. Well, gawd knows what kind of people are behind all this. So, you're not going, not on your own.' He pointed at my face. 'Look at the state of you already!'

'Well, I can't go there anyway, can I?' I retorted. 'At the moment, I've got no transport.'

'Exactly!' Ricky agreed in triumph. 'So, Maurice and I will take you. To Ivybridge.'

Morris, who'd been nodding in silent agreement all through this, added, 'In the Saab.'

'Well, I'll take you, Juno, if you want—' Becky began but Ricky cut her off.

'These are bad people, the last thing you want to do is draw attention to that LaundroMutt business of yours.'

He was right. Their old Saab was nicely anonymous.

'Okay,' I said. 'When?'

He glanced at his watch and grinned. 'No time like the present.'

CHAPTER NINETEEN

Ivybridge, on the southern edge of Dartmoor, takes its name from the medieval packhorse bridge that crosses the River Erme. The bridge is still there today, its stones picturesquely clad in ivy, and much photographed by visitors walking the Two Moors Way which begins at the edge of the town. A small town, Ivybridge has a growing population, important as a dormitory town for Plymouth.

A battle is going on there at present. As we drove along the main shopping street, red posters demanding 'Save our Shops' blared from every window. It seems the traders in the town are threatened by the arrival of a large supermarket, to be built on the existing town car park, which will rob a street of independent shops of their parking.

'Looks like a lovely bookshop,' Morris commented as we drove along.

'We're not here to look at bookshops,' Ricky told him, and he sighed.

The address we were looking for took a bit of finding, the stately old Saab not having any new-fangled accessories like satnav. The place was almost on its way out of Ivybridge, in a crescent of solid respectable houses. No. 26, like its neighbours, was red brick, with a steeply pitched red-tile roof and tall chimneys, its leaded windows picked out with white paintwork. The varnished oak front door was set back in a porch. Leafy hedges and well-tended front gardens spoke reassuringly of weekends spent mowing the lawn or washing the car in the drive, of Sunday roasts, of afternoons walking the dog. It looked like just the sort of place a dog-breeder might live, the sort of house where a contented canine mother would nurse her litter of puppies in a basket on the floor of a cosy kitchen, basking in the warmth of an Aga.

'Drive on around the block,' I instructed. 'We'll park out of sight in the road behind.'

We had formed a plan on our journey from Ashburton. Morris would be the one to go and knock on the door, as of the three of us he was the most innocent and harmless looking. Ricky's height intimidates some people, and despite the fact he's still handsome and can be charming when he wants to be, there's a lupine quality about him, as if he might suddenly transform into a werewolf. I looked like the recent victim of domestic violence, so that counted me out. But Morris, with his soft round frame, bald head, little gold specs and sweet smile, could pass for a vicar any day of the week. In fact, he's often played one during his acting days.

'Right,' he said as the Saab drew to a halt, and undid his safety-belt. 'I won't be long.'

'Hang on,' Ricky laid a hand on his arm. 'We're coming too.'

'Too right,' I agreed. 'I want to know what happens.'

'But how?' Morris asked, blinking through his specs. 'You can't just lurk about in the road.'

'We could go into next door's garden and hide behind the hedge. We'll be able to hear what goes on.'

'And we can come and rescue you,' Ricky grinned at him, 'if the householder turns nasty.'

Morris sighed as he heaved himself out of the car. 'Why don't I find that reassuring?'

There didn't seem to be anyone at home at No. 28, so Ricky and I took up our positions, crouched behind the thick laurel hedge that separated its front garden from its neighbour, as Morris opened the gate to No. 26. We heard him clear his throat nervously and then a ding-dong as he pushed the doorbell. I had to stifle a giggle.

'Good afternoon,' we heard him say in warm, well-modulated tones. 'I've come to enquire about the puppy.' There were several seconds of complete silence from whoever had answered the door. I longed to take a peek at who it was, but didn't dare move. 'I understand you have a Pomski puppy for sale,' he continued. There were a few more moments of silence.

'There's no puppy here.' It was a female voice, peevish,

high-pitched with an elderly wobble. I visualised a perm, bifocals and a cardigan.

'Oh dear. Am I too late? Has it already been sold?' Morris sounded crestfallen. 'I wanted it as a surprise for my little granddaughter, you see. She's just come out of hospital.'

I glanced at Ricky, who flicked his eyeballs skyward. 'Don't overdo it,' he muttered from the corner of his mouth.

'No. I told the man who came,' the woman responded. 'You've got the wrong address. There never have been any puppies for sale here.'

'Really? Well, this is No. 26 Haytor Crescent?'

'Yes. But as I told the man from the RSPCA, I don't breed dogs. I don't breed these . . . whatever they're called. And I told that other woman.'

'How very strange.' Morris sounded perplexed. 'It seems that I, and this other person, were both given the wrong information. I wonder how that happened.'

'I really don't know.'

'Well, I'm so sorry to have troubled you, Mrs er . . .'

'Pinfold.'

'Pinfold?' Morris sounded pleasantly surprised. 'You're not related to Mrs Angela Pinfold, by any chance, a lady who lives in Buckfast?'

'No, I'm afraid not. Although my husband's sister lives in Widecombe.'

'Widecombe?' Morris echoed. 'Such a charming village. I grew up there, you know.'

I bit back a smile. Morris grew up in Golders Green.

'Really?' Mrs Pinfold sounded delighted. 'Would you like to come in for a moment, Mr . . . er?'

'Doctor Chasuble. Thank you. If you're sure? My next bus home isn't until . . .' We heard his voice fade as he stepped inside and the door was closed behind him.

'Morris, you bleedin' idiot!' Ricky hissed as we stood up. We were both tired of crouching. 'Well, I'm not hanging about here, lurking behind this privet until he comes out.' He drew his packet of cigarettes from his pocket and pressed one between his lips. 'Let's go and wait in the car. *Dr Chasuble?*' He shook his head in disbelief. 'Let's hope she don't know Oscar Wilde.'

'Will he be all right in there, d'you think?'

'We'll give it fifteen minutes and then I'll come back, ring the doorbell and rescue him.' He lit up his fag and inhaled. 'If he's not engaged to her by then.'

I laughed. 'But she's a married woman.'

He shook his head as we exited the gate of No. 28 and set off around the corner. 'That was a widder-woman. You can tell by the voice.'

In fact, it was almost twenty minutes before a breathless and slightly agitated Morris trotted up to the car and slid into the front passenger seat. He puffed out his cheeks in a long sigh, took off his specs and polished them on his handkerchief. He looked a bit flushed.

'Are you all right?' I asked.

He nodded. 'Just give me a moment.'

'What d'you go inside for, you idiot?' Ricky demanded. 'That wasn't the plan.'

'It seemed too good an opportunity to miss.'

'I never realised you were such an old fraud,' I told him admiringly, 'Doctor Chasuble.'

He gave a coy smile. 'It's Canon Chasuble, actually, in *The Importance of* —'

'Never mind that!' Ricky snapped. 'What happened in there?'

Morris frowned suspiciously and sniffed. 'Have you been smoking in this car?'

Ricky glowered.

'All right. Well, for the first few minutes everything went swimmingly. Mrs Pinfold – Hilary – and I chatted about Widecombe and her sister-in-law. And she started to tell me about her prolapse until I explained that I was a doctor of philosophy, not a medical doctor, and she was right, there was no sign of a puppy anywhere.'

'Well, thank Gawd. You'd probably have bought it.'

'I wouldn't. You don't like dogs.' Morris's voice contained a hint of accusation.

'I don't not like dogs,' Ricky said indignantly.

'That's why we don't have one.'

'I don't not like dogs,' Ricky insisted. 'I just don't want to have to pick up their poo, all right?'

'You don't like cats either.'

'Er, gentlemen?' I tried to bring them back to the matter in hand.

'Oh yes. Well, Hilary was just about to make a cup of tea,' Morris continued, 'when the back door opened and another woman walked in with some shopping bags. I think she must have been Hilary's daughter. Her name was Fran. She seemed none too pleased to see me. Immediately suspicious. Who was I? she wanted to know. What was I doing in Hilary's house? So, I explained I'd come about the puppy. Well!' He let out a deep breath. 'She turned scarlet. I thought she was going to have apoplexy. She dragged poor Hilary off into the hall and I could hear her asking questions. She wanted to know what she had said to me. And Hilary told her: "I said what you told me to say. What I told the other person."' Morris held up a finger. 'And *then* she said, "I don't like you using my house like this, Fran. All these dogs. I don't want you to do it any more. And I don't want him coming here, either."'

'Him?' I repeated.

Ricky frowned. 'Who did she mean?'

'Well, if she was talking about the dogs,' I said, 'presumably she meant the breeder, the man Mary talked to on the phone.'

'I think so,' Morris nodded. 'Because then this Fran comes marching back into the room and starts questioning me. How had I got hold of her address? How had I heard about this puppy? Who had told me about it? She was quite aggressive.' Morris's chin wobbled at the memory. He doesn't like confrontation.

'What did you say?'

'I said I'd heard about the puppy from a friend of a friend, someone who knew I was looking for a dog for my granddaughter. I could see she didn't believe me. I apologised for wasting her time and said it was time I was going. She practically marched me out of the door. I must confess,' he added, taking out his handkerchief and polishing his specs again, 'I'm a bit concerned about poor Hilary.'

'So, what do we make of all this, then?' Ricky asked, frowning.

'I think Hilary's house is being used by her daughter – and presumably her daughter's partner – as a front,' I said. 'It's a place to convince people paying out large amounts of money for a puppy that it's been born and raised in an appropriate and loving home.'

'When in fact it hasn't,' Ricky concluded.

'When it certainly hasn't and when these *breeders* need to convince the kind of buyer who's too careful to buy a dog without seeing it with its mother . . .'

'There she is!' Morris hissed suddenly and shrunk down in his seat.

'Who?' Ricky demanded.

'The daughter. Hilary's daughter – Fran – that's her, crossing the road.'

We watched as a thin woman in ripped jeans, her straight bleached hair showing two inches of dark brown roots, emerged from a lane that must lead to the back garden of No. 26 and crossed in front of us. 'That's her daughter?' I asked incredulously. Her appearance didn't seem to fit with the house, with how I imagined her mother, Hilary. We watched as she unlocked the door of a small red car.

Ricky turned the ignition as the red Honda Jazz pulled out from its parking place.

'Let's see where she's going, shall we?'

* * *

We followed the Honda out of Ivybridge along the road towards Yelverton and soon passed the signpost for Shaugh Prior.

'Isn't that where you met Clown Head in the tunnel?' Ricky asked.

'It is.' I wondered if its proximity was significant.

The red Honda didn't turn off to Shaugh Prior, but kept on up the road to Yelverton, where it turned onto the main A386. 'Looks as if we're heading for Tavistock,' Morris said.

He was right. About fifteen minutes later we found ourselves in a long line of traffic crawling past roadworks at the edge of the town. The red car was three vehicles ahead of us, waiting for temporary traffic lights to change.

'Good job we haven't got any pressing appointments,' Ricky grumbled after we'd been waiting what seemed like ages.

'Make sure you don't lose her,' Morris warned him as the lights finally changed, 'there's a roundabout up ahead.'

'Thank you, Hercule Poirot.'

'She's not heading into town, look. She's staying on this road.'

The A386 skirts the edge of Dartmoor. We were heading north-east now, towards Okehampton. We passed the sign for Meldon Reservoir on our right, then passed the turn-off for the town of Okehampton.

'I hope she's not going to give us the complete Dartmoor tour,' Ricky complained. 'We could end up back in Ashburton at this rate.'

'Watch her,' I called from the back seat, 'she's signalling right.' The red car was turning south-east, towards Chagford down a narrow country road. There were no other vehicles between us. 'We don't want her to realise we're following her,' I said. 'Drop back a bit.'

This should have been good advice, but it wasn't. Somewhere on the road that wound towards the tiny village of Throwleigh, we lost her. Fran and her red Honda just disappeared. We turned back on ourselves, Ricky driving slowly, watching out for any turnings that we might have missed, as far back as the Okehampton turn-off, but could see nothing.

We turned back again and this time, before we reached the village, we noticed a narrow and rutted lane, scattered with stony clitter leading steeply downhill before it disappeared behind a thick hedgerow. Ricky eyed it doubtfully. 'I don't fancy risking my suspension down there.'

'Stay here,' I told him, undoing my seat belt. 'I'll have a look.'

'We're coming too,' Morris hastily fumbled to undo his.

'No. We don't want Fran catching sight of you,' Ricky told him. 'You stay here.'

'You both stay,' I told them as I got out of the car. 'Keep your engine running, we might need a quick getaway.'

'Five minutes, Juno,' Ricky warned me, 'then I'm coming after you.'

'I won't be long,' I promised and jogged off down the track.

The road behind me was soon lost from view. The track descended through rough scrub, untended land that no one had worked in a while. I came to a wooden five-bar gate, sagging on its hinges. The chain around the gatepost was old and rusty. It didn't look as if the gate could have swung open in years. Surely the red Honda could not have come this way. The words 'Cawsand Farm. Private property. Keep out' were just discernible in flaking white paint.

I just love an invitation. The gate creaked ominously under my weight as I clambered over. I jumped down on the other side, dusting my hands and looked around. The track narrowed from here and disappeared around another bend. I couldn't see what was round it. I didn't want to find myself confronted by Fran with a shotgun. Or anyone with a shotgun, if I'm honest. But I hadn't gone more than a few yards before I could tell that no vehicle had passed this way for years. The bushes on either side were so overgrown and the grass growing down the middle was long. I doubt if anyone had even trodden the track in a while. A rough bank rose up on my right, and I reckoned if I climbed it, I could get a better view. I pulled myself up, grabbing at whippy branches of hazel saplings until I reached the top. From here I had a view down the steep side of a valley. A farmhouse, stone-built and solid with a slate roof, stood in the bottom, surrounded by several outbuildings. I could see a few stunted apple trees, a vegetable patch laid out, raked earth and a rectangle of blue-green cabbages; beyond that, a polytunnel. The whole place was completely hidden from the main road. There was a track that curved around the far edge of the valley like the rim of a bowl and dropped down a slope on the opposite side, an earthen scar in the short, parched grass. The red Honda was parked at the bottom of it. But how had it got on to that track? There must be another way into this property, somewhere. As I stood staring, Fran emerged from around the side of the farmhouse with an enamel bowl in her hands and headed for the polytunnel. I jumped back down the bank on to the lane, and started making my way back the way I had come.

I hadn't gone far before I heard a lot of rustling in the bushes and a voice calling my name. 'Juno! Juno! Where the bloody hell are you?'

'I'm here!' I hissed back. 'Shut up, Ricky! I'm coming!'

I rounded the bend and there he was, picking his way with obvious distaste along the rutted lane. His relief at seeing me was obvious. 'D'you find anything?' he asked as I approached.

'No, not much,' I lied, pulling away a long green cleaver sticking to his sleeve.

'Well, you've been gone long enough. We were getting worried. I had to climb over that bleeding gate.' I grinned. That must have been a sight to see. Unfortunately for him, he had to perform this ungraceful operation all over again, the whole structure waving about unhelpfully as he clung to my proffered arm.

Back at the car Morris was looking anxious. 'Anything?' he asked.

'Nothing, just an empty farmhouse,' I told him as I slid into the back seat. 'Obviously derelict.'

I needed to come back to this place, when he and Ricky weren't with me, when I didn't have to worry about them, when they wouldn't slow me down: I'd have to wait until I had my van back, until I could be alone. I kept silent as we headed towards home, not just about the red Honda Jazz parked outside the farmhouse and seeing Fran, but about the other vehicle that Fran had parked alongside: the grey Transporter.

'Well, that was a complete waste of bleedin' time, wasn't it?' Ricky pronounced.

We'd stopped in Chagford for a well-deserved afternoon tea at The Three Crowns. I couldn't help thinking of Nutty Norman as we went inside. During the Civil War, the royalist Sir Sydney Godolphin died of his wounds in the ancient stone porch, and his ghost is said to haunt the inn to this day. I was sure that Norman and his gang had set up their equipment there more than once, although whether Sir Sydney ever honoured them with a visitation was another matter. As a ghost, he had a reputation for being uncooperative. I surveyed the plate of sandwiches and loaded cake stand and decided that the afternoon had its compensations.

'We found out about what's going on in Hilary's house,' Morris reminded him.

Ricky shot him a cynical glance. 'We think we did.'

'You know, I'm worried about Hilary,' Morris said as he dithered over selecting a sandwich. 'I don't like to think she's being forced into doing things that might be illegal by her daughter.'

Ricky slid him a glance. 'If that is her daughter.'

'Should we be ringing someone?' he went on anxiously. 'Social services or something?'

'And tell them what?'

I chewed this over, along with a dainty crab-filled finger roll. 'Tell me what she said again. Tell me what Hilary said to you about the man from the RSPCA.'

'She said that she'd told him that he'd got the wrong address, that there had never been any puppies for sale.'

'Yes, but didn't she say something about telling another woman?'

Morris nodded as he selected a cucumber sandwich. 'Yes. She said, "and I told that other woman".'

'What other woman?'

'That must have been Mary,' Ricky's long arm wavered over the table as he decided between a third sandwich or starting on the cakes, 'the woman who wanted the dog.'

'But Mary never met Hilary,' I pointed out. 'She only met Fran, or some other woman, who was claiming to be the breeder's wife. It wasn't until the RSPCA turned up that anyone knew this was Hilary's house, not hers. So, who was the other woman that Hilary spoke to?'

Ricky loaded clotted cream on to a glazed strawberry tart. 'Another customer,' he mumbled, biting into it, 'another buyer for the puppy.'

'But the breeder – the man who wanted to sell Mary the dog in the car park – only gave her the address because she refused to do business that way. He arranged for Fran, or someone, to meet her there. But it sounds as if this woman who Hilary mentioned wasn't expected. So, how had she got to hear about it? Who was she?'

Ricky shrugged. 'We'll never know.'

There were too many things I was never going to know the answer to for my liking.

'Like I said,' he repeated, 'a complete waste of time.'

'I'm sorry you feel like that about it,' I told him, reaching for a dinky tart citron, 'because if I don't get my van back in the morning, I want to waste some more of your time tomorrow.'

CHAPTER TWENTY

Riverview Developments, one of Dunston Properties' several current projects, comprised three mid-rise blocks overlooking a stretch of river in one of Plymouth's most desirable residential areas. Every one of the sixteen exclusive, two-bedroom flats would enjoy a fine view of the river from its own private balcony, as well as underground parking and landscaped gardens. Furthermore, complete security and peace of mind was guaranteed as this was to be a gated community.

Two of the glass-fronted blocks were still under construction, shrouded in tarp and scaffolding, but the completed block contained the show flat. Ricky and I had an appointment to view it that afternoon. Because it was only by viewing the show flat that we could gain access to the site, and I wanted to see the place where Phil Thomas died.

The site itself was fenced off – a muddy wasteland criss-crossed by digger tracks, edged by Portakabins and ranks of Portaloos. The long arm of a crane swung in the air high above us, like the beak of some giant waterbird, dripping chains. Cement mixers churned ceaselessly. Men in hard hats and hi-vis vests shouted at each other above the din. I gazed up at the scaffolding. The blocks were a modest four storeys tall, high enough to kill anyone who fell.

We were admitted to the site after a conversation with a hard-hat at the gate and led along a dry gravel path towards an office, housed in a Portakabin where we were met by a young woman in a suit and high heels. I recognised her from the meeting at Woodland. She had been sitting next to Alastair Dunston, her red nails clicking away at a laptop. Today her nails were pink and matched her lipstick. She handed Ricky a glossy brochure. 'Mr Steiner?' She smiled, plump, pink pout parting to show perfectly whitened teeth. 'Hello, I'm Michelle. And this is Miss . . . ?' she raised her carefully manicured eyebrows at me.

'This is my niece,' Ricky grinned, 'Belinda.'

Belinda? It was true, I didn't look like my usual self. I wore an outfit from the theatrical wardrobe, a yellow silk suit with a nipped-in waist and a tightly fitting pencil skirt, the sharply cut lapels and turned-back cuffs of the jacket embroidered with a tracery of black silk. A scarf in yellow and black silk was threaded through my curls, my black eye covered up with a skilful application of make-up. Ricky had done it, arguing that I needed a disguise. No man who could afford to buy one of those apartments would be seen abroad with a scruffy-looking bird like me, he told me. Originally this yellow outfit had been a costume worn by some vamp in an Agatha Christie play. I don't know what the name of the character was, but she certainly wasn't called Belinda. I gave him an arctic smile.

'Ah . . . your niece.' She flicked a heavily lashed glance from me to Ricky, silver-haired, handsome in his charcoal grey suit and silk tie, and drew her own conclusions. *Niece* was a euphemism for something else. Actually, the joke was on her.

'What an unusual suit,' she added, looking me up and down.

'Isn't it?' I agreed, all smiles.

'It's a Chanel original,' Ricky told her casually, and she smiled uncertainly. Men don't usually volunteer that kind of information.

She invited us to accompany her to Show Flat Number One, where we admired the light oak flooring throughout, the fashionable pale grey walls, the high-spec kitchen with its cooking island and granite worktops, the marble-tiled wet room, and walked out onto the spacious balcony where there was ample room for outdoor dining and a hot tub.

Ricky asked if it was possible to view the penthouse. Of course, Michelle would be delighted to show it to us, and whisked us up in the softly lit, smooth and silent lift, whilst she asked discreet questions about whether Uncle Ricky had an existing property to sell or whether he would require finance. He flashed her his most charming smile. He wouldn't need to sell; he wouldn't require finance. Michelle could barely conceal her excitement.

The penthouse had a great all-round view. As well as the river, it currently took in the entire construction site. When we walked out onto the balcony, we found ourselves on a level with the roof of the almost completed block opposite, the block from which Phil Thomas fell. I watched the hard-hats in their yellow vests working on the scaffolding. 'Wasn't there an accident a little while ago?' I asked Michelle.

'One of the builders fell from the scaffolding,' Michelle nodded sadly. 'Tragic, but it was a total accident.'

'So, the company wasn't found to be liable, negligent in any way?'

She looked shocked at such a question. 'Of course not.'

For a while we discussed the superiority of the penthouse, with its wonderful view of the city of Plymouth. It was particularly spectacular, Michelle assured us, at night, when all the city lights were on. I asked if there was only one lift. 'After all, Uncle Ricky, what if it breaks down?' I asked soulfully. 'At your age, do you think you would be able to manage all those stairs?'

'Of course, my darling, besides,' he flashed a smile at Michelle, 'I am sure it's very regularly maintained.'

Michelle assured him that there was a most rigorous maintenance programme and invited us to go with her to the office so that she could ensure that she had all of Ricky's details. We returned to the ground floor and to the Portakabin from which she had emerged. There was one occupant inside, seated at the desk. I found myself staring straight into the amber eyes of Louise Dunston.

'Mrs Dunston, I wasn't expecting you!' Michelle looked flustered.

'It's all right, Michelle,' she replied calmly. 'I only popped in to pick up some progress reports for Alastair.'

Michelle hastily introduced Ricky. 'This is Mr Steiner and his niece . . . er . . .'

'Belinda,' I furnished swiftly, keeping my eyes fixed on Louise.

She didn't blink, didn't miss a heartbeat. 'Charming to meet you.'

'Mr Steiner is interested in the penthouse,' Michelle told her.

Louise raised an eyebrow but managed to smile at Ricky. 'Really? Well, in that case I'll leave you in Michelle's capable hands. Good afternoon.' She inclined her head towards us in a brief nod, and left.

For the next five minutes Ricky confirmed the almost-but-not-entirely-accurate details he had given to Michelle. We bid her a warm goodbye, sure that we should see her again soon, and walked out, me holding our glossy brochure. '*At your age*,' he hissed at me as soon as Michelle was out of earshot. 'Cheeky bitch!'

The hard-hat who had let us in, let us out. 'Think you'll buy one, then?' he asked jovially as he accompanied us along the gravel path.

'Possibly,' Ricky told him. 'The apartments look good, but are they solidly built?'

'Course!' the man assured him. 'Very highest professional standards.'

'Yet I hear there was an accident here, a man fell to his death.'

The hard-hat nodded. 'Poor bloke. Terrible accident. Faulty coupling gave way. Mind you,' he added, lowering his voice, 'there wouldn't be so many accidents in this game if they didn't employ people who can't understand English.'

'Immigrant workers, you mean?' Ricky asked, frowning.

He nodded as he swung open the gate. 'Too many of 'em, if you ask me. We had an accident here about a year ago. A bloke got crushed by a digger. Didn't get out of the way quick enough 'cos he couldn't understand what was being yelled at him.'

'Was he a foreigner?' I asked. 'The man who fell?'

He gave an ironic grunt. 'Yeah, he was Welsh.'

We started to walk away. But Ricky suddenly grabbed my arm and said in a very loud voice, 'You've got something in your eye? Oh, darling, let me look!' and whipped out a handkerchief.

'What?' I hissed but he shushed me.

'When you turn around,' he whispered, making a pretence of examining my eye, 'without making it too obvious, take a good look at that chap over there, standing at the end of the row of Portakabins.'

'Why?' I tried not to flinch as he poked at my

eyeball with the corner of his handkerchief.

'Because he spotted you a moment ago and he's staring at you like he's seen a ghost,' he whispered. 'See if you recognise him.'

'Thank you so much, Uncle Ricky,' I said loudly. 'That's much better now,' and I turned to look behind me.

The man who was stood staring at me, apparently rooted to the spot, was a total stranger. Average height, clean-shaven. He meant nothing. There was nothing remarkable about him save for the intensity of his gaze.

'Don't know him at all,' I shrugged, turning away from him.

'Well, he knows you. Nearly fell over when he saw you. He's still staring now.'

We began to walk away from the fence towards the spot where Morris sat waiting in the car. Ricky cast a casual glance over his shoulder. 'He's following us.'

'What?'

'He's come right up to the wire fence for a closer look.' He slid his phone from his pocket.

'Stand there,' he muttered, turning me around. 'Smile, darling!' he called loudly, taking my photo. He clicked two or three times.

'Got him?' I asked as he opened the car door for me, and he nodded. 'Yeah. Now he's having a chat with the man on the gate. I bet he's trying to find out who we are, wants to know what we were talking about.'

I slid into the seat behind Morris, who turned around to smile at me.

'How did it go?'

226

'We didn't find out anything I didn't know already.' I smiled. 'Poor Michelle, she's going to be bitterly disappointed when Uncle Ricky decides not to buy the penthouse after all.'

Ricky was fiddling with the picture on his phone. 'Is that bloke still stood there, staring?'

I turned to look behind me. 'No, he's gone now.'

'What bloke?' Morris asked.

'Some fella that took one look at Juno and couldn't stop staring.' He showed me the picture on his screen. He'd zoomed in on the background, enlarged the face of the man standing behind the fence. 'Sure you don't know him?'

I studied the face, but it still meant nothing. 'Positive.'

'Perhaps it was love at first sight,' Morris suggested, his cheeks dimpling in a coy smile. 'Perhaps he was just transfixed by Juno's incredible beauty.'

Ricky cast a glance at me and shook his head. 'Nah, it wouldn't be that.'

I wasn't surprised to receive a phone call that evening. I hadn't mentioned to Ricky and Morris that I'd already had the pleasure of meeting Louise Dunston. There was no doubt that she must wonder what the hell I was doing, pretending to be someone I wasn't, posing as a buyer for one of the luxury apartments her husband's company was building.

'What exactly are you up to, *Belinda*?' She was keeping her voice down. I could hear music playing in the background. She was probably at home.

'I was curious to see where Phil Thomas died,' I told her.

'Why? What happened to him was an accident.'

'Are you sure?'

There was a brief silence. 'We're still awaiting the full RIDDOR report of course, but so far, the accident investigators seem satisfied.'

'Riddor?' I repeated.

She sighed. 'Reporting of Injury, Diseases and Dangerous Occurrences Regulations. It's all under proper investigation. Besides, what are you insinuating, that it wasn't an accident? There were witnesses to what happened.'

'No. I'm just wondering what Phil Thomas was doing working for your husband in the first place, considering what's gone on between them.'

'Well, I can't help you there.'

'Maybe you can. Do you know who employed him? I mean, it wouldn't have been your husband, would it? Not directly.'

'I imagine Swayne would have been responsible for that. He's in charge of recruiting builders.'

'Can you find out?'

I heard her sigh. 'Is this likely to be relevant?'

'I don't know what's likely to be relevant or not relevant at this point. But Phil Thomas died in an accident a short time after his wife was found murdered, and whilst the police might not think so, it's possible their deaths are linked.'

I heard voices in the background, excited barking, the

228

sounds of someone coming in, being welcomed by their dog. The sound of a happy dog caught at my heart.

'Look, I've got to go,' Louise hissed.

'So, will you find out about Phil?'

'I'm not making any promises, but I'll try.'

CHAPTER TWENTY-ONE

It was a fine weekend. I still hadn't got my van back but I kept myself busy, picking the late glut of blackberries in the back garden, my fingers purple-stained and peppered with tiny thorns. Sitting with Kate at the big scrubbed table in her kitchen, we washed and picked them through, discarding stalks and berries spoilt by insects or pecked at by birds. We boiled some of the blackberries up for jam, filling the kitchen with a sweet, sticky smell, setting the best aside for the freezer. Adam would use these later to make into pies and crumble for Sunflowers.

On Saturday night the clocks went back, signalling the end of summer. From now on the days would be shorter, evenings getting darker, winter would be coming on. It gave me an extra hour on Sunday morning to lie in bed, feeling wretched about the missing dogs.

The next day something horrible happened. I got a

phone call from Elaine – E.B.'s mum. Would I go around? Someone had phoned her, claiming to have found him.

'What's happened?' I asked, as soon as she opened the door.

She led me down the hall into her kitchen. 'I'll make a cup of tea,' she said, her voice shaking. She looked really distressed.

'Why don't you let me make it?' I offered. 'Sit down.'

Elaine nodded miserably and sat at the table. I could hear Alan's voice from upstairs, loud and insistent, he seemed to be talking on the phone.

'So, tell me.' I flipped the switch on the kettle. On the kitchen wall was a calendar with a large colour photograph of a miniature schnauzer, his bright eyes almost hidden by his bushy eyebrows, distressingly like E.B.

'I had this phone call – about two hours ago,' Elaine began, 'from a man, saying that he worked for an animal charity and that he thought he'd found E.B. He said he'd been knocked down by a car . . .' Elaine's voice trembled and she bit her lip. 'So, I told him our dog had been stolen. He said he didn't know anything about that, this dog had been found in the road. I wondered perhaps if he'd escaped from those dreadful men, you know, like little Schnitzel did, and been wandering around lost ever since. Anyway, he said someone had brought in one of the posters we'd had printed about our dogs being taken, and he was sure this was E.B. So, he said his charity had taken him to the vet, who was operating on him now . . .' She took in a breath. I placed a mug of tea on the table in front of her and she nodded silent thanks. I sat down opposite her.

'So, I asked him, what did the vet say?' she went on. 'Was E.B. going to be all right? And he said yes, he would be fine, but there would be the vet's bill to pay. I said, well, give us the address of this vet and we'll go straight there, sort everything out . . . And he said no, not to worry, his charity would take care of all that, but would I like to make a donation?' Elaine hesitated, twisting her hands together in her lap. 'Well, I thought that was odd, him asking for money there and then on the phone like that . . .'

Alarm bells were ringing inside my brain. 'What was the name of this charity?'

'Little Cott Animal Rescue.' Elaine gave a weak smile. 'I'd never heard of it, but with the man saying they had looked after E.B. and taken him to the vet, I didn't like to refuse. And I know what you told us the other night about these dreadful people who try to trick you out of your money, but he sounded so nice, and he'd been so kind, and he was only asking for twenty pounds, so I . . . I gave him my bank details.' She gave a hiccupping sob. 'I know I was stupid. Then, I don't know why, I just had a thought. I asked him, was he still at the vet's surgery? And he said yes. So, I asked him, could he tell me E.B.'s microchip number, because I knew they'd have scanned him for it as soon as they took him in. And for a moment he didn't say anything. Then suddenly he laughed and his voice was quite different and he said, "Sorry love, I can't do that," and he put the phone down.'

'Did you try to phone him back?' I asked.

She nodded, shamefaced. 'It was a withheld number. And I knew then,' she began to cry, 'I knew that it was all a scam, that he didn't have our little E.B. at all. Alan came home and I told him and he rang the bank straight away. And this man had taken two thousand pounds. Alan's still talking to them now. We think we can get our money back . . . but it's not that, is it?' She looked up at me, her eyes glistening with tears. 'We'd have paid all of that to get our E.B. back, but how can anyone be so evil?'

'I don't know.' I wished I did. 'Have you called the police?'

She nodded. 'They say this kind of thing happens all the time. They say what you said. These scammers prey on people who put notices up about lost pets, or put stuff on social media and all that.' She managed a sip of her tea. 'I know I was stupid, after all we talked about the other night, but when, just for a minute, I thought we were going to have our little boy back again . . .' She started to weep. 'But I wanted to tell you, Juno, so you can tell the others . . . tell them to be careful, if anyone phones up, not to be stupid like me.'

'You're not stupid. You love E.B. and that's what these evil bastards are relying on.'

She nodded, unconvinced. Alan came downstairs at that moment, sighing. 'It took a little while to get through to the right people, it being a Sunday, but they were very helpful. The bank has stopped the payment. At least we won't lose the money.'

'That's not the point,' Elaine sobbed.

'No, of course it's not,' he agreed, putting his arms around her. 'I wish I could get my hands on these cruel bastards.'

You and me both, Alan. You and me both.

'So, this person who tried to scam Elaine isn't necessarily connected to the people who kidnapped Florence,' Morris asked, frowning, 'or the men who stole the dogs from your van?'

'Not at all,' I said. 'He's probably completely independent from those bastards. A freelance bastard. I talked to Guy Mitchell at the *Gazette*, and he said that since they put in the article about what happened to the Tribe, they've fielded dozens of calls from obvious fakes trying to claim the reward.'

'But no real news?' Morris asked gently.

I'd been invited to lunch at Druid Lodge. It was not because of the dogs, but because, as Ricky put it, 'it was high time we thought about that fundraising thing you're making us do'. Earlier in the year I'd suggested they might like to hold a fundraising day for Honeysuckle Farm, encourage a few local people to rehome some of the animals, or at least sponsor them and contribute to the costs of their keep. We'd decided to do it just before Christmas, when everyone is feeling charitable. We kicked around a few ideas, but now, with the dogs missing, it didn't seem so urgent.

'No,' I sighed. 'No real news.'

* * *

I spent Sunday evening on the laptop, learning about deaths from accidents in the construction industry. Despite the health and safety measures that were in place, the statistics were truly grim. It seemed that all the hard hats and hi-vis vests in the world couldn't protect builders from the hazards they faced onsite. The most common types of accidents came from falls, like poor Phil Thomas, from unsecured ladders or scaffolding. But falling objects like bricks, tools or spare parts accounted for quite a few fatalities, especially, the report I was reading claimed, if 'communication' was poor. I thought about what the hard-hat at the gate had told me, about the poor foreign worker who couldn't understand the warning he was being given and got crushed by a digger.

Vehicles accounted for a large share of accidents, but I read some horrible stories about a man being buried under 'a large quantity of soil'; another killed by a steel girder falling from a crane. RIDDOR had investigated all of these accidents, but only in a few cases had the company director and construction manager been prosecuted and sent to prison.

I wondered about Alastair Dunston and looked his company up. I soon found myself reading about Phil Thomas and, after further digging, the foreign worker who had died the year before. Digging a bit deeper, I found two more fatal accidents on construction sites of Dunston's: four in the course of five years. I had a sudden thought, and looked up the picture that Ricky had taken on his phone, the picture of the man at the building site who had shown so much interest in me. I'd asked him to email the picture to me, although the man's face still meant nothing. I found the card that Louise Dunston had left with her contact details and sent the picture to her. *Do you know this man?* I asked her. *Who is he?*

I wasn't expecting a swift response, but her email came back to me in minutes.

Why do you want to know?

CHAPTER TWENTY-TWO

Hallowe'en came and went. It was busy in the shop, Pat's pumpkin earrings and the cute witch dolls she makes, selling like hot cakes. She'd made big, glittery spider brooches that were popular too. The town was full of kids out trick or treating. I went with Sophie to a party at a friend's house where everyone dressed up as ghosts, witches and zombies, but I really wasn't in the mood. The brightest spot in the evening came when I got a call from Dean Collins to tell me that my god-daughter, Alice, now had a baby sister. Gems had given birth shortly before midnight to a healthy baby girl. They were calling her Hannah. I was pleased for him, of course, although it would render him effectively useless as a source of police information until he came back from paternity leave. Although, thinking about it, perhaps it was just as well. The last time he was on paternity leave he managed to get himself shot. But that's another story.

Next morning, I got my van back, in time for me to start work, although the police had found nothing of any help in identifying the perpetrators of the crime. Why it always takes so long to find nothing, I'll never know. I had a lot of work to catch up on, clients to visit who I'd not been able to see. I'd been able to keep up with Tom Carter, counting the days till his operation, check in on Chloe Berkeley-Smythe's empty house and tidy her garden, dead-heading her dahlias and sweeping the paths for fallen leaves. But I'd had to miss my weekly session cleaning the Brownlows' place and Mrs Fox in Woodland, and the mountain of ironing at Simon the accountant's place was threatening to topple over. I know this makes me a very weird person, but I actually enjoy ironing, watching that towering pile of shirts get lower as I bang away with the steam iron.

I'd still been able to call on Maisie, of course, fetching her shopping and walking the obnoxious Jacko. 'Nobody's tried to steal you, I notice,' I told him that morning after I'd dragged him off the neck of an unsuspecting poodle and mollified its nearly hysterical owner.

Back at her cottage, Maisie was working her way through a pile of magazines that someone at the church had given her. Not her usual *People's Friend*, these were monthly glossies, country magazines reflecting a lifestyle that most of us can't even dream about. Houses advertised in the property section were in the millions, usually because they came complete with several acres, stables and staff cottages. 'Local' people interviewed tended to be involved in interior design, viticulture, bespoke jewellery, artisan foods or raising rare breeds of livestock. Advertisers were auctioneers, financial consultants, superior care homes and independent schools, or discreet establishments offering dental realignment and non-invasive plastic surgery. None of your scruffy junk shop owners trying to cobble together a living with cleaning and dog walking would be allowed to feature between its glossy covers. Maisie was lapping it up, enjoying being scandalised by all the prices.

'That bloke's in here,' she said by way of a greeting, as I came in loaded with her shopping, Jacko preceding me into the room, his lead trailing.

'What bloke?'

She tapped a gnarled finger on the page she was reading. 'Him what got the drink thrown over him. You know,' she added impatiently. 'Him!'

'You mean Alastair Dunston?' I put down the bags of shopping and peered over her shoulder. Sure enough, there was a double-page spread about him. *MP in the Making?* the headline queried coyly. Most of the article was composed of sycophantic drivel about the handsome and up-and-coming Mr Dunston, the contribution he had made to the business community, his links to various charities and whether or not he had political ambitions. The pictures were far more interesting. In dinner jacket and bow tie he was standing with Louise, looking stunning in a gold satin evening gown, at some charity ball. I wondered if this was the event where Sandy had confronted him. If so, this picture must have been taken prior to the Buck's Fizz being flung about. On the opposite page, as if to project an image of Dunston as an outdoors type, were pictures of him looking tanned and windswept at the wheel of a cabin cruiser. The caption told us that the boat was named *Louise*, in honour of his wife. Sweet. There was also a picture of him taken at the construction site, in yellow hi-vis jacket and hard hat, pointing into the air at nothing in particular, and looking every inch the politician.

'What do you think, Maisie?' I asked. 'If Alastair Dunston was an MP, would you vote for him?'

'No, I would not.'

'Why not?'

She sniffed in disparagement. 'I'd never vote for *that* lot. My old Bob would turn in his grave.'

It was evening before I was able to sit down, spread the map of Dartmoor out on the kitchen table and study the area around Cawsand Farm, the place where I had seen Hilary's daughter, Fran, park her red car. Where I had seen the grey Transporter.

Cawsand Farm took its name from the nearby Cawsand Beacon. The place was only a mile or so from the pretty village of Throwleigh with its old church and thatched cottages. Cordelia had taken me to that part of the high northern moor years ago, on one hot day during our long summer holidays. We'd swum in Shilley Pool, where a shallow brook, after flirting with a few frothy waterfalls, pours its water into a deep pond for bathers. Slightly to the north, and higher on to the moor, lies a scattering of hut circles, their stones all that remains of an Iron Age settlement. We camped one night, and lay flat on our backs within a circle of stone, singing and looking at the stars. Further up and higher again, is Cawsand Beacon and the treacherous Raybarrow Pool.

Bill came to give me the benefit of his advice, leaping gracefully onto the table and sniffing at the map. 'Don't sit down,' I warned him as he was about to do just that. But as I reached out to shift him, my eye was caught by the name of a place a few miles north of Okehampton: Hatherleigh. Hatherleigh, famous for being the smallest town in Devon, and because every year, on a given night between Hallowe'en and Guy Fawkes' Night, it holds a carnival.

The phone rang. It was Louise Dunston, getting back to me. She couldn't before, she explained. I wasn't sure I believed her.

'Why do you want to know, anyway, about this person?'

I explained he'd been taking what seemed an unhealthy interest in me. 'He couldn't take his eyes off me, apparently.'

'I'm not surprised. You were wearing a very alarming suit.'

That's a Chanel original, I'll have you know. I didn't bother to say it. 'Do you know who he is?'

She sounded bored. 'He's a junior member of Alastair's team. I'm not even sure what he does. I met him

241

when Alastair insisted on inviting him to dinner, along with several others on the staff. My husband likes to do this from time to time. These occasions are invariably a crashing bore. And so was this, until we found your friend lurking in the shrubbery.'

I wasn't sure I'd heard right. 'I beg your pardon?'

'That slut from the newspaper, Sandy Thomas.'

'No, I mean, this man . . . what's his name?'

'Stephen Higgs.'

'Stephen Higgs was having dinner at your house on the night Sandy was caught snooping in your garden?'

'Yes.' She thought a moment. 'Is that significant?'

'I've no idea,' I admitted. 'I've never laid eyes on Mr Higgs before I saw him at the construction site. You say you don't know what he does?'

Louise sighed down the phone, as if this conversation was also a crashing bore. 'He's something on the HR side, I believe. He's certainly not a builder.'

'I see. Thank you.'

'Is that all? Alastair will be home soon and I haven't started dinner.'

'Yes . . . just a moment,' I added before she could end the call. 'Do you remember who else was there that night?'

'Yes, Hollander. He works in finance. You would have seen him at the meeting about the Woodland development.'

'Nasty moustache?' I asked.

Louise allowed herself a soft laugh. 'Exactly.'

'And Michelle?'

Her laugh froze over. 'No. Not Michelle. One has to draw the line somewhere. Although, frankly, when it comes to socialising with the workers, I really don't think—' She stopped.

I could almost see her biting her lip, as if she'd said too much.

'What?' I asked quickly.

'I was going to say that I really don't know why Alastair feels the need to invite the likes of Eddie Swayne into our home, let alone that ghastly creature he lives with.'

'Swayne?' She'd mentioned that name before. 'Didn't you say he was involved in recruitment?'

'He's the gangmaster – recruits all the labourers. He was the one who employed Thomas, by the way.'

'Phil Thomas?'

'You did ask me to find out.'

'Yes, I did. Thank you.'

'Well, if that's all . . .' She was preparing to put the phone down.

No, it wasn't all, not by a long chalk. I wanted to ask her why her husband's company had such an appalling safety record, why there had been four fatal accidents on their construction sites in the last five years. But I doubted if asking the question would do anything other than alienate her, even if she could come up with an answer. And I wanted to keep her on side. It wasn't all. But for the moment, it was enough.

CHAPTER TWENTY-THREE

I decided to start my search for the way into Cawsand Farm at the nearby village of Throwleigh. It's a pretty village, a cluster of houses with the church and cross at its centre and a thatched, priest's house nearby. There are no shops there and not much else. The nearest pub is a mile away. It's a pleasant walk on a fine autumn day, so I decided that if I didn't find the turning I was looking for on the road between the village and the pub, then that would be a good enough reason to stop for a pint when I got there, landlords and barmaids being excellent sources of information.

But in Throwleigh itself there was only one likely source of local knowledge: the church.

St Mary the Virgin dates back to the thirteenth century. I wandered up a path through the graveyard towards a deeply recessed, carved archway and through a heavy wooden door. Inside was the sense of calm you only find in churches: a smell of incense and wood polish. It was light and airy, with glowing blues and reds pouring through three tall, narrow windows. Unfortunately, there didn't seem to be anyone about.

I was just about to make my way back outside when a quick, light footstep alerted me to the fact someone was coming in, and a moment later I found myself smiling back at a pleasant-looking grey-haired woman carrying a trug full of flowers. 'Oh hello!' she said brightly. 'Did you want to see the vicar?'

'Not necessarily,' I said. I could see her staring at my fading black eye and the scabs on my cheek, but she was too polite to ask questions.

'Oh. Well, I've only come in to arrange the flowers for the service on Sunday,' she told me, 'please feel free to look around our church.'

'Actually, I am looking for something,' I admitted after a moment's hesitation. 'I'm trying to find an address – Cawsand Farm.'

'Cawsand Farm?' she repeated, frowning as if the name meant nothing to her. 'That's not in the village.'

'No, but it's around here somewhere. I have a friend whose family used to live there, and I promised, if I was passing this way, I'd look the place up.' Is it worse if you tell lies in church, I wondered.

'What's the family's name?'

Um . . . I don't know,' I admitted, shrugging. 'I just know my friend's sister's name was Fran.'

At that moment another woman arrived, also

bearing flowers. Another of the arrangement team, obviously.

'Madge,' the first flower lady called to her. 'You don't know of a place called Cawsand Farm, only this young lady—'

'Cawsand?' The other woman frowned, first at her companion and then at me. She wore glasses and her brown eyes were magnified behind thick lenses. 'That's Swayne's old place.'

Swayne? I'd heard that name before. It was the name of Alastair Dunston's gangmaster, the person that Louise didn't welcome as a guest at her dinner table. How very interesting. Madge narrowed her eyes at me like a suspicious owl. 'Been in a fight, 'ave you?'

'No, just a slight accident.' I couldn't stop myself from dabbing at my cheek.

'You know, my dear,' First Flower Lady stared at me solicitously, 'if you've been a victim of domestic abuse, then the Church is here to help.'

'No. That's very sweet of you . . .' I said, giving a false laugh. 'I . . . er, I fell over the dog.'

They both continued to stare. 'Cawsand Farm?' I reminded them.

'What do you want to go there for?' Madge asked. 'I don't think anyone lives there now.'

'Well, I don't know.' I tried to sound as vague as possible. 'It's just my friend told me—'

''Twasn't ever a proper farm,' she went on, 'more like a smallholding. And after old man Swayne got prosecuted, he let the place go.'

'Prosecuted?' First Flower Lady raised her eyebrows in surprise. 'Whatever for?'

'Now, I don't remember the exact details 'cos it was a long time ago,' Madge said slowly, 'all I know is, he was banned from keeping animals.'

'Oh dear.' Flower Lady and I exchanged shocked glances. 'Are you sure this is the place your friend meant?'

'Friend?' Madge repeated. 'What was her name?'

'Fran,' I volunteered.

Madge was shaking her head. 'No, he didn't have no daughter called Fran. He had a son, and I suppose the place must belong to him, but I don't think he lives there.'

'Do you know how I can find it?' I asked. 'Only I promised my friend I'd take a photograph, so that she can see what the old place looks like now.'

She frowned as if she didn't think much of that for an idea. 'The best thing you can do, is walk up the road to Wonson. It's only about a mile. Call in at the Northmore Arms. They'll give you directions from there.'

'Thank you. I will.' I left them to their flower arranging, Madge unfavourably comparing the size of First Flower Lady's dahlias with the ones in her own basket.

I'd never visited the Northmore Arms but I had heard of it. In the eighteenth century it was the home of one William Northmore, Member of Parliament for Okehampton, a gambler who lost a fortune on the turn of a card, reputedly the ace of diamonds. Legend has it that he had the card painted on his bedroom wall so that he could look at it at night and repent of his folly. And a fat lot of good that did him, I'm sure.

I was ready for a drink by the time I'd walked there. It might be November, with misty mornings and heaps of rusty leaves lying deep beneath bare trees, but it was still warm during the daytime, and I was relieved to see the pub was open, a scattering of customers sitting at tables in its sunny garden. But I was heading inside, to its dim, olde world interior, with low beams and fireplace wide enough to drive a cart through.

The girl behind the bar was willing to chat as she poured me my half of cider. But she frowned when I told her I was looking for Cawsand Farm.

'I know it's up the road, not far from here,' she told me. 'But I don't really know how you get to it.'

'It doesn't seem to be signposted anywhere,' I said, remembering my ride in the Saab from the other direction.

'Hah!' came a voice from a nearby table. 'You can't expect anything as helpful as a sign.' A tanned blonde with a lot of gold jewellery weighing her down beckoned to me from a nearby table. She wore a white jumper, sandals, and sunglasses perched on top of her head. She was the kind of woman who, I imagine, is always dressed for summer. I couldn't imagine her without her toenails painted. She smiled in a friendly fashion as I sat down, obviously happy to chat. 'That place makes my blood boil, it really does!'

'You know it, then?'

'Know it? I tried to get old man Swayne to sell it for years!'

I'd have put her at about fifty, but she might have been younger, her deep laughter lines the result of too much time in the sun. 'I just hate to see a place like that going to wrack and ruin,' she went on. 'I mean, in today's market it's worth a fortune.'

'The farm, you mean?'

'The farmhouse, the barn, the lot! The long barn up by the road is worth a lot of money, just on its own. People are always looking for barn conversions.'

'Are you an estate agent by any chance?' I asked.

'Guilty as charged,' she admitted and laughed loudly. 'But I also live in Wonson and I just don't like to see places like that falling down. It's an eyesore, as much as anything, and such a waste.'

'It's picturesque, Pauline,' a man called from another table. 'You leave it alone. You'd have it done up and turned into holiday cottages, I suppose?'

'No, I'd settle for someone living in it permanently,' she countered, 'some rich old bastard like you, Henry.' He laughed. 'The problem with people around here,' she added to me in a low voice, 'is that they don't think of the local economy.'

Henry gestured towards my face with his pint. 'What happened to you?' he asked, as if he'd known me for years.

'Fell over a sheep,' I told him.

'Don't be so damn nosy, Henry!' Pauline admonished him.

I didn't want to become the focus of interest. 'I take it the old man, this Swayne, didn't want to sell?' I asked, bringing her back to the subject.

'He threatened me with a shotgun the last time I went there. But he was like that with everyone, completely paranoid.'

'How long ago did he die?'

Pauline sighed as she considered. 'About five years. His son inherited the property but has done absolutely nothing with it, despite being a builder – or so I'm led to understand. I don't think he's even there most of the time.'

'Well, someone must be living there,' Henry put in, 'cos they keep dogs there. My neighbour hears 'em barking.'

Dogs? I felt a sudden surge of excitement.

'I thought he'd been banned,' Pauline objected.

'That was the old man, not the son.'

'Oh yes. What was the son's name?'

'Eddie, like his dad.'

'Oh, that's right.' Pauline gave me a quizzical look. 'Why did you say you were looking for this place?'

'I didn't. A friend of mine from school knew someone who lived there once. As I was coming this way, I thought I'd take a look.' I shrugged. 'I'm just being nosy, really.'

'Well, if you really want to find it, it's up the road about half a mile. There's a *picturesquely* rotting barn by the side of the road,' she added, making a face at Henry. 'It's on a corner with an old track that will lead you down to the farm. But if you're planning on nosing around down there, I'd be careful. I don't know if the current Eddie Swayne is as paranoid as his father, but he probably doesn't welcome visitors.'

Henry was right about the long barn, it was picturesque. It would have made a nice painting, slates missing from its mossy roof exposing rotting rafters, its heavy stone walls green with ivy, flaky remnants of paint clinging to its sagging doors. It looked to me like a perfect haunt for barn owls, or a roost for bats. Like Henry, I was inclined to think the best thing to do with it was to leave it alone.

In its way the barn marked a boundary. On one side of it was the way back to the pub and the road down to Throwleigh; on the other side, the open moor. It stood at the corner of a wide track that left the road and carried across open moorland before it lost itself behind a stand of trees. In the distance I could see the stones of an old hut circle. There are many up here on the high, northern moor, stone rows and odd standing stones, remnants of ancient settlements going back to the Iron Age. I turned and looked around me. If Ricky, Morris and I had come another hundred yards along this road we would have seen this place; instead, we'd followed the road down into Throwleigh.

I started to walk along the track, along two clear earthen scars worn into the land by the passing of wheels, straggly grass growing between them. A few black-faced sheep grazing among the gorse watched me with mild curiosity as I passed, otherwise there was no one about. I reached the stand of trees, a few oaks and a ragged clutch of thorn and mountain ash that had rooted themselves among boulders and grown stunted and twisted by the wind. I got my first sight of the farm, below me in the bowl of the valley. The track ran around the edge of it for about a hundred yards before it dropped down the slope towards the farmhouse. I walked on a bit further. There were no more trees from here on, no cover. Anyone approaching, on foot or driving along that track, could be seen from the farmhouse below. I realised I must be sky-lining myself, clearly visible to anyone who might be looking out of the windows. It would be impossible to drive my van along here undetected. And if I was right and my Tribe had been kidnapped in that Transporter and were being kept in those outbuildings somewhere, getting them away from there undetected was going to be difficult. Assuming that anyone was at home, of course.

And someone was at home at the moment, because the red Honda was parked by the back door. Fortunately for me, perhaps, there was no sign of the grey Transporter. Step off the track, and the land dropped away sharply. It would be a clamber, a climb, rather than a walk down its steep sides towards the farm. One way or another, there was no quick way in and out of this place.

My theory about being visible soon proved right. 'Hey!' a voice yelled at me from the farmhouse door. Fran emerged, peering up at me, one hand shading her eyes from the sun. 'This is private property, you know.'

I pretended I couldn't hear her. 'I'm sorry?'

She came out to stand by her car. 'Private property!' she yelled again. 'What d'you want?'

'Oh, I'm so sorry,' I yelled back. 'I didn't realise I was trespassing.' Whenever challenged by someone potentially hostile, I always find it's best to appear to be lost or an idiot. 'Isn't this the right way to Cawsand Beacon?'

'No, it's not. Go back to the barn at the corner of the road and then strike off right towards the hut circles.'

'That way?' I asked, pointing vaguely in the direction I'd come.

'That's right. Turn around and keep going.'

'Oh, thank you so much.' A dog began barking from inside a barn near the house, a deep rumble. Then another, a high-pitched yapping, then a few more. Definitely dogs, plural. Fran glanced towards the barn uneasily. 'I don't suppose I could trouble you for a glass of water?' I asked, putting on a smile.

She hesitated. ''Fraid not, no. You'd best get going.'

Damn, I wanted to get down there for a closer look. 'I just wondered—'

'My husband will be home soon,' Fran interrupted, 'and he doesn't like strangers on his land.'

I could see then that she wasn't alone either: a figure was at work inside the polytunnel, a mere dark blur visible through the thick plastic walls.

'Yes. Right. I see. Sorry.' I gave an idiotic little wave of my fingers. 'Bye then.'

I turned around and began walking back, conscious all the time of Fran watching me.

When I reached the cluster of trees, I stopped and turned to see if she was still watching. She was.

CHAPTER TWENTY-FOUR

I was pondering what I was going to do next all the way back to Ashburton. It was almost dark by the time I got there, the sky the soft blue of twilight. I went back into the flat, but I felt restless. I decided to stroll down to the shops on North Street – the Co-op and the Spar would still be open. I needed some groceries, but more than that I needed to clear my head.

I caught sight of my reflection in the hallway mirror as I let myself out. The bruise around my eye was changing colour, purple fading to green, yellow around the edges. But without the help of Ricky's make-up, I still looked as if I'd been in a prize-fight, the scrape on my cheek a peppering of tiny scabs. No wonder Henry, Madge and the Flower Lady had been curious. But it was dark, and anyway I wasn't likely to meet anyone, except perhaps Cutty Dyer if I strayed too near the river, but even a blood-drinking demon was likely to take one look at my face and think twice about taking me on.

I opened the door. The air was still mild. Storms were threatened, remnants of some distant hurricane, brewing themselves up out over the Atlantic. They would sweep in over the coast and crash against the high tops of the moor; but they were days off yet.

What if, I wondered, Sandy Thomas had not been stalking Alastair Dunston on the night she was found in his garden? What if she was watching someone else, one of the other people gathered there for dinner? Nasty Moustache, for instance, the money man? Or Stephen Higgs, or Eddie Swayne, the gangmaster, the man who'd employed Phil Thomas? And had Phil been following Sandy's trail when he got himself work at Dunston Properties, a firm with a record of four fatal accidents? What had he been going to tell me the night before he died? Sandy told Alf she was going to see someone about a dog. What if that someone was Hilary? After all, Hilary had mentioned that another woman had come to her house enquiring about a dog.

By now I'd reached King's Bridge. If Cutty Dyer was lurking anywhere, it would be here. *Never go there at night*, Maisie warned me often, *Cutty Dyer'll have 'ee, that's what my mother used to say*. But there was only the sound of water burbling as the shallow river slid fleetingly beneath the bridge, then sneaked behind the houses on Kingsbridge Lane.

I was so wrapped in thought I didn't hear the thing that was hurtling towards me. A sudden skittering of claws on tarmac, a delighted bark and a bundle of quivering whippet threw itself against my legs, a wet nose pressing at my knee.

'Lottie!' I cried out, stooping down to give her a hug. She wriggled in my arms, trying to lick my face, snuffling joyously amongst my hair. 'Oh, Lottie!' I whispered, holding her tight. 'I do miss you.' Her lead was trailing from her collar, and I gathered it up, and after a lot more patting and hugging, and telling her what a lovely dog she was, I stood and looked about me. Where the hell was Daniel? He must be around somewhere. I couldn't see him. I crossed the road to the car park, walking through the lines of parked cars until I spotted his, parked against a wall under the spill of an old street light. The tailgate was open and he was loading in some shopping. I screamed at him. 'What the hell do you think you're doing?'

He swung around, looked shocked to see me marching towards him, Lottie trotting happily on the lead. The lamplight showed me the sharp angles of his face, the hawkish nose and high cheekbones. 'Oh Juno.' His dark brows drew together in a frown. 'What—'

'Letting Lottie run around on her own, out of your sight,' I carried on as I drew near to him. 'Haven't you heard about the dog thefts going on around here? Don't you know she could get stolen?' My voice shook angrily.

He didn't even have the grace to look uncomfortable. 'Yes, I read something about . . .' He peered at me, suddenly intent. 'What happened to your face? Are you all right, Miss B?'

The sudden concern in his voice tugged at my heart. 'Don't you bloody Miss B me!' He'd forfeited the right to that term of endearment when he'd declared our relationship at an end, when he'd slammed the door of his caravan in my face.

He began to nod slowly as understanding dawned. 'Oh, I get it! You were the woman I read about, the one in the van.' He gave a sardonic smile. 'You just can't help yourself, can you? You just can't stay out of things. You have to get involved.'

'I was not trying to get involved,' I hissed at him. 'I was driving along, minding my own business, when two dog-robbers decided they'd like to help themselves to my passengers.'

I felt my lip tremble. I could have cried afresh at the memory of what happened, but I was damned if I was going to start weeping in front of Daniel Thorncroft. I took in a deep breath. 'They dragged me out of the window.'

'Good God! Did they hurt you? I mean, apart from . . .' He reached out to touch my face.

I took a step back. 'That is none of your concern.' I threw the end of the lead towards him. 'Just look after your dog.'

I began to march away but he came after me, reaching me in two quick strides and grabbing at my wrist, twisting me around to face him. 'Don't be stupid, Juno. Of course I care what happens to you. I care too damned much. That's the very reason why—'

'Don't give me that!' I wrenched my arm away.

Suddenly I was struggling to control my trembling. 'Don't tell me that it's because of my dreadful behaviour that we cannot be together. That's bullshit!'

He frowned, his face stern as a graven image. 'Meaning?'

'Meaning that my reckless and irresponsible attitude, as you once called it, is just an excuse not to love me.'

'What are you talking about?'

'I mean that you are not ready to love anyone, Daniel, because you are still in love with Claire, and if it wasn't my dangerous behaviour that made you decide to end our relationship, it would have been something else.' Thoughts I had never voiced, not even in my head, came tumbling out. 'Claire died, and that is terribly sad, and she took a piece of your heart with her. And you could not stop her dying—'

'Now look—' He tried to interrupt me, to warn me off dangerous ground, but I didn't give him the chance.

'And your guilt won't allow you to move on, to love someone else,' I carried on inexorably. 'To love me.' Tears were streaming down my face now. I couldn't stop them and I didn't care. 'And the sad thing is that I have always known that I would never have your whole heart, Daniel, that a piece of you would always belong to Claire. But do you know what? I didn't care, because I've always thought that love was worth taking a risk.'

He stared, silent, still as a statue, his dark eyes unreadable.

I stepped closer to him. 'Listen. Do you know what I want right now? I want you to get out of my space. I want you to go away and sort your head out. Ask yourself if this is what Claire would have wanted. And if you ever feel ready to come back, well, fine! Just don't expect me to sit on my arse in my little shop, twiddling my thumbs until you do.'

I turned and marched away. He didn't come after me. Didn't call my name. Lottie barked at me, whining, willing me to come back. But I kept walking.

I was shaking when I got home. I needed a drink. But I had nothing in my flat. I only buy the occasional bottle of wine and I couldn't remember when I'd last done that. All I had was a bottle of cream liqueur that Simon the accountant had given me last Christmas. Better than nothing. I dug it out of the cupboard, fetched a large wine glass, took it through to the living room where I set it on the coffee table and poured myself a goodly glug. The front doorbell rang. I paused, the bottle in my hand beginning to tremble. I set it down and ran down the stairs. The bell rang again, the caller getting impatient. Despite everything I had just said to him, I was praying it would be Daniel. I flung open the door.

The last person I expected to see standing there was Cruella – Detective Sergeant Christine deVille. I rearranged my features accordingly.

'Good evening, Miss Browne,' she said crisply. 'I'm sorry to call so late but . . .' she frowned suddenly, 'have you been crying?'

'No,' I lied. And it's none of your business if I have. 'What can I do for you?'

'Just a few questions . . . Could I come in?' she

ventured after I'd been staring at her like an idiot for longer than necessary. Of course, Dean was on leave with his new daughter, that was why she was here. It was usually left to him to pay visits to the likes of me.

'Of course.' I led the way and she followed me up to my flat.

'I wondered if you could cast your mind back to the other day.' She paused in the living room, her eyes drawn to the bottle and the creamy beige liquid sitting in the glass.

'Want one?' I asked her.

She inclined her head to read the label on the bottle. 'No thanks. A bit too sickly for me.'

'Me too, if I'm honest.' I invited her to sit down.

'Thank you.' She was on her best behaviour. I suppose she felt she had to be whilst she was in my flat. She pulled out her notebook. 'Could you describe again what happened?'

There was no point in protesting, complaining that I'd been through it all three times at the police station already. I knew why she was asking. People often recall details later that they couldn't remember at the time, especially if they were in shock. But every night since it had happened, I'd been over and over it in the sleepless dark and remembered nothing more than I'd already told her and the inspector.

'You described your attackers as twin robots.' She looked up from her notes, her dark eyebrows raised enquiringly, disappearing into her fringe. 'Do you still think that's an accurate description?'

'They were very similar. Roughly the same height, dressed identically, dark blue overalls, baseball caps, sunglasses.'

'What kind of sunglasses?'

'Aviator type.' I closed my eyes, seeing the two of them getting out of the van, striding towards me. 'One was slightly taller than the other, bigger built.' I looked at Cruella, sitting there, pen poised. 'But that's not much help, is it?'

'You mentioned that at one point during the struggle you managed to knock the sunglasses off the face of one man. Did you get a look at him?'

'No, as I said before, once he had hold of my hair, I couldn't turn my head. He was behind me. I couldn't really see him.' All I'd got a good view of, as the two men had hauled me out through the van window, was the ground, the legs of their overalls, their shoes. Their boots. I realised something.

'What?' Cruella pounced, staring at me intently. 'What have you remembered?'

'It's nothing.'

'Oh, come on, Juno!' she snapped. 'I saw the light bulb come on over your head! You just remembered something.'

'They were wearing heavy boots, the sort that builders wear.'

'Steel toecaps?'

I nodded. I'd been lucky. Steel toecaps, the sort that builders wear. They could have kicked me to a pulp. I frowned at Cruella. Why the sudden interest?

Investigating officers often follow up on original interviews, but why now? Why tonight? 'Have there been any developments?'

She evaded the question. 'This is just routine,' she assured me.

But I'd seen the twitch of her little mouth.

'Has it happened again? Have they attacked someone else, snatched another dog?'

'No.' She shook her dark head, then gazed at me directly, her violet eyes fixed on mine. 'It hasn't happened again.' I knew she was holding out on me, there was something lurking in the violet depths of her eyes, something she wouldn't say. 'But if you should remember anything else,' she added, putting away her notebook.

'I'll let you know.'

She stood up. 'I'll see myself out.' She glanced at the bottle on the table and smirked. 'Enjoy the rest of your evening.'

I could cheerfully have punched her, but then she wasn't the saddo trying to drown her sorrows in a bottle of Christmas liqueur. 'No news on the dogs, I suppose?'

She sighed. 'I'm afraid not. But remember, these are dangerous men, so no amateur heroics on this one, Miss Browne.' She gave her odd little smile. 'I don't want to find myself investigating your murder.'

I smiled back. 'I bet you do really.'

As soon as she had gone, I was on the phone to Dean. It was late, but it wasn't that late.

'How's the baby?' I asked, when he picked up.

'Beautiful,' he responded. 'Especially when she's asleep, like now,' he added with heavy emphasis. 'What d'you want, Juno? Are you okay?'

'I've just had Cruella here,' I told him. 'Asking me more questions.'

He grunted. 'That's her job, asking questions.'

'Yes, but why tonight? Has there been another attack?'

'Not as far as I know, but I've been on leave.'

'Something's happened. Something's going on, I can sense it.'

'Like I say, I've been on leave. But I've got to go into the station tomorrow, I'll see what I can find out.'

'Good.'

'Of course,' he added with a warning note in his voice, 'if there is anything, I won't be able to tell you what it is.'

'Oh, Detective Constable Collins,' I mocked him, 'you do say the silliest things.'

CHAPTER TWENTY-FIVE

I was investigating an ominous odour emanating from the Brownlows' dishwasher next morning when my phone rang from the depths of my shoulder bag. I nearly banged my head on the dishrack getting it out of the dishwasher fast enough and reaching for my bag. I was hoping it was Dean getting back to me but when I pulled out the phone, I didn't recognise the number on the display.

'Is that the *Dartmoor Gazette*?' A woman's voice, vaguely familiar.

'Sorry?'

'This is the number I was given. That is you, isn't it, the reporter that rang up about our dog being stolen? I recognise your voice.'

'Oh yes, of course, the lady from Scorriton.' Just for a moment I'd forgotten what a liar I was. 'Mrs . . . er . . .'

'Mrs Coombes.'

'Mrs Coombes. I'm sorry. I'm out of the office at the moment . . .'

'Well, I just thought your readers might like to know that we got our Buttons back.'

I sat on the kitchen floor, all ears. 'That's wonderful. How?'

'Well, thank goodness, there are some honest people in this world. We had a phone call from a vet. She said someone had brought Buttons into the surgery. This young fella had bought him from some man outside a pub. The man said he was down on his luck, couldn't afford to keep his dog any more. The young fella felt sorry for him. Paid him a hundred pound.' She sniffed. 'He got a bargain, if he did but know it. Anyway, he took him home to his girlfriend and she told him if he'd bought a dog from someone outside a pub it was most likely stolen. She made him take him to this vet to see if he was microchipped. The vet scans him and his number comes up on a stolen dogs' list. She told the young man Buttons had to be returned to his rightful owner. He wasn't very happy about it, seeing as he'd lost a hundred pound, but the vet told him that the dog was undernourished and his coat was matted, and whoever had sold him had obviously been keeping him in dreadful conditions and should be prosecuted.'

This was interesting. Did whoever had taken Buttons resort to selling him outside a pub for far less than he was worth because the original ransom demand had been ignored? Was there a connection between the man outside the pub and Clown Head and co. in Shaugh Prior Tunnel?

'So, you've got Buttons home. How is he now?'

'Well, he looked a right mess, I can tell you. And the stink! We had to give him half a dozen baths before we got rid of the smell . . .'

'He must be happy to be home.'

'Oh, bless him! He won't stop following our Lisa around. We have to let him sleep on her bed or he howls all night.'

'And Lisa must be very happy.'

'She's over the moon.'

'Well, that's wonderful, Mrs Coombes. And I'm sure our readers will be delighted to know that Lisa and Buttons are happy together again. Just one thing, you don't remember which pub it was, where this sale took place?'

'Yes, I do. It was the Tally Ho,' she told me. 'In Hatherleigh.'

I rang Guy Mitchell as soon as I finished talking to Mrs Coombes and gave him the good news about Buttons. We both agreed it would make a heart-warming story for the readers of the *Dartmoor Gazette*. I didn't tell him I'd only got the news because I'd masqueraded as one of its reporters. 'By the way,' I asked him, 'did you ever find anything more out about the death of Phil Thomas?'

'The police seem satisfied it was an accident,' he answered. 'And there won't be any more news until the RIDDOR report comes out.'

'Did you know that there have already been four fatal accidents on Dunston's construction sites, that this is the fifth in as many years?'

I heard him chuckle down the phone. 'Juno, you've been digging. Did you know that three of them have involved immigrant workers?'

'Sounds like you've been digging too.'

'I went down to Plymouth last week, to the construction site, talked to a few labourers, asked a few questions.'

'Did you find out anything?'

'No, not really. It seems that where Phil Thomas was concerned, no one saw anything and no one heard anything.'

'Isn't that suspicious?'

'The accident happened at the end of the day – which is when most accidents happen – people are getting tired, getting careless. Everyone had come down from the scaffolding, when he remembered he'd left some tools up aloft and went back up to fetch them.'

'He was alone when he fell?'

'Apparently.'

'Should he have been allowed up there alone?'

'He probably wouldn't have been during the course of the working day, but as I say, everyone was clocking off. He'd just gone back to fetch something. The men I spoke to seemed to think it was just bad luck. Mind you, some of them were reluctant to talk. They could have been warned off saying anything. Dunston Properties wouldn't want any bad publicity. I'd only been there a few minutes and two blokes in suits came out of the office and told me to bugger off.'

I smiled. 'Funny how some people don't like reporters.'

'Isn't it?'

'D'you think they've got something to hide?'

'I don't know. I guess, after any fatal accident, they're likely to be cagey. But I took some photos through the wire fence, just to piss 'em off.'

'Can I see them?'

'The photos? Well, they're not of anything in particular – like I said, I only took them to wind these guys up.' He laughed. 'And some of those labourers are really camera-shy. They're not prepared to talk, and they certainly don't want to be photographed. Soon as I got the camera out, they went running off like rabbits.'

'Do you think they were working there illegally?'

He laughed. 'Probably self-employed tradesmen, not declaring the income they get from doing the odd job for Dunston's company. Perhaps they thought I was from Inland Revenue or the Benefit Fraud office.'

'But if they're self-employed, it won't be Dunston's responsibility, will it? It'll be theirs.'

'Hmm. Might be worth another poke around,' Mitch mused, 'try to chat to these fellas, see what I can grub up.'

'I thought you didn't want to get sued.'

'I don't. Anyway, you can see the pictures if you want. Pop by the office.'

'Thanks,' I said, 'I will.'

* * *

I reached Hatherleigh as darkness was falling. The town was packed, its narrow streets lined with excited crowds waiting for the carnival to begin. The festivities had been going on all day, starting, bizarrely, with blazing tar barrels being dragged on sleds down the steep streets at five o'clock in the morning. I have no idea why it starts so early but it's an ancient tradition that I decided to miss. It happens again in the evening, once the carnival has safely passed, and ends in a big bonfire in the marketplace. In the meantime, there had been a meeting of the local hunt, judging of decorated shop windows and a town-crier competition.

I parked Van Blanc in about the only space available, at the back of the market car park, and made my way up the steep main street as a silver band was marching down it, signalling the start of the torchlit procession. Each flaming torch, a ball of tar-soaked material about the size of a human head, was borne aloft on a long wooden pole. Golden light flickered on the faces of the onlookers and the air smelled scorched and smoky. Some torches were tied together to form elaborate fan-like frameworks and took several men to carry. Others carried crosses with torches blazing at each end. Despite the happy, good-natured crowd, it was all a bit Ku Klux Klan for my liking, and I found the resemblance of the tar-soaked balls of flame to human skulls slightly macabre. But there is something about the presence of fire. It makes me think of those Bronze Age ancestors in their stone huts, huddled around their campfires, facing into the comfort of light and warmth, the overwhelming blackness of the moor at their backs.

The sound of the marching band receded, competing with live music pouring from the open door of the Tally Ho! I planned to go in there later, see if I could find out the identity of the man who had sold Buttons. But for now, I found a spot on the pavement squashed between chattering onlookers, where I could stand looking over the heads of the children in front of me and watch the procession pass.

I didn't have to wait long for the main event, the arrival of the carnival floats. These were led by the carnival queen, a pretty teenager in a Cinderella ballgown who looked embarrassed but managed to smile and wave at the crowds in a royal fashion, along with her attendants. She was followed by a galleon in full sail, complete with a rowdy rabble of pirates brandishing their cutlasses at a delighted crowd. Then came a giant peacock, his outspread tail glowing with coloured light as he turned his head stiffly from side to side, his wings flapping with jerky clockwork movements as a cascade of bubbles poured from his beak. An underwater scene followed, tropical fish lanterns glowing, their tissue-paper bodies lit up from within, painted seahorses and giggling, waving mermaids sitting on banks of coral. Small children, streamers trailing from dome-shaped transparent umbrellas, bobbed up and down as jellyfish.

The circus float came next with acrobats and clowns; and that is where I saw him, the tiny hat perched on his bulbous pink head with its rosy cheeks and cherubic smile. Clown Head, just as I had seen him in the blackness of Shaugh Prior Tunnel. He was wearing a full clown costume this time, bright green, with a wide floppy collar and three red bobbles down its front; and ridiculously long shoes. He waved at the crowd as the float moved slowly past, throwing sweets from a bucket to the kids with their arms outstretched, screaming for his attention. I saw him. And as a torchbearer walked along beside the float, briefly illuminating the faces of onlookers, I know that he saw me. I tried to keep pace with him, moving down the street as the float rolled slowly on, forcing my way through the crowd. And although he kept on waving and throwing sweets, from time to time that great, swollen head would turn in my direction, and I could feel the stare of the man concealed within.

The procession ended at the marketplace, where the floats cleared off, out of public view, leaving the street clear for the run of blazing barrels to begin. Crowds were gathered here too, drawn by the smoky sizzle of burger and hot dog stands, or the sweet, syrupy smell of candyfloss and waffles. By the time I had forced my way through, the circus float had drawn to a standstill, the acrobats already jumping down from it and starting to disperse.

Clown Head wasn't on the float. I looked around but couldn't see him. I swore softly. Once he got out of that ridiculous costume, I wouldn't be able to recognise him. He would still be able to recognise me, of course. Not a comfortable thought.

On the underwater float, the children had jumped down and were running off with their glowing fish lanterns. The mermaids were helping each other to wriggle out of their fishy tails amid gales of hysterical giggling. The circus float was parked next to it.

I came face to face with Clown Head, just his head, abandoned on the floor of the float, along with the empty bucket that had contained the sweets. I was curious, I wanted to pick it up, find out how heavy it was, see what it looked like on the inside. But as I stretched out an arm towards it, I heard the crunch of shoes on tarmac. Someone was coming. I ducked under the float, beneath the flatbed of the lorry, breathing in the smell of hot oil and exhaust, crouched and waited.

Two pairs of legs stopped near where I was hiding, one pair clad in dark breeches and leather pirate boots, the other in green, shiny satin, the feet in ridiculous, elongated shoes. A man's voice, loud but with an edge of nervousness. 'I tell you I saw her!'

'What, the same woman?' The pirate's voice, deeper, rougher, sounded sceptical. 'That long, red-headed bint from the tunnel?'

'Yes. The dog-walker.' The long shoes came off, thrown up onto the float, landing with a thump above my head. 'The same woman who was in the van.'

I clapped a hand over my mouth, stifling a gasp.

The pirate laughed. 'Yeh, well that was coincidence, we didn't know the dog-walker would be her.'

'It doesn't matter. She's here now.' The green satin trousers fell about the man's ankles, revealing jeans underneath. He stepped out of the puddle of green material and whisked it up out of sight, stepping into beige loafers that he dropped to the floor. 'She was watching me from the crowd.'

'You're seeing things. You're seeing her everywhere.'

'She must be on to us.'

The pirate laughed. 'How can she be?'

'She turned up at the building site.'

'So what?'

'And Fran says the woman who turned up at the farm the other day was tall with red hair. It's got to be the same woman.'

'I wish she was here. I owe that bitch for biting my hand.'

It was the pirate whose hand I had bitten. I hoped he still wore my teeth marks. I hoped I'd given him rabies.

The other man lowered his voice. 'I've told you, no more violence.'

'Yeh?' There was a deep chuckle. 'It's a bit late for that, isn't it? You should have thought of that before this whole business started.'

'I wish it never had.'

'Like I say, a bit late for that. And you were the one that wanted in, you greedy bastard.'

'But what if —'

There was a sudden scuffling of feet as the pirate forced Clown Head's body against the side of the truck. 'Don't give me any what-ifs,' he hissed. 'There is nothing to worry about, understand? All you have to do is keep your nerve. You haven't been blabbing to anyone, have you?'

'Of course not.'

273

The pirate grunted, there was a moment of silence as if he was making up his mind whether to believe him. 'Yeah? Just make sure you don't.' He stepped back, releasing him. 'The boss has got no need to know about our little side-line. Understand? Now c'mon, I'm gasping for a pint.'

I crouched, holding my breath as I heard them walk away. It seemed the pirate was keeping his boots on, the cutlass hanging by his side. Perhaps he enjoyed the swagger of it.

I was trying to get my head around what I'd just heard. Florence's kidnappers and the two men who had stolen the Tribe, the men from the grey Transporter, were the same. Well, that made some kind of sense. But if Clown Head said he'd spotted me at the building site, he could only be the man Ricky had photographed, Stephen Higgs, the man who worked in HR for Dunston Properties. He was a dog thief? That didn't make any sense at all. I crawled out from under the lorry and straightened up. I had to follow him, I had to get a clear look at him, make sure he really was the man I'd seen, and try to get a look at his pirate friend.

I mustn't lose them. I began to follow them up the steep street, pushing my way through the crowds on the pavement. Walking in the road would not have been a good idea. Fiery tar barrels were roaring down the hill like blazing meteorites, trailing flares of flame. Each barrel was on a sled, its speed controlled by the men pushing it, but it was still a terrifying spectacle, difficult to believe that at any moment the barrel wouldn't charge off course, rolling, blazing, into the screaming crowd.

Up ahead, progress was impeded by a knot of bystanders gathered around a drunk who'd fallen over. As the men I was following were forced to stop, one of them turned around to look behind him. It was Stephen Higgs. His eyes locked on to mine and widened in alarm. He nudged his companion. 'There!' I couldn't hear him above the crowd but I saw his lips form the words. 'There she is!' He pointed in my direction and his companion turned to look. He was darker, a little heavier than Higgs, his face shadowed by a dark stubble that he hadn't sported when he'd dragged me struggling from my van. Perhaps he'd grown it to look like a pirate.

I didn't have time to think about it. They began to move towards me and I turned to force my way back through the crowd. My instinct was to run, to get the hell out of there, but I could only go slowly, forcing my way against the tide, shouldering roughly through the crush of people who seemed determined to block my way. Higgs and Co. were gaining on me, they'd soon be at my back. I saw an opening and stepped off the kerb, dashing across the road as a flaming barrel roared towards me. It was almost on top of me as I leapt in front of it, flinging up an arm to protect myself from its scorching heat. 'Idiot!' someone called out. 'Get out of the way!'

I sprinted along the gutter, down the steep street towards the open ground of the marketplace. Here the blazing barrels were being piled into a bonfire, sending sparks flying up into the darkness. I dodged through the queues still waiting at the burger vans, heading for the far end of the market car park, for the safety of the van. I dared to stop and look behind. Higgs and friend were standing near the bonfire, peering into the dark, looking for me. I slowed to a walk, pulling up my hood, hastily stuffing my hair inside. I kept to the shadows, weaving my way through the parked cars towards Van Blanc. Getting into it would draw attention. When I pressed the key fob to unlock, the doors would click and the lights would flash and it would give a little chirrup of welcome. I had to creep close to the door on the driver's side before I dared.

The moment I did, I saw their heads swing around in my direction. Higgs pointed. I slid into the driving seat and flipped the door locks, my hand shaking a little as I tried to put the key in the ignition. I saw the two of them racing across the car park towards a grey Transporter. My way ahead was blocked by another parked car. I thrust the gear into reverse and began to back my way slowly through the clear space behind me. As I turned the van around, the headlights of the Transporter suddenly glowed like the eyes of a waking beast, ready to give chase. The network of streets had been blocked to traffic. There was only one way out of the town, only one route I could take, one way they could follow. I didn't like to think what their intentions towards me might be if they caught me. Probably not nice. Somehow, in the darkness of the roads outside Hatherleigh, I would have to lose them.

I had a stroke of luck. The driver of one of the floats chose that moment to move his lorry, to back across the car park, effectively trapping the Transporter in its place.

It gave me the chance I needed. I sped up out of the car park as the horn of the Transporter blared in frustration, the lorry driver leaning from his cab to engage in vociferous altercation.

I got the hell out of Dodge and whizzed up the road that would take me to Okehampton and the way home. I saw no sign of the Transporter behind me. If Higgs hadn't spotted me, I'd have been able to follow them without their knowing, to see where they went. I was willing to bet it was back to the farmhouse and Fran. Was Higgs's pirate friend the notorious Eddie Swayne? I had to find out. But I couldn't go there now. They knew my van and they'd be on the lookout. Now it was time to run away, live to fight another day. To think.

The Robots who had dragged me from the van and stolen the Tribe were Higgs and his pirate buddy; definitely the same men in Shaugh Prior Tunnel. Clown Head turned out to be Stephen Higgs, one of Dunston's employees. Did his pirate friend work for Dunston too? He'd said that the boss didn't know what was going on. Did he mean Dunston? Dog theft might be big business, but it seemed unlikely to me that a man like Alastair Dunston, councillor and reputable property developer, would be involved in such a crime. Higgs had said there must be no more violence. I had the nasty feeling that meant something more serious than just clouting me in the face. I thought of Sandy, stalking Dunston to his garden, Sandy who had gone to see someone about a dog, and of Phil Thomas, of his long fall from the scaffolding, and wondered.

CHAPTER TWENTY-SIX

When I got to the office of the *Dartmoor Gazette* at lunchtime the next day, Guy Mitchell had already written up the story of Buttons' return, and there was a picture of a smiling Lisa Coombes cuddling her dog ready to grace the front page. Guy himself had been forced to go out but he'd left his photos on his laptop with instructions for Evie to let me see them if I called. 'Help yourself,' she said, inviting me to sit down. 'There's only half a dozen.'

Guy must have taken them from across the road, looking through a panel of the wire fence. She nodded at the first photo, at two men in suits, looking out of place on a muddy building site despite their hard hats. 'He says these are the two men that warned him off.'

'Well, that is Stephen Higgs,' I told her, pointing, 'he works for Dunston's company in HR. And the other one, the one with the nasty moustache, I think is called Hollander. He works in finance.'

Evie smiled as she scribbled the names down. 'How do you know all this?'

I didn't mention Louise Dunston. 'I have friends in low places.'

I scrolled on to the next picture, but it was just a general view of the building site. The only object of interest to me was the grey Transporter I could see parked beyond the fence. The next picture showed two men in working clothes standing by the door of a Portakabin. One of them looked familiar. 'Can we zoom in on this one?'

Evie got the pair in close-up, but the focus wasn't great. It looked like Higgs' pirate friend, but I couldn't be sure. 'Are there any other pictures of this man?'

We scrolled through, studying the other pictures together, but there was none clearer than the first one I'd seen. 'Can you email that to me?' I asked her. 'I want to find out who he is.' I scrolled again through the other pictures. Mitch was right about some of the labourers being camera-shy. In one photo, a young man was holding up a hand to shield his face, another turning up his coat collar.

Evie flicked me a glance. 'Juno, if there's a story in all this, will you give us an exclusive?' She sounded like Sandy. As if she read my thoughts, she added in a sad voice, 'I miss Sandy.'

'I won't be talking to anyone else,' I promised. 'And I miss her too.' A few weeks ago, I never would have thought I'd be saying that. We were both silent for a moment. 'There's no other news, I suppose?'

She shook her head.

'The last person to see her was Alf, the cleaner,' I said, 'and she told him that she was going to see someone about a dog. You still don't know what she meant?'

'No. She'd interviewed Mrs Coombes originally, when Buttons was stolen, but that was weeks before. She wouldn't have been going to see her again.'

'Perhaps she'd learnt of another victim.'

'Then why didn't she say so?' Evie bit her lip. 'I keep wondering about that last day, you know, the day she rang in sick, but wasn't at home when I called. She'd gone out. I keep thinking, perhaps I'd just missed her. Perhaps if I'd caught her, if I'd been five minutes earlier . . .'

'And I keep wondering why she'd scribbled my name on her notepad, what question she'd wanted to ask me . . .' If I'd been able to give her an answer, would it have made any difference, stopped her being murdered? Would it have stopped us feeling that we'd both let Sandy down? Well, there was only one way to make it up to her. Find her killer.

When I got home, I forwarded the photo of the pirate to Louise Dunston. *Who is this man?* I asked.

The message came back straight away. *Eddie Swayne, the gangmaster.* Louise's unwelcome dinner guest, I remembered, and his awful wife. I emailed her again.

Would his wife be a sour-faced blonde who needs her roots doing?

The reply pinged back in a moment. *Sounds like an accurate description. Her name is Frances.*

I didn't bother her with any more questions, just sent her a smiley emoji.

Lady Margaret phoned later. 'Are you doing anything tomorrow night?' she asked, as soon as we'd done the hello-how-are-you bit.

'Er . . .'

'Only my friend Betty was supposed to be coming with me, but she's had to cry off because she's got shingles, poor old sausage.'

'Coming where?' I asked.

'Ah! It's an MND fundraising dinner – for Motor Neurone Disease,' she added, just in case my acronyms weren't up to scratch. 'Alastair Dunston will be there. I thought you might like to meet him, have the opportunity of observing him at close quarters, as it were, after what happened with your friend Sandy.'

'How very astute of you, Lady Margaret,' I responded grinning. 'I would indeed.'

'Excellent. I thought you would. My treat, obviously. It's at Bovey Castle, so if you like to toddle over to Lustleigh first, then as soon as Miriam arrives . . .'

'Miriam?'

'My cleaning lady. She's coming to sit with the dogs. I'm not leaving them here on their own.' She chuckled. 'No dog-nappers are going to tangle with Miriam, believe you me. She's a good-un'.'

I couldn't wait to meet her.

'Anyway, we can drive over to Bovey Castle together,' she added.

'Good idea,' I said, searching frantically in my brain

for anything I could wear to a fundraising dinner at one of Devon's most expensive five-star hotels. It came up blank. I put the phone down in a bit of a panic. After the Chanel original, I wasn't really sure I wanted to do what I usually do, and borrow from Ricky and Morris. I wanted to blend in, not be outrageously conspicuous. But after a glance into my meagre wardrobe, I knew I had no choice. I picked up the phone and asked if they could help me out. I explained where I was going to Morris, who answered the phone, and then again to both of them after Morris had put the phone on speaker. They seemed thrilled at the opportunity to dress me up, confirming my long-held suspicion that they should have been given dollies to play with when they were boys.

'Leave it to us, Princess,' Ricky assured me. 'We've got just the thing.'

That was what I was afraid of. 'I don't want yellow,' I told him. 'And I don't want to look like Cinderella either.'

'Don't you worry your pretty little head about it,' he told me, an expression that was calculated to wind me up. 'Just bring your lippy with you and for Gawd's sake, go and buy yourself a decent pair of tights.'

It wasn't yellow, it was black, a shift dress in black velvet that skimmed my hips smoothly and ended just above the knee. It was sleeveless, but had a deep satin collar that wrapped itself around my upper arms like a shawl, leaving my shoulders bare. There was a discreet notch in this collar, strategically placed, allowing a glimpse of cleavage.

'It's beautiful,' I breathed, admiring my reflection in a long mirror, whilst Ricky, fag pressed between his lips, circled around behind me with a spray bottle, fussily spritzing my hair.

The dress wasn't just beautiful, it looked expensive. It had class. 'Where did this come from?'

'Mrs Robinson,' Morris told me, dashing in between spritzes to give the shawl a tweak.

'Who's she?'

'You remember the film of *The Graduate*? We made this dress for a stage version up in London.'

Mrs Robinson, a seriously sexy siren. I grew another inch.

I began to wish Ricky would give over with the spritzing. For one thing I wasn't sure if the stuff in the spritzer bottle was flammable. I had visions of his fag turning the whole thing into a flamethrower.

'Clutch bag!' he called imperiously, and Morris handed me a tiny black bag shaped like a shell. 'You're not going with that bloody great leather holdall dangling from your shoulder!' he told me as I frowned and peered into the tiny bag's silk-lined interior. I could just about get a lipstick, a mirror and a tissue into it.

'S'all you need,' he told me, as I voiced my objection. 'You'll have to leave your knuckledusters at home.'

'Very funny.'

'No sleuthing.' He held up a warning finger. 'And don't spill your soup.'

* * *

Once an Edwardian manor house, Bovey Castle is now a five-star luxury hotel, a long and impressively gabled building with tall mullioned windows, set in acres of grounds with its own golf course. Once renowned as a get-away for the rich and famous, it was sold a few years ago by its millionaire owner, Peter de Savary, for an estimated £17.5 million.

Its gracious public rooms boast ornate plaster ceilings, carved and decorated panelling, massive fireplaces and leaded windows. Each one of its sixty guest bedrooms is probably larger than my flat.

On this November evening, the building blazed with light and warmth. Lady Margaret and I were greeted with glasses of champagne on our arrival. As I accepted my glass from the proffered tray, I thought of Sandy Thomas. I wondered if the sight of a waitress holding a tray full of bubbling champagne glasses made Alastair Dunston nervous.

'You look gorgeous, my dear,' Margaret whispered to me as we made our way into the lounge where the guests were assembling with their aperitifs.

There were about sixty people there already. We had set out slightly later than we anticipated because of the delayed arrival of Margaret's cleaner, Miriam. The way Margaret had described her, I'd been expecting a substantial female at the least, not the wizened, bird-like little creature who ultimately arrived, and fixed me with a sharp and penetrating stare. Despite her tiny size she was intimidating.

'She was in the S.O.E. you know,' Margaret confided

to me. 'In the war. The Special Operations Executive,' she explained. She obviously had a poor view of my acronyms. 'She was parachuted into France.'

In the war? She must be ninety at least. I glanced back over my shoulder as we were leaving and found she was still fixing me with her basilisk gaze. 'Isn't she a bit old to be working as a cleaner?' I asked, once we were out of earshot. She looked too frail to be in charge of a vacuum cleaner, more in danger of being sucked up its hose.

'Of course she is!' Margaret agreed, sighing. 'But just try telling her that! I've tried to pension her off three or four times but she won't have it.'

The lounge in Bovey Castle was alive with the laughter of the well-dressed, the chatter of the well-heeled, men smart in dinner jackets, with the occasional white tuxedo, the ladies looking expensive and gorgeous, although not necessarily at the same time.

Margaret spotted the Dunstons and grabbed me by the arm. 'Come along, dear, I'll introduce you.'

We went to join a group of four that included Mr Hollander, aka Nasty Moustache, and a pleasant-looking young woman in green I assumed must be his wife. Alastair Dunston favoured the white tuxedo; Louise was one of the few women able to combine expensive and gorgeous, wearing midnight blue silk that looked stunning with her gleaming blonde hair. She caught sight of me as Margaret and I approached, and I detected a momentary hardening of her eyes and mouth. Her husband, on the other hand, greeted me with a warm handshake, an appraising gaze and no hint of recognition whatsoever. Nasty Moustache, however, was convinced he and I had met before. *Somewhere.* He was a lot less subtle with his gazing than Dunston, his eyes fixed on the strategically placed notch at my cleavage. The woman at his side, whom he eventually introduced as Jill, looked uncomfortable and slightly bored.

'Perhaps you remember me from the meeting about the new development at Woodland,' I suggested, selecting a smoked salmon canapé from a platter suddenly presented by a hovering waiter. Jill also accepted one. I noticed Louise Dunston waved them aside.

'Woodland?' A frown creased Alastair Dunston's brow. The damage to his gleaming blue Mercedes was doubtless still a sore point.

Nasty Moustache, whose name turned out to be Leslie, gave a snort of laughter. 'Don't tell me you were one of the objectors?'

'Actually, there didn't seem to be anyone at that meeting who didn't object to the development,' I pointed out, 'aside from yourselves.'

'Do you live in Woodland?' Alastair asked.

'No, I live in Ashburton.'

'Ashburton?' Leslie Hollander scowled. 'I remember now. You were with that reporter from the *Dartmoor Gazette.*'

'I wasn't with him,' I responded evenly. 'I just found myself sitting next to him.'

Alastair said nothing, but I could feel his eyes fixed on me.

'Did you know that girl, then?' Jill asked artlessly.

'The one who was murdered? What was her name?' It was an incredibly tactless question in present company, but she looked around us enquiringly, apparently in all innocence. Leslie threw her an irritated glance.

'Sandy,' I told her. 'Sandy Thomas.'

'Oh yes!' she cried brightly. 'Did they ever find out—?'

'And how are you, Lady Margaret?' Louise swiftly turned the subject. 'How are your dogs? One of them went missing, didn't he?'

'She,' Margaret corrected. 'But she's back home safely now.'

'None the worse for her adventure, I hope?'

'No, she's absolutely fine.'

Dunston also seemed keen to talk about something else. 'I thought I'd take the boat out this weekend,' he said to Hollander. 'You fancy a trip?'

Hollander smiled. 'Why not?'

'Yes, probably my last trip for this year.' He grinned. 'Then I think I'll be tying *Louise* up for the winter.'

Louise laughed, a hand at her chest 'I don't like the sound of that.'

'I hope it's the boat we're talking about,' Margaret chuckled. 'And not you, my dear.'

Jill was looking a bit crushed, sensing she'd put her foot in it. I was trying to get my head around the idea that she and Nasty Moustache were a couple. She seemed too young for him, and frankly, too nice. At close quarters he was even less prepossessing than at a distance. The weak and straggly moustache, grown on an upper lip too close to his nose to comfortably accommodate it, seemed to be an ill-judged attempt to counter a receding hairline. He'd have been better off being comfortable with his lack of follicles and forgetting the moustache altogether. I also felt that if he and Jill had been together for any length of time, she would have known about Alastair and Sandy and known not to go there. Later on, catching up with her in the gossipy and scented air of the ladies' powder room, I was to discover that she didn't know the Dunstons at all. She was the daughter of a neighbour of Hollander, and had agreed to come along with him to make up the four. 'Free dinner, no strings attached,' she confessed to me in a loud whisper as we stood in front of the mirrors primping our hair. I hoped she was right about that second bit. 'Les hasn't got a girlfriend,' she added, helping herself to a generous dollop of expensive hand lotion placed by the washbasin, 'he's divorced. Bit of a saddo, if you ask me.'

I followed her lead and depressed the pump on the bottle of hand cream. 'He works for Dunston, doesn't he? Do you know what he does?'

She shrugged as we both stood there rubbing our hands. 'I think he's some sort of accountant.'

Plenty of money and still no girlfriend. He must be a saddo.

'That Alastair is attractive, though, isn't he?' she ventured, avoiding my eye and staring at her reflection in the mirror.

I decided it was time someone filled her in on what had gone on between him and Sandy. She clapped her hand over her mouth as she listened, mortified at the faux pas she'd made, but grateful for the information.

As it turned out, this wasn't the only tête-à-tête I was to enjoy during the course of the evening. The seating plan, ten people around each circular table, separated Margaret and me from the Dunstons' party for the duration of dinner, allowing me to give my full attention to my seared scallops, celeriac remoulade, and chocolate passionfruit tart, with no interruption except for some inconsequential conversation with my neighbours. As I would be driving Margaret and myself home, I resisted any attempts to refill my wine glass. I drank lots of water instead. By the time the coffee and petits fours arrived, a precursor to the speeches and draw for the luxury raffle prizes, I was ready for my second trip to the powder room.

Louise Dunston must have been keeping watch on me. As soon as I left the table she joined me, appearing at my side on the long walk to the powder room. 'Just exactly what are you doing here?' she asked.

'I'm enjoying a very pleasant evening, thank you,' I told her blandly, 'as a guest of Lady Margaret.'

'If you're not working for me, then you're working against me,' she whispered tersely. 'Now which is it?'

'It's neither.' I stopped walking and turned to face her. 'I told you when you came to my shop, I'm not working for you. I'm not someone whose services you can hire. But I'm not trying to dig up dirt on your husband either. I just want to get to the truth. I want to know who killed Sandy.'

She stepped a little closer to me and whispered in my ear. 'I don't care who killed her.'

I drew back so that I could look at her face. Her amber eyes were cold. 'As long as it wasn't your husband?'

'Oh, I know it wasn't,' she assured me, smiling. 'And yes,' she added with a nod of satisfaction,' I'm glad she's dead.'

I stared after her as she turned and walked away from me, shocked at her malice, her callousness towards poor Sandy who could be of no threat to her any more, who never really was.

I returned to my table a few minutes later, and concentrated my attention on the prize draw. Margaret and I had purchased tickets on the way in. We couldn't avoid it really. It was for a good cause and the ticket-sellers weren't taking no for an answer. The prizes had been donated by various businesses and were definitely a cut above the usual variety. Apart from a plethora of lavishly packaged toiletries or chocolates, bottles of superior wine and exotically flavoured gins, there were vouchers for all kinds of treats. Despite buying several tickets, I managed not to win a hot-air balloon ride, various beauty treatments in several different spas, a paddle-boarding lesson, dinner for two at any expensive restaurants, or a hamper full of locally produced luxury preserves and pickles. In fact, I managed not to win anything, not even a day out at a local donkey sanctuary, the prize I probably would have enjoyed the most.

'Ricky, Morris and I are organising a fundraising day for animals at Honeysuckle Farm,' I told Margaret with a sigh. 'I wish we could get people to donate prizes like these.'

'Oh, leave it to me, my dear,' she said with an airy wave of her hand. 'I know a lot of 'em. I'll see what I can do.'

It was when we were just about to leave, and I was on my way to collect Margaret's coat from reception, that I had my final tête-à-tête of the evening.

'The famous Juno Browne,' said a voice, and I turned to find Alastair Dunston smiling at me. He was very close, giving me the full-on benefit of the twinkle in his blue eyes, the disarming grin and the expensive aftershave. 'I confess when we were introduced, I didn't immediately make the connection. I've heard your name, of course, but no one warned me how beautiful you are.'

I laughed. 'Pull the other one.'

'No, I mean it.' He waited for my response, but whatever was on offer, I wasn't buying.

'So,' he continued after a moment, 'you were a friend of Sandy Thomas?'

'I wouldn't say friends, exactly.' I felt mean, distancing myself from her, but this wasn't a casual question and I didn't want to put him on his guard more than he already was. 'More acquaintances.' And added, because I couldn't help myself. 'You probably knew her better than I did.'

His eyes narrowed slightly. 'Don't believe everything you read, especially in the *Dartmoor Gazette*. She was nothing but a pest, had a bee in her bonnet.'

'What about?'

He shrugged. 'She was like any other of these so-called reporters, trying to dig up dirt on anyone in the public eye. And if they can't find it, they'll make it up.'

'Did you know her ex-husband, Phil?' I asked.

He shook his head. 'No. I never met the man.'

'Yet he was working for you on the day he died, on one of your construction sites.'

'It was an accident.' His blue eyes were wary. 'He fell from scaffolding.'

'Why did he come to work for you,' I asked him, 'of all people?'

'Look,' he began to raise his voice, to sound irritated. 'I can't know the identity of every labourer employed on my sites. He would have been taken on by the gangmaster. I suppose he needed the work.'

'It's an odd coincidence, though, isn't it? His accident coming so soon after her murder.'

He flushed. 'What is your point exactly?'

'Ah! My dear, there you are!' Lady Margaret was suddenly bearing down on us like a ship in full sail. 'I thought you'd got lost.'

Alastair Dunston gave a curt nod to indicate that our conversation was at an end. 'Goodnight, Lady Margaret,' he said to her. 'Miss Browne,' he added, turned on his heel and walked away.

We both watched him go, Margaret sidling closer to me and speaking from the corner of her mouth. 'He seemed to be getting a bit hot under the collar.'

'He doesn't like talking about Sandy or Phil Thomas.'

'I hope you didn't provoke him too much. I imagine

he could be an unpleasant adversary.' She handed me a crisp white envelope. 'I won this in the draw. It's no earthly use to me. You'd better have it.'

I thanked her profusely. It contained a voucher for a free treatment at a spa, offering a choice of pamper packages. One of them I noticed, was for a mother and baby special. Good. I could pass it on to Kate.

CHAPTER TWENTY-SEVEN

I arrived at 26 Haytor Crescent in Ivybridge on Tuesday afternoon, having persuaded Sophie to do my shift at the shop. She had to be there working on a painting anyway, so I didn't feel too mean about it.

'Mrs Pinfold?' I asked as the front door swung open to reveal a tall, grey-haired lady. 'Mrs Hilary Pinfold?'

She was wearing an apron over her skirt and carried a tea towel as if I'd interrupted her whilst she was cooking. She frowned. 'Yes?' That single syllable contained a world of suspicion and doubt.

'I'm from the Family Alliance Against Fraud.' I allowed her the briefest flash of my ID.

a photocopy of my passport photo stuck on to my library card. 'I wonder if I could have a word?'

'Well, I . . .'

I shoved a photograph under her nose before she had

a chance to think about it. 'Have you ever seen this man?' It was a head and shoulders shot of Morris, wearing a Panama hat and looking every inch the country vicar. I'd cropped it from a picture of him standing with Ricky at a garden fete, wine glasses in hand as they tried to guess the weight of the giant marrow.

Hilary's face lit up with pleasure. 'Oh, yes! I remember him! He was charming. Doctor . . . someone.'

'Dr Chasuble?'

'That's it.'

'That's one of the aliases he uses.'

She looked disappointed. 'You mean, it's not his real name?'

'I'm afraid not. He's a notorious conman. What reason did he give you for his call?'

'He said he'd come to ask about a puppy, but as I told him at the time—'

'Did he ask you for money?'

'Well, no but our conversation was interrupted. You see, Fran came in . . .'

'What about this woman?' I thrust a picture of Sandy at her, one I had cut from the newspaper. 'She is his accomplice.'

Hilary studied the photo for a moment. 'She looks a little familiar.'

'She has a strong Welsh accent.'

'Oh yes. I remember her now! She came about a puppy too, but that was some time before the doctor came.'

So, she had been here. I nodded wisely. 'That's their modus operandi.'

'Oh dear.'

'You didn't give either of them any money?'

'Well, no,' Hilary looked confused. 'But you see, they didn't ask for any.'

'They would have got around to it, eventually. It sounds as if you had a lucky escape, Mrs Pinfold. Good morning and thank you for your time.'

'Is that all?' she asked. 'What if he comes back? Dr Chasuble, I mean.'

'I don't think he will,' I assured her, smiling. 'But if he does, don't let him in and call the police.'

'Oh, right, I will . . . Thank you,' she called after me as I made my way back up the path. She closed the door, looking confused, never questioning how I'd known the good doctor had called there or how I knew her name.

As I came out of her gate, I found myself confronted by her neighbour, lurking behind the same privet hedge that Ricky and I had lurked behind on our previous visit. 'Excuse me,' she hissed. 'Could I have a word with you?' She was a woman of roughly Hilary's age, dressed in light-coloured jacket and beige slacks. 'Only, I was coming out of my door just now and I couldn't help but overhear what you were saying. I've tried talking to the police, but they say until I've got some evidence there's nothing they can do.'

'This isn't about Doctor Chasuble?' I asked uneasily.

'No, it's about Hilary. Look, would you like to come in for a moment?'

'Certainly.' I followed her up the garden path wondering what on earth I was getting into now. From the

297

outside, her house was a mirror image of Hilary's. Inside it was all pastel colours, fitted carpets, plug-in air fresheners and silk flower arrangements. I wiped my shoes on the doormat. 'Would you like me to take them off?' It was the sort of place where you felt you should ask.

'No, that's all right. I'm Joan, by the way.'

'How can I help you, Joan?' I asked, as I took a seat in the armchair she indicated.

She sat on the sofa. 'Well, I don't know who to talk to about this,' she admitted, 'but I heard you say you were investigating a fraud and . . .' She twisted her hands, looking awkward.

'And you think Hilary might be a victim?' I asked.

'It's just a suspicion, really.'

'Please go on.'

'Well, it's that woman that comes, Fran. She's been coming for a couple of years now, since Andrew, Hilary's husband, died. Hilary had a fall and she took this Fran on to help with the shopping and some of the housework.'

'So, Fran is not related to her?'

'No, not at all. Hilary doesn't have any family, except for a nephew in Australia, and she hasn't seen him for years. And that's one of the things which makes her vulnerable, that she's got no one, and she's getting a bit confused as well. I pop in for a tea or coffee most days and I know her place as well as I know my own. I mean, you get used to seeing things about and you notice when they go missing.'

'And you think things have been going missing from Hilary's?'

'I know they have. Ornaments from the mantelpiece and the window sill, and a bracelet Andrew had given her. Hilary thought she'd lost it and we hunted high and low for it, turned the whole house over.'

'You think Fran took it?'

'Well, it seems like the only explanation, but Hilary wouldn't believe it. You see, that's the problem. Fran has really, well . . .' she frowned as if searching for the right word, '. . . *ingratiated* herself. Hilary won't hear a word against her. The other day we were out shopping and when Hilary came to pay, she didn't have enough money in her purse. And she said to me, "I'm sure I had more in there than that." Well, straight away I thought Fran must have taken it. Hilary just laughed it off, said she was going dopey in her old age. But I could see it had upset her. And that's what got to me. I think this Fran is making Hilary believe she's more confused than she is. There's a word for it . . .'

'Gaslighting,' I supplied.

Joan nodded. 'That's it. Trouble is, I can't prove anything.'

'Hilary gets no other visitors?'

'No regular ones.'

'Has Fran ever brought anyone else to the house, do you know?'

'Yes, as a matter of fact. There's a dark-haired man, bit of a rough-looking sort, that I've seen her arrive with more than once. I asked Hilary who he was and she said it was Fran's husband, although I don't know what business he has going in there.'

'This is going to sound like an odd question,' I said after a moment, 'but Hilary doesn't have any pets, does she?'

'No.' Joan shook her head. 'But I've seen that Fran take dogs in there. She brings them in through the back garden.'

'More than one?'

'She seems to have several. Each time I see her she seems to be with a different one. Although, to be honest, I'm not too keen on dogs myself, so I really wouldn't know.'

No, I could imagine that Joan wouldn't like dog-hair or muddy pawprints on her scatter cushions.

'I don't think Hilary minds the dogs,' she went on, 'at least not much. But what worries me is that I'm sure Fran is setting out to rob her. I popped in there one day and she was standing in the kitchen with a bank statement of Hilary's in her hand. Hilary must have left it on the table.'

'Perhaps she was just being nosy. Leaving mail around is an open invitation to some people, they just can't help themselves.'

'You don't think I should do anything, then? The police say that unless Hilary actually reports something stolen, they can't do anything.'

'Leave it with me for the moment,' I said. 'I'll see if I can find out a little more about this Fran. You don't know her surname, or where she lives?'

'I'm afraid not.'

'Or how Hilary got hold of her? I mean, did she advertise for a helper or go to an agency?'

'Oh, I know that. She put an advert in the newsagent's window.'

'And when Fran answered the ad, Hilary didn't ask for references or a CRB check?'

'Oh, I don't think so. I don't think Hilary would have thought of that.'

'Well, thank you, Joan. You've been most helpful.'

'Do you think you'll be able to find out anything?'

'I'll do my best.'

'Do you have a business card?'

I pretended to search for one in my bag. I could hardly give her one with *Juno Browne Domestic Goddess* written on it. 'I seem to have run out.' I scribbled my phone number on a piece of paper. 'There,' I handed it to her and smiled. 'Just in case you think of anything else.'

I phoned Becky when I got back home. 'Your client's friend, Mary, the one who went to that house in Ivybridge to buy the puppy, she reported her suspicions to the RSPCA. You don't know if she reported it to the *Dartmoor Gazette*?'

'No, I don't know. I could try to find out, I suppose. Why, is it important?'

'It could be. Sandy Thomas went there.'

'The reporter who was murdered?' Becky sounded shocked. 'Wouldn't her office know if someone had reported it?'

'All they know is that before she disappeared, she was going to see someone about a dog.'

'And you think that's where she went?'

'I know she went there,' I said. 'What I don't know is whether that's what led to her death.'

But I'm going to bloody find out.

CHAPTER TWENTY-EIGHT

It seemed so strange, next morning, getting up to walk Schnitzel by himself. It was lovely to have him back again, to have him safe, but somehow his presence made the absence of the others even more painful. I missed them and I know he did. He trotted along busily enough, but kept looking up at me, questioning me with his bright eyes. I walked him through the woods, under trees weeping their autumn leaves. I had promised his mum I wouldn't let him off the lead, that I wouldn't lose him, let him disappear into the undergrowth never to be seen again. I was sorry I couldn't give him the freedom to go snuffling among the ferns and deep leaf litter in the way he loved, but I wasn't going to take the risk, I was just grateful his mum had sufficient trust in me to allow me to walk him at all.

The weather was changing, wind rushing through the

trees, swaying branches, whirling the falling leaves into a blizzard: the first sign of the promised storms. I turned up the collar of my coat. Schnitzel, his floppy ears blown inside out by the wind, decided that if he couldn't chase the leaves, the least he could do was bark at them, and ran in excited circles, as far as his lead would let him. But then he found treasure, a stick, short and stubby, and carried it in his mouth as if it was a cigar.

The wind got wilder as the day went on, turned hooligan. It howled up and down the streets of Ashburton, slamming over cafe boards, shoving bins along the pavement, tearing hats off heads and mussing up hair, pushing people from behind, sending them running, clutching at their flapping coats. It buffeted parked cars, whipped around corners, and whistled up Shadow Lane, setting the sign above *Old Nick's* door swinging. Then the rain came, flung in fitful volleys against the windows by the hammering wind.

'Brilliant,' I muttered as I watched it from inside the shop. 'Just what I want. Brilliant.'

Of course, the sensible thing to do, I told myself as I watched fat raindrops bouncing off the shining cobbles, would be to delay my planned excursion until next day. But I couldn't.

The rain eased off in the middle of the afternoon, soggy clouds clearing from a washed-out sky. I made my escape from the shop, leaving Sophie to lock up. At home I changed into warm clothes, put a rainproof jacket, my walking boots and the rucksack I had packed earlier into the back of the van, and headed for

Throwleigh. I drew in at a lay-by, just up the road from the Northmore Arms, near the long barn and the track that led down to the farmhouse.

I was waiting for the grey Transporter. I didn't want to drive along that track and find it following me, trapping me in front of it. I wanted the Transporter to go first, leaving me with a way to back out. I just hoped that the wild weather wouldn't mean that the men on the construction site couldn't work, that Higgs and Swayne had gone home early, that I'd already missed them. I sat for half an hour, whilst the sky darkened and the rain began again, beating a relentless tattoo on the roof of the van. I rubbed mist from the inside of the windscreen with a cloth, shrugged myself into my coat, and waited. I began to think longingly of the nutty bar I'd packed in my rucksack. I was just about to give in, switch the engine on and get the benefit of the heater and the radio, when the Transporter came racing towards me, going too fast, headlights on, windscreen wipers thrashing. It passed me in a flash and I started up the engine, my wheels spinning on wet gravel as I turned in the road and made off after it. I probably had the foul weather to thank for the fact that whoever was driving hadn't seen me, lurking with my lights off in the lay-by.

As I passed the long barn and turned into the track I could see the tail lights of the Transporter ahead, two small red eyes glowing in the dark. I turned my own lights off and crawled along like a snail. I didn't want anyone in the vehicle in front to see my lights in his mirrors. I pulled up when I reached the stand of trees and looked down on the farmhouse, its dark shape lit by the glow from a downstairs window and a lantern over its door.

The Transporter, hidden for a moment by a bend, swung back into view, bumping down the slope on the far side of the valley. It stopped outside of the farmhouse. Swayne got out of the driving seat and slammed his door. He knocked on the farmhouse door, his face lit briefly by the lantern hanging above him. The lower half of his face was in shadow, perhaps he had decided to keep the pirate stubble. The door opened. Light spilt out and fell on the ground in a golden oblong. Swayne slid open the side door of the Transporter and yelled to someone inside. A man got out, quickly followed by another and another. Three men, all silent, shoulders hunched against the weather. With a jerk of the head, Swayne motioned them inside. They looked like workers from the building site, like men I'd seen on those photographs, hiding their faces. What were they doing here? I swore under my breath. I'd reckoned on Swayne being there, with Fran and Higgs, but not a whole gang of them. Where was Higgs, anyway? I hadn't seen him get out of the Transporter. Perhaps he wasn't coming. He and Swayne might be partners in crime, but a suit from HR probably didn't live with the workers. Swayne cast a glance around him into the darkness, then shut the door.

I sat and considered. If any of my Tribe were being held in those outhouses, I wasn't leaving here without them. I was taking them home. There were more men here than I'd anticipated, but they were all safely inside the farmhouse for now, and the foul weather should work in my favour. They wouldn't hear me moving about above the storm, and if anyone should come out, or peer through the windows into the rain and dark, there was less risk of them spotting me. It was possible I could fall arse over end on the steep, slippery ground, break some part of me on a rock, but that, I told myself as I laced my feet into my walking boots, was a risk I was going to have to take. I zipped up my coat, tucked my hair inside my hood, grabbed a torch and phone from my rucksack, and cracked open the van door.

The wind flung it wide, wrenching the handle from my grasp. As I clambered out, it buffeted my back, pelting my shoulders with rain as I struggled to control the door and push it closed. Within a few seconds I was breathless and my hands were wet and cold.

The wind was roaring through the valley like wildfire. As I turned to face the farm buildings, it swept back my hood and drilled rain into my eyes. I tugged it back over my head, stepped off the track and began to inch my way cautiously down the steep slope before me. Chunks of rock showed up pale in the gloom, but I could make out no other features on the rough and rutted ground, and placed each step with care. Despite the rain and dark I dared not, within sight of the farmhouse windows, switch on the torch.

Before me and below me, I could make out the outhouses, shapes denser than the surrounding dark, and the slightly paler tube of the polytunnel. I hurried, slithering on wet grass until, unable to slow my own momentum, I ran into the wall of the nearest outhouse.

I stopped for a moment, sheltering under the eaves of its low roof, and got my breath back. Rain drizzled from leaky guttering, inches from my face. At least here I couldn't be seen, and I dared to flick the torch on. Its slender beam of light showed me an even blacker dark, a rectangle in the wall, where once there would have been a door. I aimed the light inside. It slid over rough stone walls, bales of straw and sacks of animal feed.

I stepped in. After the wild and wet outside, the shelter was a relief. I turned slowly around, letting the light play over the walls. Despite the rain outside, in here there was a dry, musty smell. As I turned, drops of rain dripped from the edge of my waterproof jacket, spotting the dry floor. There was an inner door, with scratches in its peeling paintwork, an old Bakelite knob for a handle. I turned it slowly. The door, sticking at the top right corner, needed a little encouragement from my shoulder before it juddered open. A different smell then, sweeter, wetter. I played the torch around the walls and almost dropped it, clapping a hand over my mouth to stop a cry.

Clown Head was smiling at me in the dark, his swollen face pink in the torchlight. He was leaning against the wall, but not quite on the ground, balanced on the shoulders of something slumped in the corner, something with arms and legs, something in a suit. I felt sick, forced to swallow back the acid bile that rose up from my insides. I took a deep breath, the sweet, wet smell catching at the back of my throat. I crouched, playing the torch beam over the body. There was a dark stain on the whiteness of the shirt, a darker wetness on the midriff, a wound at which pale hands clutched. With no real sense of hope, I placed my fingers on the wrist of the hand nearest to me. No pulse, and the flesh was already cold. I stood up slowly, casting around me with the torch.

I found a small wooden crate, picked it up and placed it down in front of the body, balancing the torch on top of it. I would need both hands to lift the clown's head. I didn't want to look at what it was hiding but I had to. I took a breath, trying to steady the beating of my heart, placed my hands over Clown Head's ears, and lifted the head from the suited shoulders. It felt surprisingly light, not heavy at all.

Stephen Higgs stared into the brightness of the torch beam; but dead eyes are not dazzled, do not blink. I stared back, unbelieving, fighting a reeling sense of shock. When I could gather my wits enough, I moved back, placing the clown's head on the floor, my hands trembling as I laid it down. I wasn't going to put it back on a murdered man, cover his dead face with that obscenely smiling thing.

I had to call the police, right now. I felt for the phone in my pocket. My fingers, wet and cold, fumbled and I almost dropped it. I tried to dry my hands on my jeans, but the denim legs were sodden. I went back into the outer room and checked for a signal. Outside the wind had calmed, the rain thinning to a drizzle. Then a sound came to me from the barn near to the farmhouse. The sound of barking.

I slid the phone back into my pocket, clutched the

torch to my chest, and ran for it. Across the open ground, slithering on mud and wet grass, to the shelter of the building's overhanging roof. I stayed still, leaning against the wall, getting my breath, and listened, straining my ears. There was no more barking, no sound at all. Had I really heard a dog? I crept towards the wooden door and opened it softly.

The smell of dog poo nearly knocked me off my feet. I turned my face away, took a deep breath, then turned back and stepped inside, closing the door behind me. It was black as a coffin inside. But I knew at once I wasn't alone. The air was fetid, warmed by the heat of animal bodies, by the breath of living creatures, creatures that shifted and scratched and whined. I flicked on my torch. The light played on metal bars, on bright animal eyes shining back at me. But there was no light coming in from outside, no windows to let light in or let it out. I played my torch beam over the walls, discovered a switch by the door and flipped it on.

A dismal fluorescent strip hummed and blinked overhead. I found myself standing on a concrete floor, the walls around me lined with kennels, some proper cages with metal bars, others simple pens made from chicken wire, about ten in all, and imprisoned within them perhaps twenty dogs or more. At the sight of me, some of them began to pad to the doors of their prisons, to wag their tails and whine, craving human touch; others hung back, afraid. A Rottweiler barked, deep in his throat, and I shushed him, crouching before the bars of his cell, letting him sniff my hand through the wire mesh. 'Quiet,' I told him, keeping my voice soft. 'There's a good dog.'

There was an impatient woof behind me and I turned. A long-haired German Shepherd with one ear up straight and the other flopping forward, was wagging his tail at me. 'Dylan!' I cried as he began to paw at the chicken wire. 'Oh, Dylan! You lovely boy!' I wanted to let him out, to hug him, bury my face in his fur, but the door of his cage was padlocked, and I could only splay my hands against the wire, letting him lick them through the mesh, his nose squashed tight up against it. His kennel, like all the others, was filthy with dog mess, with no bedding, a bowl half-full of water, and a tiny saucer, licked clean, that I supposed was for food. In the kennel next to his, a poor, thin spaniel lay trembling in the corner, gazing at me from wretched eyes. I tried a soft hello, but he didn't respond, just sighed and rested his head on his paws. I walked along the row. A Staffordshire Bull Terrier hung his head as I went by, avoiding my eye and licking his chops nervously. Next to him, three smaller dogs were crammed into one cage, one of them scrabbling frantically at the wire with his paws, whining for my attention. 'E.B.!' I cried. 'Hello E.B.!'

He kept on scrabbling, woofing softly, demanding to be let out. 'Soon,' I promised him, poking a finger through the wire mesh so that I could tickle his furry head. 'Very soon.'

I had my back to the door and didn't see it open, only felt a cold draught of fresh air as it swung wide and the click as it closed softly. I turned.

A boy of about fourteen was looking at me, dark-haired, slim in jeans and a hoodie. For a moment we regarded each other, both still, silent with shock. He gave me a long-lashed stare from beautiful dark eyes as I rose slowly to my feet, and spoke. 'What happened to the other lady?'

CHAPTER TWENTY-NINE

Before I could answer, a shrill voice penetrated from outside. 'Adil? Adil!' It was a woman's voice, must be Fran. 'Adil, where the hell are you?'

'Quick!' The boy darted forward, grabbing my hand and leading me between the kennels to a stack of fertiliser bags at the end. 'In here!' There was a narrow corridor of space between the pile of sacks and the wall. 'Hide here! Quick!'

I squeezed my body between the sacks and the wall. There was a stool in the corner, an old tin full of candle stubs, a blanket. This secret space was someone's den.

'Adil, are you in with those dogs again?'

'I'm here, Fran,' he called back, then turned to me and laid a finger against his lips.

I heard the door swing open, a blast of windy weather, and then the sound of it swinging shut.

'What are you doing in here?'

'I come to tell dogs goodnight.'

For a moment there was an edge of softness, almost of sympathy in Fran's sharp voice. 'I told you, it's no good getting fond of 'em.' Then she added, 'And you haven't finished your chores.'

'A few more minutes,' Adil pleaded.

'All right,' she agreed grudgingly, 'but no running off.' I heard the door click shut again as she left.

'Is safe now,' he whispered after a moment, and I eased out from my hiding place.

'Thank you. Adil, that's your name?'

He nodded, jerking a thumb towards E.B. 'Is dog yours?'

'And him,' I added, pointing at Dylan. I scanned the dog pens, a sudden sense of panic rising. 'And there are two others I can't see.'

'There is other shed,' he told me. 'More dogs. Blue Eyes, she is yours? She came with these.'

'Blue Eyes? A husky?' I asked. Adil frowned. 'Grey fur,' I added, 'and a curly tail.'

He nodded. 'I call her Blue Eyes.'

'And there is another. A boxer . . .' He shrugged, not understanding. 'Um . . . no tail,' I went on, 'squashed in face . . . she's brindle with white,' I put a hand to my chest, 'here.'

'Yes, in other shed.' He pointed. 'On other side of house.'

I let out a breath, almost a laugh, of relief. I'd been so afraid that they might not all be here, that they might have been sold on, that I might be too late.

'They keep them, always, for time.' Adil's dark eyes were solemn. 'More time, owners pay more to get them back.'

'But why have they put them in a different shed?' I asked, 'Do they separate the boys from the girls, is that it?'

He nodded.

'Adil, what are you doing here?' He was only a boy. At a guess I'd have said of middle eastern origin. He couldn't be a relative of Fran's. 'Do you live here?'

He didn't answer.

'Are there many dogs here?' I tried.

He shrugged. 'I do not know how many.'

'What happens to them?'

'Some owners pay to get them back. Others . . .' he looked at his feet. 'If no one want them, if they cannot sell them, they take them away in van.'

'Take them where?' I asked, my heart thumping with misgiving.

'Anywhere, far from here. Let them out on road.'

'You mean, they're just abandoned?'

He shrugged. 'Fran say someone will find them.'

I looked around me and my heart sank. I might be able to take the Tribe away with me, but there was no way I would be able to rescue all of these dogs. Some of them looked thin, woebegone, so pitiful, and they all seemed to have their eyes fixed earnestly on me. I glanced across at Dylan, he whined and his tail wagged slowly, begging me to let him out.

'You said another lady came here?'

Adil pulled up the stool and gestured I should sit, before he sat cross-legged on the floor. 'She promised she come back.'

'Who was she? What was her name?'

He shook his head. 'I don't remember.'

'Well, what did she look like?'

He thought a moment, searching for words. 'Not tall as you. Her hair was colour like Fran but not straight. More . . .' he pointed at my dripping curls. 'And her voice was . . .' he smiled a moment, 'like song.'

Like song? Sing-song? *Welsh.* 'I think her name was Sandy,' I said slowly.

'Yes. Yes. Sandy,' he answered excitedly. 'I remember. She said she work for newspaper. She take pictures of this place on phone.'

'Adil,' I began sadly, 'I'm afraid Sandy won't be coming back.'

He stared at me for a moment, then nodded, as if my words had confirmed a suspicion. 'Eddie, he see her here, talking with me. They fight. He chase her in van.'

'He chased her, in the Transporter? Are you sure?'

'Yes. She run to her car, drive away. He drive after her.'

'When was this?'

He frowned in an effort to remember. 'Long time. I wait, I hope she come back.'

'Did she say why she had come? Had she come because of the dogs?'

He looked confused. 'Dogs, yes, but . . . she knew about Khaled . . . she said she would come back, bring help.'

'Khaled?' I repeated.

'Adil!' a voice shrilled from outside. 'Get your arse back in here, right now!'

'I must go.' He got to his feet. 'Stay here. Wait, please! I will come back, few minutes.'

He hurried to the door, and giving an apologetic shrug, flipped out the light. 'I'm coming!'

I heard him yell as he ran off outside.

I sat in the dark listening to the dogs sighing, snuffling, scratching. How much light did these poor animals see? Were they locked in the dark all day, as well as all night, in this stinking, fetid place? I flipped on my torch, shone it around. Was one of the poor, shivering little dogs, fur matted with excrement, the shih-tzu that had been stolen? It was difficult to tell. In a cage in the corner a small terrier was obsessively licking a front paw over and over. He had worn away the fur, leaving a bald, sore patch of skin. Typical stress behaviour. I wondered how long the poor little mutt had been here.

I made my way over to Dylan's cage and inspected the padlock in the torchlight. I had a penknife in my pocket. Could I undo the padlock, get Dylan out, get him and E.B. safely into my van, then go back to the other shed to find Nookie and Boog? What were my chances of getting them away undetected? I knew I couldn't try to leave yet. I had to stay, talk to Adil, find out everything he knew. He was a witness to the fact that Sandy had found her way here, and that Eddie Swayne had seen her, that he had chased her. Had he pursued her all the way back to Ashburton, to the woods? Stephen Higgs had been worried about violence, that things had gone too far. Now he lay dead in a storage shed, shot in the stomach. Someone had killed him and in cruel mockery placed that smiling clown's head on his shoulders. Could Swayne have murdered Sandy and then Higgs just to cover up a dog theft racket? Or was something worse going on here, something that had led also to the death of Phil Thomas? A boy like Adil did not belong in a place like this. I thought of the three men in the Transporter. They had gone into the farmhouse and had not yet come out. Did they live here too? Khaled, Adil had mentioned someone called Khaled . . .

The phone rang in my pocket, making me jump like a startled rabbit. I fumbled for it and hit answer. It was Dean. 'Juno, where the hell are you?' he demanded. 'Are you okay?' He was yelling down the phone so loudly I was scared they would hear him in the farmhouse.

'Stop shouting,' I whispered fiercely. 'What's the matter?'

'I'm not supposed to tell you this but . . .' his voice suddenly faded. The signal must be patchy. '. . . is the reason she came round.'

'What?'

'Cruella . . . asking more questions . . . I thought you ought to know . . .' He sounded like a muffled robot, his voice fading in and out. '. . . so you don't . . . any . . . stupid.'

'Dean, I can't hear. I can't make out what you're saying.'

'They found a DNA match,' his voice was suddenly

318

clear again. 'The man you bit was the man who killed Sandy Thomas. There were traces of his DNA on her body.'

Then there was nothing. Silence. 'Dean! Dean!' I yelled as loudly as I dared. I tried to call him back, to tell him that Swayne was here, to tell him about Higgs. If I could get through to him, the cavalry would be here in minutes. But my phone was showing almost no signal. If I wanted to make a call, I was going to have to get out of here. And I wasn't ready to do that yet.

One thing was for sure. Whatever I did, if I didn't want to end up like Sandy Thomas, I had to be damn certain that Swayne couldn't follow me, that the bastard couldn't get away. I opened the door a crack, then stepped outside.

The storm had blown itself out, the rain stopped, the wind nothing but a ragged whisper of its former self. It was dark. I could glimpse stars between fast-moving masses of black cloud.

I crept down the slope to the hardstanding where the Transporter and the red Honda were parked, scurried around the back of the Transporter and plunged my penknife into a back tyre. Heart thumping, I proceeded to massacre the other three, all the time keeping my eyes fixed on the door of the farmhouse. I ran to do the same to the Honda. A light flicked on in an upstairs window and for a moment I froze, staring up at a blurry image behind frosted glass. I dodged back behind the bulk of the van. A toilet flushed, I heard water running in the downpipe. When I dared to peer out again, the light had gone out. I quickly stabbed the Honda's tyres. I hesitated. I should go back to the barn, wait for Adil. No. I must find Nookie and Boog.

Adil had said they were in a shed on the other side of the farmhouse. I crept down the side of the building, ducking low under the ledge of a lighted window and branched off along a path to another dark building. This time I was ready for the stench as I opened the door. Or I thought I was. It was as bad, if not worse, than the other shed. And like the other shed, completely black inside. I let the door close to behind me before I flipped on the torch. I shone the beam around, looking for a light switch and found one by the door. No flickering fluorescent strip this time but a single low-wattage bulb that cast a dim yellow glow, barely lighting up the centre of the room and leaving the corners in shadow. There were a dozen or so pens around the walls. I shone the torch into each one. In the first, a Jack Russell terrier, her white fur smeared with filth, was nursing three tiny pups. In the next were more puppies, too small to have been taken from their mother. They lay asleep on the concrete floor with no bedding, six of them, little black and white things, bundled together for warmth and comfort. An insistent whining behind me told me that I had found Boog. I turned and there she was, excited to see me, wagging her whole rear end and trying to lick me through the mesh of the pen. She looked thin. 'I'm going to get you out of here, Boogie,' I promised her. 'Very soon.' I shone light into three more cages, another full of mewling puppies, before I found Nookie, the last of the Tribe, unharmed, but far from safe. She was panting in distress. Of all of the Tribe she probably suffered the most from incarceration inside, in this stifling dark. I needed the keys to these cages.

I heard a door bang somewhere close by. Flicking off the light and my torch. I opened the door to the shed a crack. I could see no one. Perhaps a door had just banged in the wind. I waited, to be sure, before I slipped out, closing the shed door quietly behind me. I ran through the dark, back towards the barn. It was time to get back to Adil. I was pretty sure he didn't have the keys, but maybe he could get them.

'Khaled was my brother,' Adil told me softly. I had come back to the barn and waited for almost an hour, time to think about how to get the dogs out and to realise I couldn't do it on my own; time in which to consider that the man who had brutally murdered Sandy Thomas, Eddie Swayne, was in that farmhouse, just a few yards away.

Fran and Eddie believed Adil was in bed. He had been forced to wait until he was sure it was safe, then climbed out of the window of the attic that served as his bedroom. Something he often did, he told me with a smile. There was a handy drainpipe for him to climb down. We sat together by the light of a candle stub. He liked to spend time in here with the dogs, he told me. Around us, in the shadows, some of them were sleeping, not the contented sleep of a well-fed, happy hound, but the restless, shifting doze of a starving, miserable one.

'Back home in Syria,' he went on, 'Khaled was

student, training to be doctor. My father was college professor and my mother, she was teacher too. I had two sisters, younger than me. One day, Khaled go on protest, against government. Next day, police come to our house to look for him. We know it was not safe any more for him to live at home. He hide with friends. I take messages. And food. Every day. I had to be sure, every time, police do not follow me. I take him message that day, the day the bombs came, fell on our street, our house – killed everyone but Khaled and me.' The flickering light of the candle played on his features as he remembered, turning his sadness into shadows. 'There was nothing left. Our street, our town, nothing but . . . rocks, stones . . .' he frowned, searching for a word.

'Rubble?'

'Rubble,' he repeated bitterly, 'and dust. No water, no food. We could not stay. We had to come. To England. Our grandfather, grandmother, our cousin . . . they live many years, in Bradford.' He looked up at me, his black eyes questioning. 'Is very far, Bradford?'

'It's quite far from here. But not as far as you've already come,' I added hastily as his face fell in disappointment. 'How did you get here?'

'We walk to refugee camp in Turkey. Held there many months. Then we get away – Greece, boat to Italy – lorry, walk, lorry,' he shrugged. 'I forget.' His gaze was far away as he relived it all. 'We must stop many times, find work, for food, for money to travel to England. We must have money for boat. Khaled, he dig ditches, pick fruit, work for farmer – all to make money. Then we come to camp in France, and we wait. Wait to find boat, wait for chance to come.'

I imagined some fragile inflatable craft, crammed, weighed down almost to the waterline with desperate refugees, struggling to stay afloat as it drifted helplessly across the Channel.

'Khaled find man who say he will take us, in boat, for two thousand pounds each. We come.'

'In one of those inflatable boats?' I asked.

He shook his head. 'No. Good boat. Small, but with proper engine. Cabin.'

'A cabin cruiser?'

He shrugged and shook his head. 'I do not know. We were in hold, all of us. All sick . . . rough weather, smell of petrol. But when we get on boat, man says is not two thousand pounds now, but ten thousand we must pay. None of us have enough.'

'How many of you were in this boat?'

'Eight. The man say we owe him money. We must pay off debt. We must work for him until debt paid off, before we can be free. But I am too young, so Khaled, he goes, but I work here.'

'Where did Khaled go?'

'To building site. Every day. They promise he soon pay off debt and then they let him go. He can claim asylum. But many times, he does not get money. They take for food, for to live here, for van to take to work and back. They take money for everything.'

'Just let me get this straight,' I said, rubbing my forehead. 'You and your brother were brought here from the boat and kept here. You are forced to live here, and your brother is forced to work, and is taken backwards and forwards to the building site in the Transporter, for little or no pay. And, since you landed here, you've never been free to go anywhere else?'

'Yes.'

'And your brother, or any of the others, they've never tried to contact the authorities or the police?'

'Police put us in detention centre. Send us back.'

'But this is slavery, Adil. Have you never tried to run away?'

Tears sprang to his eyes suddenly. 'Run from here? Where is here?' he cried angrily. 'I do not know where here is. They do not tell us. We land on shore. Is England. But where? One day I run to top of hill. I walk. I get lost in mist, the ground it sinks, like water beneath my feet. I get stuck. I am frightened. I run back. But I am lost. Is everywhere wilderness. Broken rocks, broken houses, like after bombing. I see the road, but I know I must not go on road. Fran tells me, soldiers patrol road. If they catch me, they shoot me.'

How must he have felt, lost and alone up there on the moor in the mist? The land is bleak, scattered with rocky clitter, a few stunted thorn trees. It sounded as if he had wandered dangerously close to Raybarrow Pool, a treacherous bog that would have sucked him down and gulped him whole.

'That's Dartmoor, Adil. Those ruins you saw, are from the villages of ancient people. They lived here thousands of years ago. They weren't bombed.'

'Fran say place is haunted with evil spirits.'

'She's lying to you, to keep you from running away.'

He was shaking his head. 'I see spirit at night. Out there! Beyond the trees. It floats.'

'Like a big head?' I gestured with my hands, showing its size, and he nodded. 'It's a trick, Adil. It's nothing but a mask.' No wonder he was afraid. The poor kid was brought here in darkness. He has no idea what part of the country he's in, doesn't know there's a village just down the road, a pub he could have run to, where he could have found people who would have listened to his story, who could have helped him; if he hadn't been scared away from the road by Fran telling him stories about soldiers. 'It's all lies, Adil.'

'But I hear guns.'

'Yes, the army – the soldiers – train on parts of the moor,' I explained. 'There are firing ranges, places where some days it's not safe for people to go. They fly red flags on those days. You may hear gunfire sometimes if the wind is in the right direction. But these are only training exercises. The soldiers are not shooting at people. And they are certainly not out on the road looking for you.'

He stared. I wasn't sure he believed me.

'Those men in the house,' I went on, 'are they prisoners here too?'

'They come in boat. They are locked in room at night, like me.'

'And where is Khaled?'

Tears shone in his eyes. 'Khaled is dead.' His voice broke pathetically. 'They say there is accident on building site. But I know they kill him because he fight with Eddie.'

'I'm so sorry.' I reached out for his hand, but he withdrew it, used it to dash away his tears. I thought for a moment. 'When he died, on the building site, there must have been an investigation. Every accident is investigated. What happened then? Weren't the authorities suspicious?'

'The others tell me, they put false papers on his body. Give him other man's name.'

'When was this?' I asked. 'How long ago?'

'A year.'

'And you're still here, all alone?'

'I work in house. In garden. Do chores.'

I realised it was probably Adil whose blurred figure I had seen through the walls of the polytunnel when I was speaking to Fran.

'Eddie says I do not earn my keep. He want to sell me, to make money, but Fran not let him. So I stay here. When I am old enough, I work on building site,' he said miserably. 'I must pay off my debt, and Khaled's too.'

'No, Adil. I promise you, that's not what is going to happen.'

He shook his head, as if he knew whatever I said, his fate was sealed.

'But you like to come in here,' I asked, 'to be with the dogs?'

'Fran does not give them enough food. They are always hungry.'

I could see that. They were fed just enough to keep them alive.

'Does Fran keep the keys to the cages?'

'Yes.'

'Forgive me for asking, but you are a Muslim, aren't you?' I said tentatively. 'Aren't dogs considered unclean in your religion?'

'Dogs are impure,' he admitted, nodding. 'But the Quran tells us that we must be merciful to all creatures. I cannot help them. I cannot set them free. But I come to talk to them,' he added softly, 'because I know they are lonely.' For a moment he stared from eyes that showed me the depth of his own loneliness. Then he blinked and looked away and I found my own eyes pricked with tears.

'Listen, Adil, when Sandy came here, you said she knew about Khaled. She knew his death was not an accident?'

'I do not know all she knew. But she knew about boat.'

'This man on the boat, do you know who he was?'

'Was not Eddie. He and Stephen wait for us on beach, take us in van.'

'And you've no idea where you came ashore?'

'It was dark. I remember sand, rocks, that is all.'

That was no help. There were hundreds of isolated coves along the south Devon coast where a small boat could land undetected. 'Do you remember anything about the boat? You didn't see a name? It would have been painted on the side.'

Adil frowned. 'I see word painted. I remember, I ask Khaled, because I do not know word, do not know how to say it.'

He grabbed my hand suddenly, and with his forefinger began to trace letters on my palm. I said them out loud. 'L . . . O . . . U . . . Louise!' I almost shouted. 'The boat was called Louise.' They were all in it, then. Dunston brought the refugees to England in his boat. No wonder his company was doing well, when a quick pop across the Channel would net him eighty thousand pounds' worth of free labour. Adil said that Sandy had known about Khaled. She must have found out about this illegal trade. But was it a story about slave labour, or about stolen dogs that had brought her to this place?

I realised Adil was watching me anxiously. 'All this must end,' I told him. 'If you and the men in that farmhouse are not going to be slaves forever, then we must tell the police.'

His eyes flared in alarm. 'They will send me back,' he cried.

'No. I don't think they will. Khaled would have been able to claim political asylum for you both. And you have family here that you can go to. But it is a risk you must be willing to take, Adil, if you are going to be free, if you are to be with your grandparents.'

He thought for a while, and then he nodded solemnly.

'Yes?' I asked.

'Yes,' he said. Reluctantly. Then he looked up at me. 'What is your name, lady?'

'Juno.' I smiled and put out my hand.

'Juno,' he repeated, shaking it awkwardly.

I pulled out my phone. 'We must find somewhere where I can get a better signal. We'll go outside and up the hill to the track. My van's parked there, behind the trees. I'll make the call and then we'll wait in the van for help to arrive. Understand?'

'What about the dogs?'

'Don't worry. They won't get left behind. I promise.'

'Wait,' he said, 'there is something,' and disappeared behind the stack of fertiliser sacks.

He came back and held something out towards me. 'She drop it, when she run from Eddie. I keep it safe.' It was a mobile phone.

'This is Sandy's?' I breathed. I looked up at him. 'Do you know what's on it?'

He shook his head. 'I cannot get into it. Do not know password. But she took many photographs on it.'

I took it from him. What else was on this phone? Messages? Evidence of her affair with Dunston? Photographs of this place, and what else? 'Adil. This could be very important. You have done the right thing, keeping it safe.'

He nodded. 'You take it now.'

I slid it into my pocket and zipped it up. 'We must go.'

As we reached the door, I turned around to look at the dogs, at Dylan and E.B., at all of them. 'I'll come back for you. I promise,' I told them in a whisper. But leaving them, closing the door on those anxiously watching faces, was hard. I couldn't bring myself to meet their eyes again.

Outside, I crept to the corner of the building, Adil close behind me, and peeped around to see if the coast was clear. I was just in time to see the figure of Eddie

Swayne climbing the slope opposite. I swore beneath my breath. 'What's he up to?'

He was heading for the storage shed. Was he going to check on Higgs' body, to move it maybe? He'd see that I'd taken off the clown's head, know that someone had been there. I watched him disappear inside. 'Quick!' I grabbed Adil's hand. 'Let's move now, before he comes out.' We began to run up the slope towards the track. But before we'd gone more than a few steps we heard Swayne's bellow from inside the shed and he appeared in the doorway.

'Down!' I hissed at Adil, and we flung ourselves onto the ground, hoping that the darkness and scattered rocks would hide us.

'Adil!' he yelled. 'Where are you, you little bastard? Adil!'

I could hear him grunting as he strode down the slope towards the farmhouse. Then the bang of the door and Fran's voice. 'What's all the shouting about? What's the matter? Adil's in bed.'

'Go and look in his room,' Eddie told her. 'He's been messing about in that shed. It can only be him.'

Eddie disappeared inside and we crawled further up the slope, through mud, through cold, slick, wet grass, keeping low. The door banged again, and we froze. I dared a quick look. Eddie stood outside of the door, staring around him, the light shining down on his head and shoulders, and glinting on the twin barrels of the shotgun he carried. I stifled a moan.

Fran appeared in the doorway behind him. 'He's not

in his room. Oh, no, Eddie!' she screamed when she saw the gun in his hands. 'Not the boy, please!'

'He's found the body.'

'Body?' Adil whispered.

'Higgs,' I mouthed at him and he took in a shocked breath.

Swayne began trudging slowly up the slope, training the shotgun in slow arcs as he looked from side to side. We couldn't move from where we lay hidden without him seeing us. I began to inch the phone from my pocket and hit emergency call.

'You make call,' Adil hissed. And before I realised what he meant to do, he leapt to his feet and started running, down the slope right in front of Eddie. I watched in horror as Eddie took aim. But as he pulled the trigger, Fran cannoned into him, throwing the whole weight of her body against his shoulder and knocking him off balance. She screamed as the gunshot echoed around the valley, but he had fired harmlessly into the air. Eddie knocked her to the ground and Adil disappeared behind the storage shed.

'Police!' I hissed into the phone. 'There's a man with a shotgun. One man dead.'

'Can you repeat that, caller?'

I scrabbled a few more feet up the slope and said it again. At that moment, Eddie took aim a second time and fired, chipping the corner of the shed and sending splinters of wood flying into the dark. At least the controller on the phone heard it. 'Was that a gunshot, caller?'

Eddie cursed and reloaded as I gabbled my location, the phone clutched in one muddy hand.

I clawed my way up the slope, my boots slithering on the ground. Terror stole my breath. It came in gasps. My chest ached. I had to make it to the van, get inside. I had to drive along the track and pick up Adil.

Eddie saw me and fired. Something scorched the air a foot above my head and I screamed.

I flung myself over the brink of the slope and rolled onto the track. He realised what I was about and tossed the gun away with a curse, turned and headed for the Transporter. I picked myself up, hands shaking as I unlocked the van and climbed into the driver's seat. By now Eddie had discovered what I'd done to his tyres. I heard him yelling at Fran to get into the other car, and despite my desperate fumbling of the key into the ignition, I laughed.

I drove slowly around the rim of the valley until I spotted Adil, crouching behind the shed. I stopped and flashed my lights, sounded my horn. He turned to look up the slope towards the track as I leant across and opened the passenger door. He ran, at first keeping low, up the side of the hill towards me. But the ground was littered with rocks, and he was forced to slow down, to pick his way. Eddie and Fran were screaming at one another down by the car. In a lighted upstairs window, I could see the silhouette of three men looking out, three men imprisoned there, wondering what the hell was going on. Eddie caught sight of Adil and came striding over the ground towards him, stopping to pick up the empty gun by its barrel, wielding it like a club. I got out of the driver's seat and ran round to the passenger side, knelt at the edge of the track and screamed at Adil to keep going. But the ground was so steep here he was forced to clamber from rock to rock. I leant down over the edge of the track, my arm at full stretch, hand reaching out, ready to catch his, to pull him up to safety. Eddie was gaining on him, almost at his feet. His hand clutched at mine, slipped, clutched again. I got my other hand around his wrist. I hauled. I felt the muscles of my neck and shoulders tearing with the effort. But Eddie was at the base of the rock now. He stretched up and grabbed at Adil's dangling foot, gripping him around his ankle. 'Gotcha, you little bastard!'

Adil screamed and kicked out uselessly with his free leg. He was like a cracker being pulled between Eddie and me. Only he couldn't be torn apart, he would have to go one way or the other. I shifted my weight, heaving a leg over the edge of the track and kicked out hard. My walking boot struck Eddie on the forehead and he fell back with a grunt, letting go of Adil's ankle and rolling back down the slope. For a moment we dangled perilously, clinging on to each other. Then I flung my weight backwards, and Adil was over the edge of the track and rolling in the mud beside me.

'Get in the van!' I screamed at him as I saw Eddie rising groggily to his feet.

Adil slid into the passenger seat and I climbed into the driver's side, slamming the door shut.

I flung the gearstick into reverse and put my foot

down. We swerved back along the track. Blue lights were flashing through the trees, coming towards us.

'Is that the police?' Adil asked, frightened.

'No,' I told him and smiled. 'It's the cavalry.'

CHAPTER THIRTY

They arrived mob-handed. First an armed response unit, coming in answer to my call about the shotgun. They arrested Eddie for attempted murder, and then, following my directions to the corpse of Stephen Higgs, arrested him some more. Further calls were made when the three men imprisoned in the house were discovered, in a padlocked room with three mattresses on the floor, and Mike Swift and his Anti-Slavery Unit arrived from Plymouth.

They arrested Fran. I can't understand her. She obviously had some compassion, for a young boy, for Adil, enough to save him from being sold by Eddie into God-knows-what. How could she have so little pity for the wretched animals kept in her charge? A specially trained officer was sent to interview Adil, who refused to say anything unless I was allowed to remain with him. Eventually, someone called the RSPCA.

It was almost dawn when I got home, exhausted, caked in mud. I felt like a traitor, leaving Adil, but he had to be taken into care by social services. 'What will happen to him?' I asked Mike Swift.

'He's a minor. He will be very sympathetically treated,' he assured me. 'They all will.'

'But will he be allowed to stay, to join his grandparents?'

'It's not my decision, I'm afraid. His application for asylum will have to be processed, but I'm pretty sure he will.'

And for the time being, I had to be content with that.

They wouldn't let me bring the Tribe home. I cried when they were all brought safely out of their prisons. Cried and hugged all four of them, sobbing into their fur. I didn't care how filthy and smelly they were. But it was the responsibility of the RSPCA to return them to their legal owners, and I understood that. So, I gave the officers their names and addresses and waved as I watched them being loaded into a van. There were thirty dogs imprisoned in all, not counting the puppies, and judging by the emaciated state of some of them, they'd been there some time. I didn't know whether they'd ever be reunited with their proper families, but at least they'd be looked after, and rehomed. They'd all be checked over by a vet before anything else, the nice lady from the RSPCA told me. It looked like the vet was in for a busy night.

Despite how late it was, I rang Elaine and Alan and told them E.B. was safe and where he could be picked up from next morning. They promised they'd phone the others at once.

I let myself into the house as quietly as I could, to avoid waking Adam and Kate. I'd taken off my muddy walking boots and changed back into trainers, carrying my boots by their laces, but the rest of me was wet, my clothes felt clammy and stiff with mud. As I crossed the threshold, I stepped on something white lying on the floor in the hall, something that must have been slipped under the door. An envelope. I bent to pick it up. I turned it over, but in the gloom, I couldn't read the name on it and flipped on the lamp on the hall table to see who it was addressed to. *Miss Browne with an 'e'* was handwritten in black ink. I felt a shock like I'd been thrown into cold water. After a moment of staring stupidly at the handwriting, I tore the envelope open and unfolded the single sheet of paper inside. The message was brief.

My Dear Miss B,

You are right, of course, in what you said. None of what has taken place between us is your fault. The fault is all mine and I hope you can forgive me. You were a bright and shining moment in my life, but I seem to have fallen back into the dark again. When I saw you the other evening, so beautiful and so angry, like some flame-haired avenging angel, I wanted to tell you I loved you. But I was turned to stone, paralysed by some part of myself I do not understand. And you were right about Claire, this is not what she would have wanted. So, I have decided to do what you advise. I am getting out of your space and going to get my head sorted out. This may take some time. Please do not waste your own by waiting for me.

Take care of yourself, Miss Browne with an 'e'.

Daniel.

The paper began to shake in my hand. I let it fall to the floor as I headed for the door, not bothering to close it behind me. I got into the van and drove, tearing up the road towards Halsanger Common. I was blinded by tears, forced to keep blinking them away. I didn't know what I was going to say to Daniel, only that I had to talk to him again, to beg him not to go, to tell him that we could fight the dark together.

The sky was lightening as I drove on to the common, turning pink in the east with the promise of sunrise. There was no sign of Daniel's car. I ran up to the caravan and rattled the door. It was locked, in darkness. I tried banging with my fist, but the emptiness inside it echoed. I thumped on the door of the farmhouse, walked around the building, peering in all the downstairs windows, but I knew I was too late. Daniel had gone.

I stood and watched the sun come up, chilled by the wind that blew through me in my wet and muddy clothes.

CHAPTER THIRTY-ONE

There is nothing quite like a walk on a winter's afternoon, just as the golden light of the sun is fading and you know it will be dark soon. It was a month since that day when I received Daniel's letter. The blazing glory of autumn had faded. I walked along a lane where most of the trees were bare. No leaves, just a few shrivelled fragments clinging to the branches. Their time was over. Now was the time of the husk, the seed pod and the shrivelled berry. The only green was the green of holly and dark fir, the only gloss, the gloss of ivy and of ferns that poked like green tongues among the bushes. I stopped to look at scarlet berries of black bryony hanging in clusters from a necklace of strong stems woven into the hedgerow. There was burdock here too, its sticky seed cases like little bombs covered in tiny hooks.

A lot had happened in a month. On that day, that

new day, new life had begun. I'd barely washed the mud off under a long, hot shower before Adam was yelling up the stairs at me and I was driving him and Kate to the hospital in the back of the van. Baby Noah arrived in time for breakfast, complete with a healthy pair of lungs and a fine head of black hair. He sometimes wears the grumpy look of his father, but is nuzzly and snuggly and adorable. Bill doesn't know what to make of him at all.

Sandy had been cleverer than anybody knew. She'd made unpleasant discoveries during her affair with Dunston, and her phone, once the police boffins had managed to unlock its secrets, was full of incriminating evidence: messages, photographs, recorded conversations – incriminating Dunston, Higgs and Swayne, also Hollander. I knew that moustache was nasty.

Alastair Dunston was arrested that same day, and charged with people trafficking and, ultimately, conspiracy to murder. He tried to distance himself, deny all knowledge of what his underlings had been up to. There were several tiers of management between him and the labourers his firm employed, he claimed, and it was the gangmaster who was responsible for recruitment. He couldn't be held responsible. But computers, laptops and phones seized by the police showed that he was part of a network supplying illegal labour to the building trade throughout the West Country, and there was enough evidence on the *Louise* to damn him, including the testimony of Adil and the others, who identified him as the man who had brought them to these shores. 'Human trafficking is rife down here,'

Mike Swift had told me later. 'It's just too easy to land a small boat around this coast. Migrants get brought here, charged exorbitant prices for their journey. They start off in debt to some unscrupulous employer. And because many of them don't speak English and don't understand the law, they can be trapped for years, forced to accept whatever cash-in-hand payments their employer gives them. And even if they run away, they can't get legitimate work without visas and they're too frightened to go to the authorities.'

As for Louise, the real Louise, how much she knew of what was going on is difficult to say. I can't believe she would have tried to involve me if she'd known what her husband was guilty of, known what I might find out. She might be a cold woman, have nursed vengeful feelings towards Sandy and other women her husband had cheated on her with, but there was no evidence that she knew of his darker crimes. Perhaps she didn't want to know, turned a blind eye. I think, in her heart of hearts, she knew something terrible was going on, and wanted to be free of it, free to protect her children, and that is why she came to me.

How much the workmen on Dunston's building site, the home-grown ones, knew about the immigrant workers, is under investigation too. Most of them admitted to knowing that the foreign labourers didn't have all the paperwork they should, that maybe they had arrived in the country illegally, but they'd turned a blind eye. It was none of their business, the men worked hard, so why should they cause them trouble? They claimed to know nothing about those being held in captivity by Swayne, just thought he was giving them a lift home to their lodgings every night. But once they realised Eddie Swayne was under arrest, they became a lot more forthcoming about the death of Phil Thomas. Two of them admitted to having seen Swayne come down from the scaffolding after Phil had fallen. But they'd been too scared to say anything.

In the end, Eddie admitted to killing Sandy. He knew the DNA evidence on her body would damn him. It seems when he had chased her away from Cawsand Farm, he'd lost her. She'd given the Transporter the slip, somewhere on the road between Chagford and Ashburton. But he knew who Sandy was, and called Alastair Dunston, who had told him where she lived. And as far as I'm concerned, that made him as guilty of killing her as Swayne. And whilst Sandy was taking the long road home, trying to make sure Eddie wasn't following her, he'd driven straight to her place and lain in wait on that lonely road, ready to cut her off before she got there. When she'd seen that Transporter blocking her road, then she'd got out of her car and bolted into the woods.

Fran was fairly talkative too. She and Eddie had been involved in dog theft for years. They'd already been fined twice and banned from keeping animals. For Eddie, of course, the dog trade was just a side-line to the main business of trafficking in people, a side-line he kept secret from Dunston. Stephen Higgs, who was, coincidentally, Fran's cousin, and up to his neck in the cross-Channel slave labour imports, found out about the dogs' racket and wanted a share of that too. The trouble was, that whilst the forced labour could be controlled merely by threats of violence, Higgs himself was a bit windy when it came to dishing out the real thing. According to Fran, he must have got cold feet or grown a conscience. Either way, Eddie decided he'd become a liability and had to be got rid of.

At least with Fran and Eddie out of the way, I could tell Joan not to worry about Hilary. I paid her a visit, in Ivybridge, and between the two of us we fixed up a regular carer for Hilary, a pleasant lady with glowing references from social services who would pop in on her every day.

Exactly what had brought Sandy to Cawsand Farm on the day she died is not clear. Had she been following Eddie Swayne from the building site? She'd told Alf she was going to see someone about a dog, and we know she'd been to Hilary's house. Had she found her way to Cawsand Farm the same way I had, following up the story of the puppies for sale and tracking Fran from there? Whether she realised the two crimes were linked before she found Adil is something else that we'll never know. Nor what Phil Thomas had said to her, what it was he was going to tell me. Had he found out about forced labour on the building site? Perhaps he went to work for Dunston so he could see for himself, to track down Sandy's killer. Perhaps he just asked too many questions.

One question has been answered. I found out what it was that Sandy had wanted to ask me, when she scribbled my name on her notepad. On the day of her funeral, attended by most of Ashburton judging by the people packed into St Andrew's Church, I found myself chatting to one of her neighbours.

'I wanted you to walk my dog for me whilst I was away for a couple of days on a course,' she told me. 'It was Sandy who suggested you, said she knew you. I kept asking her to ask you if you could do it, but she kept forgetting. I said, "For God's sake, Sandy, ask her. Write it down," but I don't think she ever did. I had to get someone else to do it in the end.'

Was that it, then, the reason for that heavily ringed message on her notepad? *Ask Juno Browne.* Ask me if I could walk a dog? Nothing secret or important, no dramatic revelation, no clue to her murder, just a simple enquiry about walking a dog. Somehow, the very ordinariness of it made me want to cry.

In all the excitement I completely forgot about the auction of the Della Robbia pottery that Lady Margaret had given me, until the auctioneer phoned me to tell me how well I had done. I hadn't made megabucks, but I had Lady Margaret's generosity – or gratitude as she preferred me to call it – for the fact all the bills were taken care of for a few months and I could start looking around for some really nice stock for *Old Nick's*. 'Don't forget there's still a lot of other stuff in that loft,' she reminded me.

'Don't worry,' I promised her. 'I won't.'

I haven't heard from Daniel. I've tried leaving messages on his phone obviously, but there's been no response. The only person I had told about his letter to me was Elizabeth.

'I don't think Daniel is ready to move on,' she agreed. 'But the point is, Juno, are you?'

'What do you mean?'

'You know what I mean. Will you move on, or will you always be secretly hoping that Daniel will come back?'

'I don't know,' I answered honestly. 'I'm afraid that a part of me always will. And there's that house of his up on Halsanger Common, he can't just abandon it, surely?'

'That nice-looking detective has been in this shop twice now,' she added. 'He's obviously smitten. And you've been decidedly cool with him.'

She meant Mike Swift. He's popped into the shop twice to give me news of Adil. Elizabeth is right. He is very nice. He brought Adil to say goodbye to me before he took him up to Bradford, to be reunited with his family whilst his application for asylum is pending. And Adil sent me a beautiful photograph of himself, with his grandparents, standing proudly between them in his new school uniform.

As I walked along the lane, the phone rang in my coat pocket.

'You haven't forgotten that you're coming to tea, have you, Princess?' Ricky's voice demanded. 'Only Mag-bags is here already.'

'No, I'm on my way.'

'Well, get a move on, then,' he told me. 'She's started on the gin already.'

346

I returned the phone to my pocket. I was going to Druid Lodge to help sort out the final details for the Honeysuckle Farm fundraising day. There were still lots of things to discuss. I hoped it wasn't going to turn into a party. I mustn't stay late. In the morning, I'd have to be up early to walk the Tribe.

As I shoved my phone back in my jeans, my fingers brushed against something that felt like cardboard. I pulled it out. It was a business card, a bit soft and wrinkly where it had been through the wash a few times. *Mike Swift, Anti-Slavery Unit,* it read, and a telephone number. I studied it for a moment and then put it back in my pocket. I sighed, and my breath made a cloud in the chilly air.

There is nothing like a walk on a winter's afternoon when there's a slight chill in the air, when the golden light of the sun is fading, you know it will be dark soon, and you have friends waiting.

ACKNOWLEDGEMENTS

I would like to thank my good friends Katy and Phil Richards for sharing with me some of their experiences as hosts of the excellent Work Away scheme. Truth, as they say, is stranger than fiction. I should also thank Peter Hyland for his excellent book, *Della Robbia Pottery, Birkenhead 1894–1906*. As for the volunteers of the charity 'Dog Lost' who work so hard to re-unite lost and stolen dogs with their owners, please keep up the wonderful work you do.

Thanks to all the usual suspects: Susie, Fliss, Fiona and Libby at Allison and Busby, my brilliant agent, Teresa Chris, my dear book-buddy Di, and to Martin, always, for his love and unfailing support.

STEPHANIE AUSTIN has enjoyed a varied career, working as an artist and an antiques trader, but also for the Devon Schools Library Service. When not writing she is actively involved in amateur theatre as a director and actor, and attempts to be a competent gardener and cook. She lives in Devon.

stephanieaustin.co.uk